Beyond Bethlehem

Beyond Bethlehem

Margaret Horsfield
Peter Horsfield

CBC Enterprises
Les Entreprises Radio-Canada

Excerpts from THE NEW JERUSALEM BIBLE, copyright 1985 by Darton, Longman and Todd, Ltd., and Doubleday, a division of Bantam Doubleday Dell Publishing Group, Inc. Reprinted by permission of the publisher.

Excerpts from THE BIRTH OF THE MESSIAH by Raymond Brown, copyright 1977 by Raymond Brown. Reprinted by permission of Doubleday, a division of Bantam Doubleday Dell Publishing Group, Inc.

Excerpts from JOSEPHUS: THE JEWISH WARS by Gaalya Cornfeld, copyright 1982 by Massada Ltd., Publishers, Givatayim and Gaalya Cornfeld, Tel Aviv. Used by permission of Zondervan Publishing House.

Canadian Cataloguing in Publication Data

Horsfield, Margaret
    Beyond Bethlehem

Based on a CBC radio Ideas program.
Includes bibliographical references.
ISBN 0-88794-361-6

1. Jesus Christ – Nativity.   I. Horsfield, Peter
II. CBC Enterprises.   III. Title.

BT 315.2.H67 1990   232.9′21   C 89-095281-7

Editor: Jill Burrows
Design: Linda Gustafson

Printed and bound in Canada
93 92 91 90 89   5 4 3 2 1

For Anne and for Elizabeth, with love

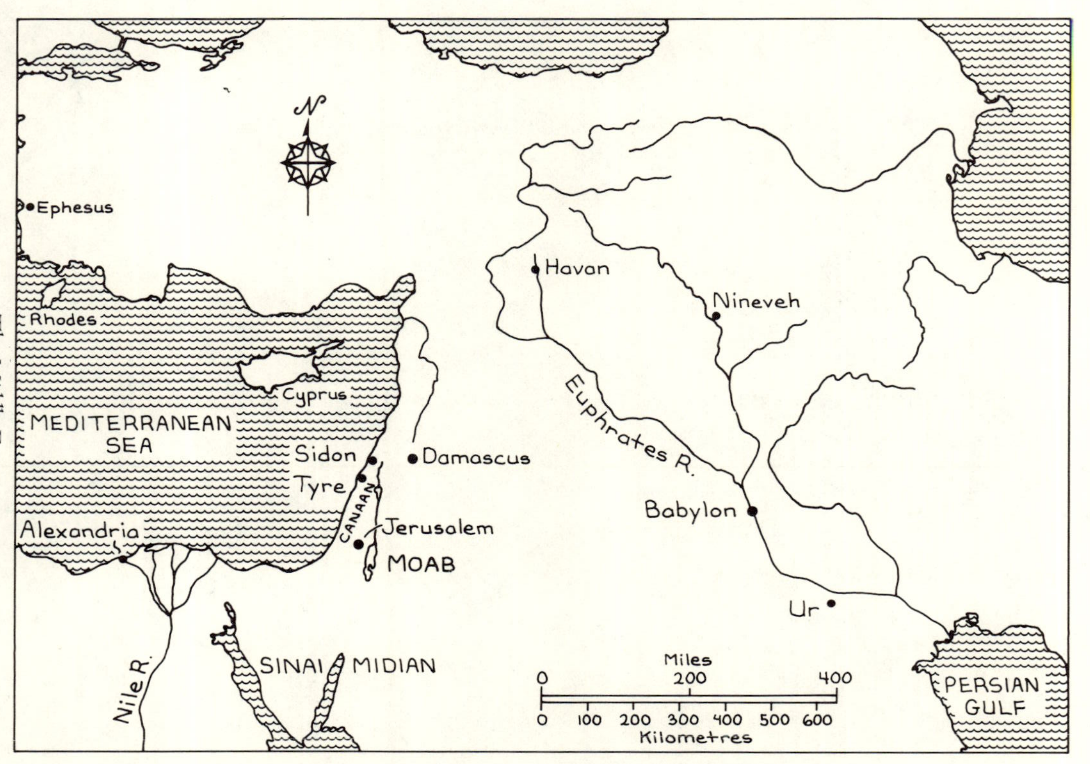

The Middle East

N
Sidon
Dan
Tyre
Damascus
MEDITERRANEAN SEA
GALILEE
Nazareth
SEA OF GALILEE
CANAAN
SYRIA
Samaria
Shiloh
River Jordan
Bethel
Jamnia
?Ramah
Jericho
Jerusalem
Bethlehem
DEAD SEA
JUDAH
MOAB
Beersheba
Miles
0   10   20   30   40   50
0   50   100
Kilometres

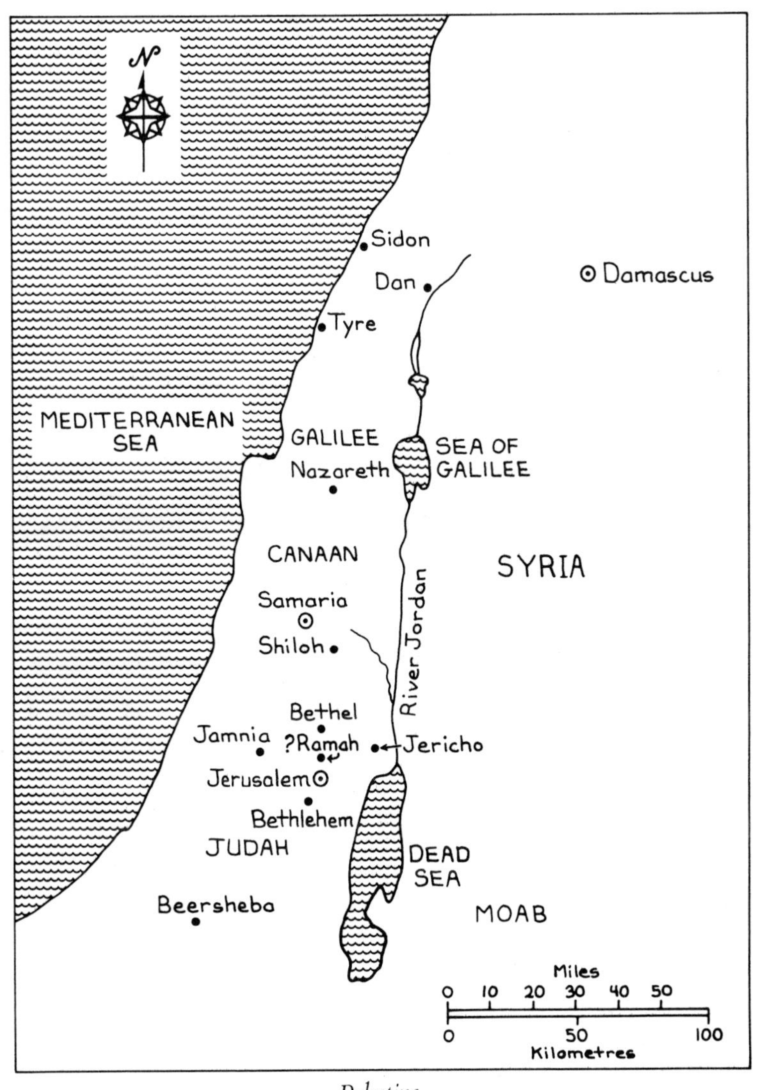

Palestine

Contents

The idea for this book can be traced to a Christmas visit with my family a few years ago, and a casual conversation about Christmas-cards. Looking around the living room, I was struck by all the magi: those solemn, glossy magi who populate so many cards, with their camels and their rapt expressions, following stars highlighted in gold paint somewhere in the upper-right-hand section of the sky. I wondered aloud about the magi, and what on earth the story was really all about. 'The magi' my father said, 'they came marching right out of the Old Testament. Didn't you know?' I didn't know, but I was about to learn. My father was then giving a series of lectures to an ecumenical study group about the background of the Christmas stories, or the Birth Narratives as they are technically known. I was able to sit in on some of his lectures, and in a very short time I found myself immersed in the subject.

The more I learned about the stories of the birth of Jesus the more I wanted to know. When the Ideas series of CBC Radio asked me to make two radio documentaries about the Birth Narratives, my research intensified. I read widely; I talked to and then interviewed many leading scholars; I borrowed my father's lecture notes and I discussed the project with him in detail. Following the Ideas broadcasts, the BBC World Service in London asked me to do another radio documentary on the same subject and the national network of BBC Radio 3 wanted yet another. The subject was evidently popular. People seemed intrigued. This book is the result of all that interest.

In writing this book, my father and I have worked together from start to finish. We have learned a great deal. Neither of us claims to be an expert in biblical scholarship, but we share a fascination for the work of the experts in biblical scholarship, and we hope that we have made some aspects of their work accessible and interesting. Discovering the background to the stories of the birth of Jesus is an intriguing process. In *Beyond Bethlehem* we want to show the stories of Jesus's birth are much more than familiar Christmas-card scenes. They are complex and lively stories that are part of a complex and lively tradition. They deserve the best kind of attention.

MARGARET HORSFIELD

London, England
September 1989

Introduction

In *Beyond Bethlehem* we try to address some very basic questions about what is popularly known as 'The Christmas Story'. Who are the main characters of this story? What do we know of them, and how do we know it? How has their story reached us? Who are the people who wrote the story, and what was their background? Above all, what are the origins of this story?

Such questions are not new. We make no pretence at offering radical new conclusions of our own; what we are presenting covers well-known territory in modern biblical scholarship. The problem is that modern biblical scholarship is not well-known territory. Far from it. Biblical scholarship exists in an enclosed academic world largely unknown to outsiders, and its influence is limited. Even though scholars have a lot to say about the birth narratives, few people hear it. Most of us carry on assuming we know the stories of the birth of Jesus, completely unaware of the scholarly work that is going on. The Christmas stories do not seem like serious texts worth taking seriously; they are pretty passages from the Bible, telling an attractive story about the baby Jesus in the manger in Bethlehem;

stories that have mutated on to Christmas-cards and wrapping paper. Even if we want to consider the texts seriously there is a problem. Books on this subject are usually very uninviting. They tend to be specialized, or obscure, or pious, or all three. Any enthusiastic, lively interest in the Christmas story dies a quick death when faced with the literature of the experts; a problem common to many academic disciplines.

We hope we are offering something different. Beyond Bethlehem is a title we have chosen because for both of us it means trying to reach beyond the pretty pictures and the clichés about the Christmas story, to the background and roots of the stories. We have tried to do so in a way reflecting what we have found to be the most helpful elements of current scholarship. This has meant looking closely at the biblical stories of the birth of Jesus, and then turning to look closely at connected stories from the Old Testament, or the Hebrew Scriptures as that section of the Bible is also called. There are countless stories in the Hebrew Scriptures that are closely related to the birth stories in the gospels. We will be quoting many passages from many such stories in the following pages. We will be placing related passages alongside each other so that the connections are easy to see. In looking at all these related biblical passages, an extraordinary pattern of storytelling emerges, and a great deal of evidence is revealed about how the birth stories were written.

Assessing this kind of evidence is something each individual can do to his or her own satisfaction. Some background information may be needed and some assistance in finding the related stories; that is what we are offering in *Beyond Bethlehem*.

Throughout this book all biblical passages quoted are from the New Jerusalem Bible (NJB) unless otherwise indicated. We think that it is important to turn to a good modern translation like the NJB when reading well-known biblical passages. The NJB is one of the best available, and it is accompanied by very helpful notes and introductions.

The dating system we are using in the book may be unfamiliar. Traditionally the years since the time of Jesus have been noted as AD or *anno domini*, meaning 'year of the Lord'. The system is now changing, and scholars are increasingly referring to the Common Era for numbering the years in the Christian centuries. This gives rise to the initials BCE (Before the Common Era) for the years before Jesus, and CE (Common Era) for the years since his birth. We shall be using this system of notation throughout the book.

In *Beyond Bethlehem* we are referring to the Old Testament as the Hebrew Scriptures. This designation is becoming widely used, and it is acceptable to Jews and Christians alike.

Whenever we provide dates for biblical passages it is worth noting two points about how such dates are determined. The first is that ancient dates are always subject to different theories and different estimates. We have tried to provide the most widely accepted dates, and to keep them consistent with one another. The second point is that two types of dates are often involved. There is the date of the person or the event in question, and then there are the dates of the records about that person or event. Particularly in the earlier scriptures these dates can be many centuries apart. The Chronology should help with all the dates we give.

Any errors in this book are our own. We shall be surprised if there are none; we hope only that their number is small.

MARGARET HORSFIELD
PETER HORSFIELD

Protection Island
August 1989

The Stories

> This is how Jesus Christ came to be born. His mother Mary was betrothed to Joseph; but before they came to live together she was found to be with child through the Holy Spirit. Her husband Joseph, being an upright man and wanting to spare her disgrace, decided to divorce her informally.
>
> *Matthew 1:18-19*

This is the opening of the story of the birth of Jesus in one of its more widespread modern English translations. It is not a very promising start for one of the world's great religious leaders, but two thousand years later the story still seems to be flourishing. It permeates the language and imagination of Western society. Around the time of the northern winter solstice the story is inescapable, and no amount of evasive action is any use. Every Christmas we are assaulted by countless different versions of the nativity of Jesus. It is sung on every radio, and told on every television network. It is retold in every newspaper, acted and re-enacted in schools, and carolled by choirs in cathedrals and in supermarkets alike. It has inspired poets and artists, and even advertising agencies, to great heights of inventiveness.

The power of this story is clearly evident in any great art gallery where paintings depicting the nativity of Jesus are found on every wall. In London, in the National Gallery, a quick scan of the collection reveals the following: eleven annunciations, thirty-eight adorations of magi or of shepherds, sixteen nativities, seven flights into Egypt, and thirty-seven madonnas with child. It is the same wherever you go. Most of the great masters of the European tradition were able to create something of lasting beauty from the stories of the birth of Jesus. The modern Christmas-card industry would be lost without them. Along with the icons of the Eastern European tradition, the lavish statuary of Spain and Latin America, and the stained glass of medieval artists, these great paintings have given us an outstanding visual heritage telling of the birth of Jesus. Whatever we may choose to think of the story, or to believe about it, most of us can probably visualize it.

Whether we imagine the scene as a Filippo Lippi painting, or as a plastic crèche beside the Christmas tree, there are certain constants. Mary and the baby are always there, stage centre. Mary is almost always earing blue – blue because that was the most expensive pigment the early Italian masters could get their hands on, more expensive even than gold leaf. It was ground from lapis lazuli, which came a great distance, from what is now Afghanistan. The tradition of Mary wearing blue has persisted long beyond the days of precious pigments, and it has been inherited by Sunday-school pageants and Christmas wrapping paper alike.

Also in the usual nativity scene is Joseph; slightly in the background, wearing something that more often than not manages to look like a brown dressing-gown. Joseph is frequently portrayed as much older than Mary, and once again this is due to artistic representations of an earlier age. Medieval painters were insistent that Joseph was an old man. Only by showing him as old, and sometimes as completely uninterested in the baby, could the idea be transmitted that Joseph was not the father of this child. Physically, he had to be seen to be past it, an old man quite incapable of having become a father.

There are a lot of optional extras in the nativity scene; all those shepherds and magi and angels and animals; the ox and ass, possibly a star or two, and maybe a distant palm tree. The whole thing is vaguely set in some kind of stable. The trouble with all of this is that so much of it is rooted in nothing but popular imagination. A great deal of what is thought to be part of the Christmas story does not appear in the biblical accounts at all, and the popular nativity scene is an odd mixture of biblical stories and artistic licence. Mary in blue, Joseph as an older man, the ox and the ass, and even the stable itself; these are details that do not appear in the Bible, but they have become part of a concoction of popular imagery and biblical allusion. To try to get beyond this concoction of familiar imagery means going back to the original texts, the primary sources, and examining closely what they really say.

All of the primary sources of information about Jesus are found in the New Testament. This specifically Christian section of the Bible usually has twenty-seven books, although this can vary according to which translation of the Bible is being used. These twenty-seven books include the four gospels, giving four different accounts of the life of Jesus. Only two of these gospels, Matthew and Luke, have anything to say about the birth of Jesus. In the rest of the New Testament not one of the other writers has anything to say about it. Even in the gospels of Matthew and Luke, which taken together have fifty-two chapters, only four chapters touch on the birth of Jesus. This raises intriguing questions. The Christmas story is extremely well known; it is influential, widely circulated and unavoidable, yet in the foundation documents of the Christian religion most of the writers simply ignore the birth of Jesus.

The first writer in the New Testament is Paul. He was writing as early as the year 50 CE, not yet a generation after the death of Jesus.[1] He had been a Jewish religious leader, a well educated Pharisee and probably a rabbi, who had been active among those Jews who wanted to stamp out Christianity by force. When he was converted to Christianity Paul became an equally forceful leader of the new religion. He travelled extensively all over the eastern Mediterranean, establishing new Christian communities. He then kept in touch with these communities by letter, instructing them, advising them, and often admonishing them. Some of Paul's letters have survived to become the largest collection of teaching material

1 For a discussion of Paul's dates see NJB, Introduction to Paul pp 1849-1865.

in the New Testament. He has a great deal to say about the new Christian religion, but he says nothing about the origins of its leader, nothing about the birth of Jesus or about his parents, nothing at all about that famous nativity.

Chronologically, the next part of the New Testament to be written was the gospel of Mark. His is the earliest and the shortest of the four gospels. According to some of the earliest church authorities Mark was an assistant to Peter in Rome around the time of Peter's death in 64 CE, and his gospel was written very near that time.[2] Mark, like Paul, says nothing at all about the birth of Jesus. His gospel opens with an account of the baptism of the adult Jesus by John the Baptist, and he never looks back to the infancy. In Mark, the lack of a birth story is conspicuous because the three gospels of Mark and Matthew and Luke are usually very closely related. They are known as the synoptic gospels. New Testament scholars are nearly unanimous that Matthew and Luke both drew on Mark's earlier gospel. Yet in their birth narratives Matthew and Luke cannot turn to Mark, for he provides them with no material.

So both Mark and Paul are silent about the birth of Jesus, and in many ways this is characteristic of each of them. Paul was a teacher, more interested in establishing early Christian doctrine than in telling stories about the life of Jesus. He rarely tells any stories at all. Mark was probably working out of Rome at a time of severe persecution of both Christians and Jews. In such circumstances it is not surprising that compared with the other gospels his account of Jesus's life and ministry is short, and sometimes abrupt. Mark never wastes words on non-essential material. Given the nature of their writings it is understandable that neither Mark nor Paul tells of the birth of Jesus. Stories of the birth may not have been known to them, or they simply may not have been interested.

The two writers who were interested are Matthew and Luke. Their two gospels were written later in the first century, probably between the years 75 and 85 CE.[3] Matthew's gospel is the first to appear in the New Testament. He opens with what can be best described as a lengthy family tree, showing just who Jesus was.

2 See NJB, p. 1603.
3 See chapter 4, pp. 33–47, for discussion of when and where Matthew's and Luke's gospels were written.

Matthew seems to be clearing his throat, and setting the record straight as his gospel begins:

> Roll of the genealogy of Jesus Christ, son of David, son of Abraham . . .
>
> *Matthew 1:1*

After the genealogical roll call Matthew goes on to tell the story of Joseph and Mary and the birth of Jesus. He tells of the magi arriving to pay homage to the child, and this is followed by the story of the murderous Herod killing all the first-born babies in Bethlehem, and an account of how Jesus is saved from this fate by the flight into Egypt. In Matthew's gospel Joseph plays a prominent role, and makes all the important decisions. He decides to stand by Mary; he decides they should flee to Egypt to escape Herod, and he decides when they should return. All of these actions are dictated by an angel in a series of dreams. Once the family has returned from Egypt, Matthew has no more to say about Joseph or Mary or the childhood of Jesus. Without any transition he skips some thirty years and starts telling the story of John the Baptist and the baptism of Jesus.

Luke's account of the birth of Jesus is notably different. He starts his gospel with the story of the miraculous conception of John the Baptist, who seems to have been some sort of cousin to Jesus. John's parents, Elizabeth and Zechariah, are too old to expect children but an angel appears to Zechariah to announce an impending pregnancy and is greeted with incredulity. About six months later the same angel appears to Mary to announce her equally unexpected pregnancy. Luke's gospel records Mary's reaction to the announcement, her amazement and her doubts and in the end her great song of praise to God. In due course John the Baptist is born to Elizabeth and Zechariah, with great rejoicing. A few months later, when Mary and Joseph are visiting Bethlehem where Joseph has come to register for a census, Jesus is born and is laid in a manger, and shepherds come to pay homage. We then hear about a visit to Jerusalem where Jesus is presented at the temple. After that we hear nothing until Jesus is twelve years old when the family again visits the temple at Jerusalem, and then there is silence, as in Matthew's gospel, until about the year 30 CE. Luke does not neglect to provide a genealogy, to identify Jesus and to provide him with an honourable family tree, but this comes later, following the baptism of Jesus by John the Baptist.

The birth narratives of Luke and Matthew are clearly not the same. Matthew has the magi, stars, and dreams; he has the flight into Egypt, and a prominent role for Joseph. Luke has shepherds, songs, and angel choirs; he has the birth in a manger, and he concentrates on Mary rather than on Joseph. But on certain points the two gospels do agree with each other, or at least they accommodate each other's versions of the story. Both Matthew and Luke maintain, against all normal expectations, that Mary was a virgin when Jesus was born. Celestial portents appear in both gospels: in Matthew to the magi, in Luke to the shepherds. Angelic announcements about the birth are made in each gospel, in Matthew to Joseph, in Luke to Mary:

> 'Mary, do not be afraid; you have won God's favour. Look! You are to conceive in your womb and bear a son, and you must name him Jesus...'
>
> *Luke 1:31-32*

In Matthew's gospel the angel addresses Joseph:

> '...Joseph son of David, do not be afraid to take Mary home as your wife, because she has conceived what is in her by the Holy Spirit. She will give birth to a son and you must name him Jesus,...'
>
> *Matthew 1:20-21*

These angelic speeches provide the only point at which the two birth stories can be compared almost word for word. Other close textual parallels do not exist.

Despite all the differences between the two gospels, the basic framework of the story of the birth of Jesus does seem to be roughly the same in both gospels. Matthew and Luke do agree on the questions of time and place and people, but such agreement is never as clear as it first appears.

Both Matthew and Luke date the birth of Jesus by using the accepted historical method of the time, referring to contemporary political figures. The most that can be said for the results is that the two gospels manage to place the birth within the same decade. Matthew dates the story in the days of Herod the Great:

> After Jesus had been born at Bethlehem in Judaea during the reign of King Herod...
>
> *Matthew 2:1*

Near the beginning of his gospel, Luke appears to agree with this:

> In the days of King Herod of Judaea there lived a priest called Zechariah...
>
> *Luke 1:5*

So far, so good; Matthew and Luke agree that Herod was king. But Luke goes on to complicate matters in chapter 2.

> Now it happened that at this time Caesar Augustus issued a decree that a census should be made of the whole inhabited world. This census — the first — took place while Quirinius was governor of Syria, and everyone went to be registered, each to his own town.
>
> *Luke 2:1*

Luke's mention of Quirinius has always fascinated and puzzled anyone who wishes to date the birth of Jesus exactly. It seems simple enough. All that is needed is to find out when Herod was king, and when Quirinius was governor in Syria, and that should provide a fixed point for the date. The trouble is that Quirinius was the Syrian governor in the year 6 CE, some ten years after the time of King Herod, who had died in the year 4 BCE. The two men did not overlap at all. According to Professor Ed Sanders, of Oxford University, Luke just made a mistake.[4]

4 *The Birth Narratives* (1987), p. 16; see also chapter 10, pp. 135-7, for further discussion of Luke's census; compare chapter 8, p. 110.

He was writing possibly as late in the century as the year 85 CE, looking back eighty years or more to the birth of Jesus. During this time Palestine had been devastated and Jerusalem destroyed in the war between the Jewish people and the occupying Roman forces. Many valuable historical records had been lost. By the time Luke was telling the story of Jesus's birth anyone who had known Jesus or his family or anything about the details of his origins would have died. The exact date of the birth remains debatable, but most scholars now believe that Luke got it wrong and that Jesus was born in the latter days of Herod's reign, which means at the latest by the year 4 BCE.

Matthew and Luke seem more clearly united on the question of where Jesus was born. Bethlehem is not in dispute as the birthplace.

> After Jesus had been born at Bethlehem in Judaea during the reign of King Herod, suddenly some wise men came to Jerusalem from the east . . .
>
> *Matthew 2:1*

> . . . Joseph set out from the town of Nazareth in Galilee for Judaea, to David's town called Bethlehem, since he was of David's House and line, in order to be registered together with Mary, his betrothed, who was with child. Now it happened that, while they were there, the time came for her to have her child, and she gave birth to a son, her first-born.
>
> *Luke 2:4-6*

However, this apparent agreement about Bethlehem is not complete. Matthew's gospel suggests that Mary and Joseph lived in Bethlehem, and that after the flight into Egypt they went back not to Bethlehem but to Nazareth. Luke has them living in Nazareth before going to Bethlehem for the birth of Jesus and then returning to Nazareth after the birth. Nazareth and Bethlehem are nearly eighty miles apart, which is quite a long walk.

When it comes to the main characters in the birth stories, there is complete agreement between Matthew and Luke about the names. Mary is the mother; Joseph is the putative father and Jesus is the name of the child. This agreement falls apart, however, in the genealogies. Matthew and Luke each take pains to establish the ancestry of Jesus, but they provide conflicting lists of ancestors. Only some of the names are the same, and the lists go in opposite directions, Luke going from Joseph into the past while Matthew goes towards Joseph from the past. But even though they do not tell the same story about Jesus's ancestors, both Matthew and Luke stress that Jesus is in the direct line of the royal house of the ancient kings of Israel, and that the great King David is his ancestor.

These lists of ancestors and the process of identifying Jesus through the genealogies are easily overlooked. They seem to be the most boring sections of the gospels, but there is more here than meets the eye. To understand anything about how the birth narratives are written this biblical Who's Who' is the real point of departure. All these 'begettings', as they are called in many biblical translations, are extremely important for Matthew and Luke. Buried within the lists of Jesus's forebears are great personalities and great stories, which establish Jesus's ancestral credentials, and which set the stage for the stories of his birth. So we begin with the begets.

II

Identification: The Women

According to Matthew, there need be no doubt at all about who's who in the story of Jesus. He goes straight to the point, setting out a detailed family tree, and because his gospel is placed first in the New Testament, these are the words that open the Christian section of the Bible.

> Roll of the genealogy of Jesus Christ, son of David, son of Abraham:
> Abraham fathered Isaac,
> Isaac fathered Jacob,
> Jacob fathered Judah and his brothers,
> Judah fathered Perez and Zerah, whose mother was Tamar, . . .
>
> *Matthew 1:1-3*

This is pretty tedious stuff, and there is much more. Both Matthew and Luke provide lengthy genealogies for Jesus. Matthew's is the longer, and the more prominent, and the more interesting of the two, because it contains several surprises. Because of these surprises and this prominence, any discussion of the genealogies in the birth narratives looks first of all to Matthew.

Matthew's genealogy takes up more than half of his first chapter; sixteen long verses describing forty-two generations. He traces the lineage of Jesus right back to Abraham in a dogged and determined way, providing a resounding roll-call of names both famous and infamous in the history of the people of Israel. Like all the other genealogies in the Bible this seems a mystifying exercise which is included in the text for reasons known only to the author with little or no meaning for a modern reader.

By Matthew's time, in the last quarter of the first century, many of the followers of the new Christian religion were sure that Jesus was the messiah, the holy one, the anointed of God who would soon come to redeem Israel and the whole world. This messiah was known from many writings in the Hebrew Scriptures, and whatever else was said about him, the messiah was above all defined as a son of the house of David. David is the man usually credited with founding the kingdom of Israel, some thousand years before the time of Jesus. It was David who had finally succeeded in bringing together the twelve disparate tribes of Israel, consolidating them into a nation and establishing a royal line of kings. Even though that line of kings had foundered long before the time of Jesus, to be of the house of David was still of great consequence. It meant to be of royal blood, and of a noble line of religious and political leaders. To validate the claims Christians were making about Jesus, Matthew knew that the first thing to do was to show that Jesus had descended directly from David.

In the late first century, to an audience of Christians who were mostly well grounded in the Hebrew Scriptures, and who could be expected to know the history of the kingdom of Israel, Matthew's list of the ancestors of Jesus made perfectly good sense. The names were those of well-known political and religious leaders whose exploits rang out in the history of the Jewish people. The list would have called to mind wonderful stories about the great and the good of the past. That was the purpose of a genealogy. Yet if that was the idea, Matthew seems to have slipped up a few times, particularly when it comes to the women.

Some five generations into the genealogy Matthew mentions a woman for the first time. In itself that is notable because such biblical lists do not often mention women. In most genealogies in the

Hebrew Scriptures, the impression is given that no women are involved in the generational process at all. But Matthew mentions four women in a list that names some forty-two men.

The first woman is Tamar whose story is found in the thirty-eighth chapter of Genesis. This is the first book in the Hebrew Scriptures, and it is also the first book of the Jewish Torah or Law, and the first book in the Christian Bible. Tamar's story is an ancient one, which can be traced back at least as far as 1700 BCE, and the writing of this part of the book of Genesis could well date back to 950 BCE.[1]

Tamar makes her first appearance when she marries:

> Judah took a wife for his first-born Er, and her name was Tamar. But Er, Judah's first-born, offended Yahweh, and Yahweh killed him.[2]
>
> *Genesis 38:6-7*

This is a rough start for Tamar but worse is yet to come. Tribal custom required that a widow must be taken as wife by one of the deceased's brothers. Er had a brother called Onan.

> ...Judah said to Onan, 'Take your brother's wife, and do your duty as her brother-in-law, to maintain your brother's line.' But Onan, knowing that the line would not count as his, spilt his seed on the ground every time he slept with his brother's wife, to avoid providing offspring for his brother. What he did was offensive to Yahweh, who killed him too.
>
> *Genesis 38:8-10*

So Tamar is twice widowed, and still childless. In the eyes of the world she has failed to carry on the line of Er, the son of Judah. Judah, her father-in-law, sends her back to her own father's tents, quieting her objections by telling her she will have to wait only till

1 See Introduction, p. XII, on the dating of the Hebrew Scriptures.
2 Yahweh, or Jehovah, is one of the many names in the Hebrew Scriptures that means God. Others include El, Elohim, Shaddai, Adonai, and Yahweh Sabaoth. See Exodus 6:2-4 where Yahweh explains his name to Moses; see also NJB, pp. 8-9, 85n.

his younger son Shelah is old enough for her. Judah was a man of great power and authority; the leader of one of the twelve tribes of Israel. Tamar obeys Judah, and goes back to her father for 'a long time', and seems to have been quietly forgotten, at least by the men of the family. Shelah grows to manhood, but Tamar remains a childless widow, deprived of her right to bear children of the line of Judah. She is not happy about this. One day she hears that Judah is coming to a nearby place called Timnah for the sheep shearing, and she decides to take charge. She changes out of her widow's clothes, disguises herself with a veil, and sets out to intercept her father-in-law:

> Judah, seeing her, took her for a prostitute, since her face was veiled. Going up to her on the road, he said. 'Here, let me sleep with you.' He did not know that she was his daughter-in-law. 'What will you give me for sleeping with you?' she asked. 'I will send you a kid from the flock,' he said. 'Agreed, if you will give me a pledge until you send it,' she replied. 'What pledge shall I give you?' he asked. 'Your seal and cord and the staff you are holding,' she replied.
>
> *Genesis 38:15-18*

The transaction is completed and in due course Judah sends a friend around with the kid, expecting to retrieve his pledges. Meanwhile Tamar has resumed her ordinary clothes and her role as widow. The prostitute has vanished and the pledges with her. Inquiries made by Judah and his friend lead nowhere. Tamar waits.

> About three months later, Judah was told, 'Your daughter-in-law has played the harlot; furthermore, she is pregnant, as a result of her misconduct.' 'Bring her out,' Judah ordered, and let her be burnt alive!' But as she was being led off, she sent word to her father-in-law, 'It is the owner of these who made me pregnant. Please verify', she said, 'whose seal and cord and staff these are.'

Judah recognized them and said, 'She was right and I was wrong, since I did not give her to my son Shelah.'

Genesis 38:26

From this encounter Tamar bears twin sons, Perez and Zerah, who in turn carry on the tribal line. Hundreds of years later, in the book of Ruth, the family of Tamar is praised and held up as an example.

'...may your family be like the family of Perez, whom Tamar bore to Judah.'

Ruth 4:12

Several generations beyond Tamar, Ruth herself appears in Matthew's list of Jesus's ancestors. Obed whose mother was Ruth' is the entry, and behind this stands another story. Ruth is famous in the Hebrew Scriptures, which include a short book of her biography in her own name.

The background to Ruth's story is that a Jewish family with two sons moves to the Gentile region of Moab. The sons grow up in this region, and when the time comes they marry local women. After about ten years the father and the two sons all die, leaving behind the mother, Naomi, and the two gentile daughters-in-law, one of whom is Ruth. Naomi decides to go back to the land of Judah, but she urges the two younger women to stay in their native Moab. One of them agrees to remain; the other insists on going with Naomi:

But Ruth said, 'Do not press me to leave you and to stop going with you, for
   wherever you go, I shall go,
   wherever you live, I shall live.
   Your people will be my people,
   and your God will be my God.
   Where you die, I shall die
   and there I shall be buried.
   Let Yahweh bring unnameable ills on me
   and worse ills, too,

> if anything but death
> should part me from you!'
>
> *Ruth 1:16-17*

When Ruth and Naomi reach the land of Judah they arrive in Bethlehem at the time of the barley harvest. They are destitute. Ruth goes gleaning in the fields of Boaz, a wealthy relative of the father of her dead husband. Boaz notices her and tells the reapers to let some of the grain fall so Ruth can glean it more easily. She continues to glean in the fields till the harvest is over. Then there is a celebration of the harvest, and afterwards everyone goes to sleep in the field. Ruth lies down at the feet of Boaz:

> In the middle of the night, he woke up with a shock and looked about him; and there lying at his feet was a woman. Who are you?' he said; and she replied, 'I am your servant Ruth. Spread the skirt of your cloak over your servant for you have the right of redemption over me.' 'May Yahweh bless you, daughter,' he said, 'for this second act of faithful love of yours is greater than the first, . . .'
>
> *Ruth 3:8-10*

The rest is history. According to Matthew's genealogy, Ruth was the great-grandmother of David, so it is not hard to understand why Matthew mentions her.

It is much harder to see any reason for the next woman on Matthew's list. She appears more obliquely: 'Solomon, whose mother had been Uriah's wife'. The name of Uriah's wife was Bathsheba, and her story was a national scandal in Israel.

> It happened towards evening when David had got up from resting and was strolling on the palace roof, that from the roof he saw a woman bathing; the woman was very beautiful. David made inquiries about this woman and was told, 'Why, that is Bathsheba daughter of Eliam and wife of Uriah the Hittite.' David then sent messengers to fetch her . . .
>
> *2 Samuel 11:2-4*

Uriah the Hittite is away at the wars, and Bathsheba is soon pregnant with David's child. To get rid of the unwanted husband, King David arranges for Uriah to be killed in battle. The only trouble is that a prophet called Nathan hears about all these goings-on, and he is outraged. He confronts David, pronouncing God's judgment on the king for the disgrace he has brought upon his nation:

> Yahweh, God of Israel, says this,
> "I annointed you king of Israel, I saved you from Saul's clutches, I gave you your master's household and your master's wives into your arms, I gave you the House of Israel and the House of Judah; and, if this is still too little, I shall give you other things as well. Why did you show contempt for Yahweh, by doing what displeases him? You put Uriah the Hittite to the sword, you took his wife to be your wife, causing his death by the sowrd of the Ammonites. For this, your household will never be free of the sword, since you showed contempt for me and took the wife of Uriah the Hittite, to make her your wife."
> *2 Samuel 12:7-10*

The first child of David and Bathsheba dies, but in time the wrath of Yahweh is appeased, and their next child becomes the wise and great King Solomon. This story of David and Bathsheba has inspired many artists, but it is not a story the ancient Jewish people were proud of. It showed the great King David in a bad light and it had been kept reasonably quiet for the best part of ten centuries. It is odd that Matthew draws attention to the story by referring to Bathsheba in the list of Jesus's ancestors.

But this is not all. There is one more woman on the list: Rahab, mother of Boaz. Like her daughter-in-law Ruth, Rahab was a Gentile, and, even worse, she was a prostitute. Hers is another name that resonates in the Hebrew Scriptures. She lived in the city of Jericho during a time when the Israelites led by Joshua were infiltrating the land of Canaan.

> From Shittim, Joshua son of Nun secretly sent two men to reconnoitre. He said, 'Go and explore the country and Jeri-

cho.' They left; they went into the house of a prostitute called Rahab, to spend the night there. The king of Jericho was told.' Some men have come here tonight from the Israelites, to reconnoitre the country.' The king of Jericho then sent a message to Rahab, 'Send out the men who came to you and are lodging in your house, for they have come to reconnoitre the whole country.' But the woman took the two men and hid them.

Joshua 2:1-4

Rahab hides the two men on the roof under a pile of flax stalks, and sends the king's soldiers chasing across the country looking for them. She then lowers the men from her window by a rope, and tells them to make for the hills, where they will be safe. Later the Israelites spare Rahab and all her house when the city is conquered and pillaged. She ties a scarlet cord to her window as a sign and by this the soldiers know who she is and do her no harm. Rahab goes on to marry an Israelite called Salmon and she becomes a thoroughly respectable matron and the mother of Boaz.

Rahab and Ruth, Bathsheba and Tamar are all famous mothers in Israel, and they are all remarkable women. They each contribute to the line of David in courageous, as well as outrageous ways. Two of them, the two gentiles Ruth and Rahab were the great-, and the great-great-grandmothers of David, but even this distinction does not really explain why Matthew took the unusual step of naming them in his list. There had been, after all, many outstanding women in the history of Israel who had never been named in any genealogies.

One of the more succinct comments on the place of the women in Matthew's genealogy comes not in a considered scholarly argument, of which there are many on the subject, but in a poem written by Michael Goulder, which he includes in his book on Matthew. It sums up the arguments as well as any other commentary could:

Exceedingly odd is the means by which God
Has provided our path to the heavenly shore —
Of the girls from whose line the true light was to shine
There was one an adulteress, one was a whore:

There was Tamar who bore-what we all should deplore—
A fine pair of twins to her father-in-law,
And Rahab the harlot, her sins were as scarlet,
As red as the thread that she hung from the door;
Yet alone of her nation she came to salvation
And lived to be mother of Boaz of yore —
And he married Ruth, a Gentile uncouth,
In a manner quite counter to biblical lore:
And of her there did spring blessed David the King,
Who walked on his palace one evening and saw
The wife of Uriah, from whom he did sire
A baby that died-oh, and princes a score:
And a mother unmarried it was too that carried
God's Son, and him laid in a manger of straw,
That the moral might wait at the heavenly gate
While the sinners and publicans go in before,
Who have not earned their place, but received it by grace,
And have found them a righteousness not of the law.[3]

At the end of Matthew's genealogy there is a fifth woman. Like the four other women, her virtue has been questioned, and her story has given rise to much controversy. Like the four other women, her name is outstanding in the genealogy, even though it is nearly buried in a ponderous list of male names. Matthew could have avoided mentioning the first four women in the genealogy if he had wished, but they do help to introduce this fifth woman, and Matthew had no choice but to include her. Her name is Mary:

After the deportation to Babylon:
    Jechoniah fathered Shealtiel,
    Shealtiel fathered Zerubbabel,
    Zerubbabel father Abiud,
    Abiud fathered Eliakim,
    Eliakim fathered Azor,
    Azor fathered Zadok,
    Zadok fathered Achim,

3 Quoted in *Goulder* (1974), p. 232.

Achim fathered Eliud,
Eliud fathered Eleazar,
Eleazar fathered Matthan,
Mattham fathered Jacob;
and Jacob fathered Joseph the husband of Mary;
of her was born Jesus, who is called Christ.
Matthew 1:12-16

III

Identification:
The Men

Matthew's Men

...and Jacob fathered Joseph, the husband of Mary;
of her was born Jesus who is called Christ.

The sum of generations is therefore: fourteen from
Abraham to David; fourteen from David to the Babylonian deportation; and fourteen from the Babylonian deportation to Christ.

Matthew 1:16-17

Right to the very end, Matthew's genealogy is systematic and highly
organized. He runs through the forty-two generations of Jesus's
predecessors in a businesslike fashion, not pausing to explain anything about all the unpronounceable names rolling past. In his time
no explanations were necessary. The names and the stories behind
the names were easily identifiable. The genealogy was a kind of
shorthand, each name coded with its own vivid history. The four
women stand out among the names; their stories are unexpected and
highly memorable. It is the same with many of the men.

Once he has run through all the generations, in verse 16 of his first chapter, Matthew explains the system he has been following, and this system is helpful in understanding who's who among the men. Matthew outlines three periods of the history of Israel, the first from the greatest patriarch to the greatest king, the next from the greatest king to the time of the great exile in Babylon, and the third from the time of the exile to the birth of Jesus.

The first section of the genealogy starts with Abraham. Abraham is the leading patriarch of three major world religions. Jews, Christians and Muslims all claim to be children of Abraham and acknowledge him as one of the greatest of their leaders. All three of these religions rely on the Hebrew Scriptures for their primary information about Abraham. The chief source is the book of Genesis and, in Genesis, Abraham is always having visions.

Abraham lived some years before Hammurabi, the great-law-giver of the first Babylonian Empire. The usual date suggested is about 1850 BCE, very near the edge of recorded history. His family is said to have come from Ur of the Chaldaeans and to have settled in Haran, a long way from Ur, up the one of the tributaries of the Euphrates river. In Chapter 12 of Genesis, Abraham has a conversation with Yahweh in which he is told to leave Haran in favour of 'a country which I shall show you' where 'I shall make you a great nation'. The Genesis text makes it clear that Abraham and his people lived in tents and migrated with their herds. They headed for this promised land, a country they called Canaan, which today is usually called Palestine, a land still claimed by competing groups of people, all of whom say they are children of Abraham.

In the saga of Abraham and Sarah his wife, they start out with different names. They are called Abram and Sarai until they change their names in response to one of Abram's visions. These visions are troubling, because Abram and Sarai are repeatedly promised a great number of descendants, but they are getting old and have no children:

Some time later, the word of Yahweh came to Abram in a vision:
Do not be afraid, Abram!
I am your shield

and shall give you a very great reward.

'Lord Yahweh,' Abram replied, 'what use are your gifts, as I am going on my way childless? . . . Since you have given me no offspring,' Abram continued, 'a member of my household will be my heir.' Then Yahweh's word came to him in reply, 'Such a one will not be your heir; no, your heir will be the issue of your own body.' Then taking him outside, he said, 'Look up at the sky and count the stars if you can. Just so will your descendants be,' he told him.

Genesis 15:1-5

Sarah is past the age of childbearing when she has a son called Isaac, the second name in Matthew's list. Later, they nearly lose Isaac because Abraham is sure that his god, like all the others in the neighbourhood, requires the first born to be sacrificed. As he reaches for the knife to kill Isaac, a voice speaks:

> . . . the angel of Yahweh called to him from heaven. 'Abraham, Abraham!' he said. 'Here I am', he replied. 'Do not raise your hand against the boy,' the angel said. 'Do not harm him, for now I know you fear God. You have not refused me your own beloved son.' Then looking up, Abraham saw a ram caught by its horns in a bush. Abraham took the ram and offered it as a burnt offering in place of his son.

Genesis 22:11-13

The new dynasty is saved, and from then on the children of Abraham are different from their neighbours because, despite some backslidings, they reject human sacrifice. Having been spared this untimely end, Isaac goes on to father Jacob. Jacob, like his grandfather, changes his name:

> God said to him, 'Your name is Jacob, but from now on you will be called not Jacob, but Israel.' Thus he came by the name Israel. God said to him, 'I am El-Shaddai. Be fruitful and multiply. A nation, indeed an assembly of nations, will descend from you, and kings will issue from your loins.'

Genesis 35:10-11

So Jacob becomes Israel. His twelve sons become the patriarchs of the twelve tribes that eventually merge to form the kingdom of Israel. One of these sons is Judah, the father-in-law of Tamar, and Judah is a name central to the genealogy, because the line of Judah becomes the most influential of the twelve patriarchal lines. Most of the early parts of the scriptures were recorded by scribes of what are usually known as the prophetic schools of Judah. This means that nearly all of the record keeping of ancient Israel that has survived favours the descendants of Judah.

As Matthew's genealogy shows, many generations passed before a successful king emerged for the tribes of Israel. The kingdom of Israel was finally formed shortly before 1000 BCE. It lasted only two generations, then there was a rebellion and the kingdom split in two. The larger part in the north was called Israel, the smaller southern part which included Jerusalem was called Judah because it included the territory that long before had been assigned to the patriarch Judah. These 'divided kingdoms' lasted until the year 720 BCE when the Assyrians conquered the northern kingdom. The kingdom of Judah to the south struggled on until it was conquered by the neo-Babylonian Empire in 587 BCE. The land of the kingdom of Judah was known as Judaea; today the religion is called Judaism and the people are called Jews. All these names are derived from Judah.

The first successful king of the original, unified kingdom of Israel was David. David heads the second section of Matthew's genealogy. He was chosen to be king by Samuel, the seer or prophet, who was deputed by Yahweh to find the new king: 'Fill your horn with oil and go. I am sending you to Jesse of Bethlehem, for I have found myself a king from among his sons.' Samuel did as he was told, and went to Bethlehem complete with a heifer. Once there he arranged a sacrifice to Yahweh, and he invited Jesse and his sons to the feast. He interviewed each of the sons in turn, and rejected seven of them:

> He then asked Jesse, 'Are these all the sons you have?' Jesse replied, 'There is still one left, the youngest; he is looking after the sheep.' Samuel then said to Jesse, 'Send for him, for

1 For the story of David and Bathsheba, see chapter 2, pp. 15-16.

we shall not sit down to eat until he arrives.' Jesse had him sent for; he had ruddy cheeks, with fine eyes and an attractive appearance. Yahweh said, 'Get up and anoint him: he is the one!'

At this, Samuel took the horn of oil and anointed him, surrounded by his brothers; and the spirit of Yahweh seized on David from that day onwards.

1 Samuel 16:11-13

David goes on to enjoy an illustrious career. He starts by slaying Goliath the giant, and ends by ruling the twelve tribes of Israel. His reign lasted for forty years and by the time of his death his small kingdom was a power to be reckoned with. This is a period of Israelite history always recalled with great pride.

Matthew's third section of genealogy starts with a man called Jechoniah. Abraham and David are reasonably familiar names, but Jechoniah enjoys no such fame. Yet he is given first place in one of Matthew's three historical sections and, so far, these sections have been anything but random. Abraham heads a list of the all-but-prehistoric patriarchs, and David heads a list of the kings of Israel and Judah. Abraham had established a religion and a people; David, a kingdom. Jechoniah did not establish anything, and by his time everything was going very wrong. First the united kingdom of Israel had split, then the northern part of the divided kingdom was destroyed by the Assyrians, and gradually the remaining southern kingdom of Judah started to fall apart. When the unfortunate Jechoniah appeared, the kingdom collapsed. There are even problems over the man's name. He started out as Eliakim, and in different places in the text he can appear as Jehoiakim, Jechoniah, or Coniah; and with even more variations of spelling. These indignities stem from his status as a puppet of the superpowers of the day: Pharaoh Necho of Egypt, and King Nebuchadnezzar of Babylon.

Pharaoh Necho then made Eliakim son of Josiah king in succession to Josiah his father, and changed his name to Jehoiakim.

2 Kings 23:34

Jehoiachin was eighteen years old when he came to the throne, and he reigned for three months and ten days in Jerusalem. He did what is displeasing to Yahweh. At the turn of the year, King Nebuchadnezzar sent for him and had him taken to Babylon, with the valuables belonging to the Temple of Yahweh, . . .

2 Chronicles 36:9-10

The keeping of records and telling of stories about the kings of Judah degenerated with the failure of the kingdom. In his genealogy Matthew seems to follow and to amend a revisionist history called Chronicles which was compiled over a period of many years, starting around 350 BCE. An earlier and equally revisionist version of the history of the kings of Judah is found in the books called Kings.[2]

Jechoniah is not quite the last of the kings of Judah, but the others are all eaten up by the superpowers, and Matthew pays them no attention. He does mention Jechoniah's son Shealtiel, but only because Shealtiel fathered one Zerubbabel. Zerubbabel is renowned for his achievements in Jerusalem seventy years after it had been conquered and destroyed by King Nebuchadnezzar of Babylon. In some accounts Zerubbabel is mentioned as governor of Judaea under the Babylonian empire, while in others he is associated with the rebuilding and resettling of Jerusalem after the Babylonian exile. There is one anecdote that shows him as a leader of great courage. The Jews who had been deported to Babylon were coming back to Jerusalem and trying to resettle in the face of heavy local opposition:

Then Jeshua son of Jozadak, with his brother priests, and Zerubbabel son of Shealtiel, with his brothers, set about rebuilding the altar of the God of Israel, to offer burnt offerings on it as prescribed in the Law of Moses, man of God. They erected the altar on its old site, despite their fear of the people of the country, and on it they presented burnt offerings to Yahweh, burnt offerings morning and evening:

Ezra 3:2-3

2 For further discussion of the books of Kings and Chronicles, see chapter 11, pp. 150-155.

In the latter part of Matthew's genealogy he moves from a list of kings into a list of priests by way of Jechoniah/Jehoiakim. By the time Zerubbabel appears, the list has entered priestly ranks. The line of kings has ended. After the events of 587 BCE when Nebuchadnezzar destroyed Jerusalem, the kingdom was effectively finished. There was a brief period of near independence about 160 BCE, and in our own time since 1948 CE the state of Israel has been established, but there have been no more kings. In Matthew's time, except for the Herods who did not count because they were agents of the occupying Romans, it was possible to see nothing but a line of ruling priests for the past five hundred years in what had once been the kingdom of Judah. These ruling priests held and exercised varying degrees of political power, but they were generally just the agents of occupying forces. Ruling priests in puppet regimes make dreary history, and they do not provide much for a genealogist to record with pride. In Matthew's list there is one priestly exception, and that is Matthan.

Matthan is likely an abbreviation of Mattathias, and Mattathias was a priest about the year 170 BCE. By that time the Greeks were occupying Judaea and the Greek king was trying systematically to suppress the Jews. At first, Mattathias left Jerusalem to avoid trouble, but trouble followed him to a place called Modein where the Greek army found him and ordered him to sacrifice to the Greek gods:

> The king's commissioners who were enforcing the apostasy came to the town of Modein for the sacrifices. Many Israelites gathered round them, but Mattathias and his sons drew apart. The king's commissioners then addressed Mattathias as follows: 'You are a respected leader, a great man in this town; you have sons and brothers to support you. Be the first to step forward and conform to the king's decree, as all nations have done, and the leaders of Judah and the survivors in Jerusalem; you and your sons shall be reckoned among the Friends of the King, you and your sons will be honoured with gold and silver and many presents.'
> Raising his voice, Mattathias retorted: 'Even if every nation living in the king's dominions obeys him, each forsaking its

ancestral religion to conform to his decrees, I, my sons and my brothers will still follow the covenant of our ancestors. May Heaven preserve us from forsaking the Law and its observances. As for the king's orders, we will not follow them: we shall not swerve from our own religion either to right or to left.' As he finished speaking, a Jew came forward in the sight of all to offer sacrifice on the altar in Modein as the royal edict required. When Mattathias saw this, he was fired with zeal; stirred to the depth of his being, he gave vent to his legitimate anger, threw himself on the man and slaughtered him on the altar. At the same time he killed the king's commissioner who was there to enforce the sacrifice, and tore down the altar.

1 Maccabees 2:15-25[3]

This scene was the start of the Maccabean revolt which lasted many years and gave the Jewish people their only period of anything approaching independent statehood between the years 587 BCE and 1948 CE. This rebellion was still a vivid folk memory at the time of Matthew.

There is one problem with Matthew's genealogy that cannot be overlooked, and that is the arithmetic of the three sections. Matthew is very emphatic about there being three sections of fourteen generations each, but this is simply not the case. Matthew seems to have miscounted, and what he really provides is two groups of fourteen generations, and one of thirteen generations. A lot of speculation has centred around this, much of it based on very loose theories about the importance of the numerology involved. The mysterious nature of numbers has compelled and fascinated people throughout recorded history and it continues to do so, but the numerological analysis that has been focused on Matthew's lists of generations has not yielded anything of substance. In Raymond Brown's authoritative study of the birth narratives, *The Birth of the Messiah*, he offers an exhaustive study of the text, but when he comes to discuss Matthew's numbering, in a chapter entitled 'Could

---

3 The books of the Maccabees are only found in Bibles which contain the Apocrypha.

Matthew Count?' he considers all the complex arguments and concludes rather reproachfully:

> With ingenuity, one can salvage Matthew's reputation as a mathematician. But from the viewpoint of a modern reader he certainly could have been of more assistance in clarifying the 3 x 14 pattern of generations that he claims...[4]

It is not until verse 16 of chapter 1 that Matthew's genealogy finally leaves the ranks of patriarchs, kings and priests, and arrives at Joseph:

> Matthan fathered Jacob;
> and Jacob fathered Joseph the husband of Mary;
> of her was born Jesus who is called Christ.
>
> *Matthew 1:15-16*

Matthew here moves away from the normal wording of a genealogy. He does not present Joseph as the natural father of Jesus; nowhere does he claim that Joseph actually sired Jesus. This gives rise to some very puzzling questions. If Joseph is not the father of Jesus, why bother with the long genealogy that sets out to show that Jesus is of the line of David through Joseph? A great many scholars have spent a great deal of time trying to understand this from a legal point of view. Many would argue that legally Joseph was the father of Jesus because of his marriage to Mary and his acceptance of the child. Thus, with Joseph as his legal father, Jesus would be of the house of David, even though Joseph was not his natural father. Other scholars are less than happy with this argument, and fragments of early documents feed this debate. Geza Vermes is an eminent historian of the period, and he has done extensive research into the Jewish ancestry of Jesus. In his book *Jesus the Jew* he discusses the final verse of Matthew's genealogy in detail, explaining that there are different early Greek and Latin versions of this passage. He also mentions an old Syriac gospel found in a monastery on Mount Sinai which gives the following version of Matthew 1:16:

4 *Brown* (1979), p. 219.

...Mattan begot Jacob, and Jacob begot Joseph. Joseph, to whom was betrothed Mary, the virgin, begot Jesus who is called the Messiah.[5]

The different versions of this final verse of the genealogy give rise to a very lively debate about the paternity of Jesus. This debate is unlikely to be resolved easily or to go away quickly.[6]

Luke's Men

Luke writes a very different genealogy. He starts with Joseph and goes back in time all the way to Adam, the first man in the Hebrew Scriptures, whom Luke calls son of God'. He mentions no women at all, and the list of male names is substantially different from Matthew's. The two gospels do have some names in common in their lists, like the great patriarchs of Israel, and some of the personalities mentioned above, including Shealtiel and Zerubbabel and Jesse and Boaz, but between the last two sections of Matthew's genealogy and Luke's corresponding list, they have only two names in common.[7]

The two genealogies are completely at odds about the immediate forebears of Joseph. Luke says this:

When he began, Jesus was about thirty years old, being the son, as it was thought, of Joseph son of Heli, son of Matthat, son of Levi, . . .

Luke 3:23-24

The father and grandfathers of Joseph named here are entirely different from those in Matthew's list, but in both versions these men are in a line of priests. Priests were very influential at the time of Matthew and Luke, and many priestly names figure in both genealo-

5 Quoted and discussed in *Vermes* (1973), pp. 215-17.
6 For further discussion of this passage and the debate it gives to, see chapter 5, p.61.
7 For further discussion of the relationship of the two genealogies, see NJB , p. 1609. It is worth remembering that Luke may be using some of the same names as Matthew, but with different spellings.

gies. By naming Heli, or Eli, as the name is frequently written, Luke is drawing in one of the key priestly figures in the scriptures. Joseph's father may or may not have been a priest of that name; what is important here is that Eli is a prototype of priests, his is an old and honourable name that carries authority and recalls a famous story. The original Eli appears in the story of the prophet Samuel:

> Now, the boy Samuel was serving Yahweh in the presence of Eli; in those days it was rare for Yahweh to speak; visions were uncommon. One day, it happened that Eli was lying down in his room. His eyes were beginning to grow dim; he could no longer see. The lamp of God had not yet gone out, and Samuel was lying in Yahweh's sanctuary, where the ark of God was, when Yahweh called, Samuel! Samuel!' He answered, 'Here I am', and, running to Eli, he said, 'Here I am, as you called me.' Eli said, 'I did not call. Go back and lie down.' So he went and lay down. And again Yahweh called, 'Samuel! Samuel!' He got up and went to Eli and said, 'Here I am as you called me.' He replied, 'I did not call, my son, go back and lie down.' As yet Samuel had no knowledge of Yahweh and the word of Yahweh had not yet been revealed to him. Again Yahweh called, the third time. He got up and went to Eli and said, 'Here I am as you called me.' Eli then understood that Yahweh was calling the child, and he said to Samuel, 'Go and lie down, and if someone calls say "Speak, Yahweh; for your servant is listening."' So Samuel went and lay down in his place.
>
> *1 Samuel 3:1-9*

Through mentioning a priest called Eli, Luke alludes to this story of the wise and famous priest, and of the young boy who will become a great seer and prophet in Israel. Prophets are very influential figures in the Hebrew Scriptures, and several prophets appear in Luke's genealogy. The greatest among them is Amos, whose name is given to one of the earliest prophetic books in the Bible. He was an orchardist and shepherd who lived in the southern kingdom of Judah, in the hill country towards the Dead Sea from Jerusalem. This was around 750 BCE, a time of prosperity in the northern kingdom of Israel, and Amos went north to prophesy at the sanctuary called Bethel, which was across the border between the kingdoms. No one there cared for what he said:

> Amaziah the priest of Bethel then sent word to Jeroboam king of Israel as follows, 'Amos is plotting against you in the heart of the House of Israel; the country cannot tolerate his speeches. For this is what Amos says. "Jeroboam is going to die by the sword, and Israel will go into captivity far from its native land."' To Amos himself Amaziah said, 'Go away, seer, take yourself off to Judah, earn your living there, and there you can prophesy! But never again will you prophesy at Bethel, for this is a royal sanctuary, a national temple.' 'I am not a prophet,' Amos replied to Amaziah, 'nor do I belong to a prophetic brotherhood. I am merely a herdsman and dresser of sycamore-figs. But Yahweh took me as I followed the flock, and Yahweh said to me, "Go and prophesy to my people Israel."'
>
> *Amos 7:10-15*

Amos was right. He foresaw the downfall of the kingdom of Israel. He was a great, if rather gloomy, figure, an orchardist anyone would be proud to list in a family tree.

Still farther back in Luke's genealogy come the patriarchs. Like Matthew he has a sonorous list giving all the greatest names: Abraham, Isaac, Jacob and Judah, as well as many others not so well known. One that Luke alone mentions is Lamech. Lamech pre-dates even Abraham, which puts him just beyond the hazy limits of what can be called history. He makes only a brief appearance in the Hebrew Scriptures in a lyric which comes in the earliest section of the book of Genesis. Lamech had two wives, Adah and Zillah:

> Adah and Zillah, hear my voice,
> Wives of Lamech, listen to what I say:
> I killed a man for wounding me,
> a boy for striking me.

Sevenfold vengeance for Cain,
but seventy-sevenfold for Lamech.

Genesis 4:23-4

The importance of Lamech in Luke's list is his great antiquity. He links history with prehistory, and carries the genealogy back to the stories of Cain, and thence to Adam. Luke's final words in his genealogy, as he reaches farther and farther back in time, are 'son of Seth, son of Adam, son of God'.

In Matthew's genealogy, everyone on the list descends from Abraham; they are all acknowledged as children of Abraham. In Luke's genealogy, everyone on the list descends from God; they are all acknowledged as children of God. It could be argued that in this way Luke resolves the question of the paternity of Jesus with a certain finesse. This is entirely characteristic: Luke always writes with finesse. Immediately before he begins his version of the genealogy of Jesus, which comes at the end of his birth story, Luke tells of the baptism of the adult Jesus. The connections between the baptism and the genealogy are made very clear. Both passages stress the identity of Jesus, and his relationship with his God:

Now it happened that when all the people had been baptized and while Jesus after his own baptism was at prayer, heaven opened and the Holy Spirit descended on him in a physical form, like a dove. And a voice came from heaven, *'You are my Son; today I have fathered you.'*

Luke 3:21-22

IV

The Writers

One way of trying to understand the differences between the birth stories of Matthew and Luke is to try to
learn more about the two men credited with writing
these gospels, and about the world they inhabited. This is easier said
than done for in looking back over nineteen centuries, the available
evidence is at best imperfect. It is impossible to be absolutely certain
about Matthew and Luke. No one knows exactly who these men
were, or where they lived, or how they worked. Although absolute
certainties are hard to come by, the existing evidence about
Matthew and Luke does give rise to some very strong probabilities.
Most of the evidence is internal, from within the gospels themselves,
and it is open to widely different interpretations. It is also open to all
the problems of textual corruption.

There are no well-preserved first-century manuscripts of the
gospels handwritten by Matthew or by Luke. Instead, the earliest
texts of the gospels are a collection of crumbling, fragmentary bits of
papyrus or vellum which have turned up over many centuries, in various states of preservation. These early fragments, which continue
to be unearthed, date from as early as a generation or so after the time

of writing to three or four centuries later. Nothing that can claim to be an original document has survived. To complicate matters further, other hands were involved in the writing, not just the two men called Matthew and Luke. Scribes copied their stories and teachings, posibly adding editorial variations to what Matthew and Luke actually said and wrote and preached. Many scribes were involved in the copying of texts in the ancient world, often working in shifts, taking dictation from a reader. This process left a lot of room for error in the transmission of any text, and this is an inevitable feature of every form of ancient literature.

The earliest complete manuscript versions of the gospels are now preserved in the British Museum, the Louvre, and the Vatican. They are contained in large volumes called 'codices'. These codices are full editions of the Bible, dating from the fifth century CE. In the British Museum there are two of them; the Codex Siniaticus and the Codex Alexandrinus, side by side in a glass case. The gospels are extremely well preserved in these volumes, although by the fifth century they had been copied and recopied many times and inevitably had been affected by the copying process.

Despite all the alterations and corruptions that almost certainly affected the gospels as they were recorded and re-recorded, the personalities of Matthew and of Luke do emerge. Two entirely distinct minds can be seen at work in the two gospels, and two very different characters. They are influenced by different educational traditions and they express themselves in entirely different styles. Matthew's gospel speaks with a stern voice, stressing law and authority, wasting no time on frivolous or colourful detail. Luke's gospel is the work of a great storyteller, providing both detail and colour. He speaks with a gentler voice than Matthew. When the two gospels tell the same stories about Jesus, as they often do, the tone of these stories is never the same. The parable of the lost sheep is a good example. Matthew says:

> 'Tell me. Suppose a man has a hundred sheep and one of
> them strays; will he not leave the ninety-nine on the hillside
> and go in search of the stray? In truth I tell you, if he finds it,
> it gives him more joy than do the ninety-nine that did not

stray at all. Similarly it is never the will of your Father in heaven that one of these little ones should be lost.'

Matthew 18:12-14

Luke says:

> 'Which one of you with a hundred sheep, if he lost one, would fail to leave the ninety-nine in the desert and go after the missing one till he found it? And when he found it, would he not joyfully take it on his shoulders and then, when he got home, call together his friends and neighbours saying to them, "Rejoice with me, I have found my sheep that was lost." In the same way, I tell you, there will be more rejoicing in heaven over one sinner repenting than over ninety-nine upright people who have no need of repentance.'

Luke 15:4-7

It is entirely typical of Luke that the shepherd would lift the lost sheep on to his shoulder, and share his joy so openly with his friends and neighbours. Matthew's story is essentially the same but it lacks the kindly, personal touch of Luke's version. Throughout their gospels, this same type of comparison can be made. It is no accident that in the birth stories Luke has the angel choirs, and the songs of joy, and the memorable description of the birth in a manger, while Matthew emphasizes legal lineage, and warning dreams, and political plots.

Like all forms of literature the gospels reflect not only the personalities of the writers, but the world around them. They are the products of particular environments, containing the stories that were told and the message that was preached by the leaders of early Christian congregations. Matthew and Luke were writing for different sorts of people, at different times, and in different places. Their congregations had specific concerns and needs, and the gospels respond to and reflect these concerns and needs. A great deal can be understood about these early Christian congregations simply by reading the gospels carefully, for Matthew and Luke drop many hints in their texts about where they were writing, and for whom.

Interpreting these hints involves a certain amount of speculation, and it is a process subject to many different theories. None the less, the process of trying to decode the various clues that Matthew and Luke provide about their congregations and communities is worth the effort, because it helps to build a vivid picture of what was going on in the larger political and religious scene of the time. This brings the late first century to life, admittedly in a patchy and incomplete fashion, but also in a very vital way. This vitality, this sense of being in a real world, full of change and tension and excitement, is essential to understanding the gospels of Matthew and Luke.

First we turn to Matthew, and what is usually understood about Matthew. Most scholars agree that he was a Greek-speaking Jew, who wrote in the '80s from an area vaguely referred to as Syria, where he led a community of Christian converts, most of whom were Jews. He was probably a well-educated Jewish teacher. This means a synagogue teacher who received considerable training for the job, but who did not have the more extensive education of a rabbi. The type of synagogue in which he taught may well have been a dual-purpose building used for worship and as a teaching centre. Here reading and writing would be taught, the scriptures would be studied, and the writings of the law and the prophets of Israel would be discussed and debated.

The exact location of Matthew's community gives rise to a lot of scholarly discussion and a great many theories, none of them conclusive. To say he was in Syria is a very general statement, because 'Syria' could include anything from Damascus to Jerusalem. There is a strong possibility that Matthew's synagogue was in a town somewhere between what is now the Gaza Strip and Lebanon. One particularly interesting theory favours a town called Jamnia, which was west of Jerusalem, near the sea.[1]

Matthew's gospel was written ten to fifteen years after the destruction of Jerusalem. That destruction had taken place in August of the year 70 CE. It is not possible to understand the New Testament adequately without allowing for that terrible event in the history of the Jews. It was cataclysmic. It shaped the religious

1 See below, pp. 42–43.

history of both the Jews and the Christians, and exacerbated the already bitter divisions which continue to this day.

Most of the writings of the New Testament reveal undercurrents of the political unrest which was part of everyday life throughout the first century in Palestine. This unrest surrounds Jesus and all his reported activities. It was still going strong when the gospels were being written, fifty or sixty years after the death of Jesus. The unrest was centuries old. It had bled from one period of Jewish history into another, from one kind of political domination to another. From at least the time of Alexander the Great, who died in 323 BCE, the Jews had resented their Greek conquerors. There were frequent unsuccessful uprisings. The suppression that followed these uprisings bred further unrest until about two hundred years before Matthew's time, when a rebellion did, at last, succeed. This was the rebellion started by the priest Mattathias at Modein, which is chronicled in the books of the Maccabees.[2]

After the death of Mattathias his sons took over the leadership of what by then was a guerrilla campaign against the Greeks. The most famous son of Mattathias was the one called Judas Maccabeus. He was such a brilliant guerrilla fighter that when, in our century, the Jewish people rebelled against the British, one of their best guerilla leaders, Moshe Dayan, is rumoured to have used the books of the Maccabees as an inspiration for his campaign. In the days of Matthew and Luke, Judas Maccabeus was still a popular hero, and he provided just the sort of role model the Jews expected the long-awaited messiah to follow. 'Judas' and 'Jesus' are variant forms of the same name.

With this history of heroic unrest it is not too surprising that in the first century there was a major rebellion against the Romans, who had succeeded the Greeks as overlords of Palestine and of the Jews. It started in 67 CE, which is shortly after Mark wrote his gospel and twelve years or so before Matthew wrote his. At first the rebellion was surprisingly successful. The Jews held off the Romans, then the greatest military power of all time, for three years. The story of this war is told in the writings of Flavius Josephus, the

2 See chapter 3, p. 27.

first-century Jewish historian who was commissioned by the
Romans to write the history of the rebellion. Josephus' account of
the rebellion is compelling and terrible, especially near the end
when the fighting reached the temple itself:

> While the Temple was ablaze, the attackers plundered it,
> and countless people who were caught by them were
> slaughtered. There was no pity for age and no regard was
> accorded rank; children and old men, laymen and priests
> alike were butchered; every class was pursued and crushed
> in the grip of war, whether they cried out for mercy or
> offered resistance.
>
> The Temple Mount, everywhere enveloped in flames,
> seemed to be boiling over from its base, yet the blood
> seemed more abundant than the flames and the numbers of
> the slain greater than those of the slayers. The ground could
> not be seen anywhere between the corpses, the soldiers
> climbed over heaps of bodies as they chased the fugitives.[3]

In the end the Romans not only conquered Jerusalem, they
destroyed it. They levelled all the wonderful buildings, including
the enormous temple complex rebuilt by Herod the Great at the
beginning of the century. This destruction of the temple was a
crushing blow aimed at the Jewish people, a purposeful and wanton
sacrilege of the most holy place in Judaism. According to Josephus,
the Romans even levelled the land where the walls of the temple had
stood, and thereafter no Jew was allowed to live anywhere near the
site:

> There were no more victims for the army to kill or plunder,
> and no soul on which to vent their rage; for mercy would
> never have made them keep their hands off anyone as long
> as there was work to be done. Caesar consequently ordered
> them to raze the whole city and the Temple, leaving only

3 Book 6, chapter 5, verses 272, 276-7, *Josephus* (1982), p. 423.

the loftiest of the towers... and the stretch of wall enclosing the city on the west.

All the rest of the wall encircling the city was so completely levelled to the ground that no future visitors would believe it had once been inhabited. This, then, was the end to which the mad folly of revolutionaries brought Jerusalem, that magnificent city renowned throughout the world.[4]

The results of all this were devastating. There had been all the usual rapine, starvation, disease and death of wartime, but the destruction of the temple overshadowed it all. It was an event that was to shape the future of Judaism. The temple at Jerusalem was gone and with it the ancient tradition of regular daily sacrifice. Even more important, the temple had been the focus of an annual pilgrimage. Every year at Passover, Jews had flocked to the city to offer sacrifices at the temple. Their numbers were vast. Josephus provides the figure of 2.7 million pilgrims coming for the Passover of 67 CE, and even allowing for exaggeration, that is an extraordinary number of visitors. Jerusalem was made extremely wealthy and powerful by this religious tourist traffic to the temple. Now it was wiped off the face of the map. Judaism had to regroup, and re-form.

The destruction of Jerusalem also affected the emerging Jewish sect called Christians. All the evidence that has survived indicates that until the rebellion in 67 CE Christians tended to organize themselves in small groups within Jewish synagogues. This was so all over the Mediterranean world, not just in Palestine. Jews were dispersed at least as far as Babylon to the east and Spain to the west and so were their synagogues, many of them with Christian groups attached.

The Christian groups within the synagogues often made themselves very unpopular, by the age-old religious tendency of insisting they were right and everyone else was wrong. In the book of Acts, which was written by Luke, probably sometime around the year 80

4 Book 7, chapter 1, verses 1, 3–4, Josephus (1982), p. 454.

CE, he tells the story of Paul and Barnabas, and what had happened nearly a generation earlier when they preached at a synagogue in Antioch:

> The next Sabbath almost the whole town assembled to hear the word of God. When they saw the crowds, the Jews, filled with jealousy, used blasphemies to contradict everything Paul said. Then Paul and Barnabas spoke out fearlessly. 'We had to proclaim the word of God to you first, but since you have rejected it, since you do not think yourselves worthy of eternal life, here and now we turn to the gentiles.'
>
> *Acts 13:44-6*

Early Christian leaders like this must have been very irritating people to have around, preaching in the parent synagogue yet scorning its authorities, and declaring through their own interpretation of the Hebrew Scriptures that Jesus was the messiah. By the time the gospels were being written, such Christians were no longer at ease within the Jewish establishment, and they had come to expect, quite understandably, nothing but trouble from the authorities. This can be seen even in the earliest gospel:

> 'Be on your guard: you will be handed over to sanhedrins; you will be beaten in synagogues, and you will be brought before governors and kings for my sake, . . .'
>
> *Mark 13:9*

In the late 60s, as the rebellion against Rome gained strength, the sufferings and dislocations of the political situation became worse. At the same time the tensions between Jews and Christians grew much more marked and after the destruction of Jerusalem in 70 CE these tensions developed into serious divisions. The whole of Judaism had been rocked by the loss of the temple at Jerusalem and badly needed to re-establish some kind of equilibrium. It is hardly surprising that the unsettling beliefs and ideas of Christians were treated with hostility and often anger. The growing number of Christians came to be seen as a threat to the already beleaguered

Jewish authorities and a strong reaction against the Christians set in. By the time Matthew and Luke were writing, they perceived what was to them a persecution of Christians:

> 'Blessed are you when people abuse you and persecute you and speak all kinds of calumny against you falsely on my account. Rejoice and be glad, for your reward will be great in heaven; this is how they persecuted the prophets before you.'
>
> *Matthew 5:11*

> 'Blessed are you when people hate you, drive you out, abuse you, denounce your name as a criminal, on account of the Son of man. Rejoice when that day comes and dance for joy, look! — your reward will be great in heaven. This was the way their ancestors treated the prophets.'
>
> *Luke 6:22-3*

This process of turning against Christian groups in the synagogues probably began as a series of more or less isolated events, slowly becoming more widespread in the years 70 to 80 CE and later. All of the gospels refer in different ways to a growing rift between Christians and Jews. By the mid-nineties, John, in his gospel, could write:

> ... there were many who did believe in him, even among the leading men, but they did not admit it, because of the Pharisees and for fear of being banned from the synagogue: ...
>
> *John 12:42*

This refers to what was going on in Ephesus, probably some time before the writing of John's gospel.

As the dislocations between Christians and Jews became worse, the problem began to find formal expression among the Jewish authorities, when the rabbis and other representatives of the synagogues met in various councils. A school had been set up not long after the destruction of Jerusalem to try to undo some of the damage caused by the war. It was at the town called variously Jamnia, Jabneel or Jabneh. This town was near the sea and close to Jerusalem. It became the headquarters for many leading rabbis and teachers in the late first century. Around the year 85 CE the Jewish authorities at Jamnia issued what is known as the *Birkhath-ha-Minim*. This was a reformulated version of an existing prayer, one of the eighteen benedictions that were principal prayers in the synagogue at the time. In its new form this *Birkhath-ha-Minim* became a curse on all *minim*, or heretics, particularly Christians.

> For persecutors let there be no hope, and the dominion of arrogance do thou speedily root out in our days; and let Christians and minim perish in a moment, let them be blotted out of the book of the living and let them be not written with the righteous. Twelfth Benediction of the *Birkhath-ha-Minim*[5]

Matthew was probably writing before the publication of this curse against heretics, at a time when some Christians in some groups were being persecuted in a random way. Luke would have been writing some time after the curse had been circulated, perhaps before it had taken full effect.

The *Birkhath-ha-minim* was a way of dealing with an increasingly unmanageable problem. The early Christians were a substantial threat to the Jewish authorities, because their numbers were increasing rapidly, and they were becoming more insistent that Jesus was the messiah. The Jewish authorities could not share this belief, and could not ignore the growing Christian presence in their midst, so they banished the Christians from their congregations. It was the end of any kind of unity between Jews and Christians, and the formal beginning of a long and tragic history of strife.

This tragedy starts to play itself out just under the surface in the New Testament. It shows very clearly in Matthew's gospel and the way it is expressed reveals a great deal about both Matthew and the community he served. The time is right, for however one decides the date for Matthew's gospel it comes out somewhere around ten

5 Quoted in *Ellis* (1974), p. 5.

years after the fall of Jerusalem, not much earlier than 80 CE and not much later than 85 CE. This coincides with the date of the *Birkhath-ha-minim*, in so far as it can be determined. The place is also right, particularly when it is argued that Matthew's gospel comes from Jamnia.[6] Jamnia became the heart of Judaism after the destruction of the temple. This was where the rabbis set up a temporary headquarters, where they re-established their schools, and where they met for their councils. This would have been a very likely place to find a well-educated synagogue teacher such as Matthew. It is easy to understand what a scandal it would have been for the Jews if one of their teachers in this town had formally changed allegiance to become the leader of one of the first independent Christian churches. That church, if it had been in Jamnia, would naturally have had a difficult time with the Jewish authorities. There can be no certainty that Matthew's church was there, but such a reconstruction is plausible.[7]

Wherever Matthew's church was, there had been acute difficulties for the Christian congregation. It is abundantly clear that Matthew has an axe to grind with the Jewish authorities. This shows in his repeated and vehement denunciations of the scribes and the Pharisees and the priests for what he sees as their lack of understanding and their bad behaviour. Matthew has a sharp and legalistic mind, and he knows the Jewish law inside out. In his gospel he often indulges in lengthy, rather obscure debates about the law, debates in which the Jewish leaders are always shown in a bad light. A great many of the comments Matthew attributes to Jesus reveal Matthew's own preoccupations with the Jewish authorities.

This explains much of what we find in his birth story. Matthew is anxious to show that Christianity is the culmination of everything in the Hebrew Scriptures. This is why the genealogy is so carefully modelled on the Hebrew Scriptures and so definitively sets out the authority and the identity of Jesus. It also explains the careful way Matthew follows the pattern of the book of Genesis throughout his birth story, recalling stories of the great patriarchs and law-givers of Israel. A church just expelled from the synagogue could be

6 See *Ellis* (1974), pp. 5-6.
7 For accounts of Matthew's church, see *Goulder* (1974), pp. 8ff., and *Ellis* (1974), pp. 4-6.

expected to be even more careful than the parent synagogue in the reading and interpretation of the Hebrew Scriptures. These scriptures were read aloud regularly in synagogue, and this system of reading was carried over into the Christian church. Its leader would try to select what was needed from familiar readings to give support to the new religious beliefs. Matthew continually turns to the scriptures in this way.

But in all this, what of Luke? The gospels of Luke and Matthew emerge from very different sets of circumstances. Not for Luke the beleaguered, defensive world of Matthew, so dominated by the aftermath of the destruction of Jerusalem. Luke was writing later than Matthew, possibly by as much as ten years, and in every sense he is farther away from Jerusalem. His church is generally thought to have been Greek. This does not necessarily mean it was entirely gentile because there were many Greek speaking Jews, so it could have been a Greek speaking church bringing both Jews and gentiles together. It was probably situated either in Greece or in the south-western part of what is now Turkey.

Luke was not Jewish, but Greek. As the Greek leader of a church in Greece or Asia Minor, Luke would have been less pressured than Matthew by the weight of Jewish tradition. He is less inclined to discuss Jewish law than Matthew, and he invokes scriptural authority much less obviously. Yet Luke clearly knows the Hebrew Scriptures well, and he uses them brilliantly in telling his stories about Jesus. He frequently refers back to scriptural passages that strike him as suitable or helpful, alluding to them, quoting them, and building on them in his own stories. There are also indications that Luke was able to refer to Matthew's earlier gospel, and that he built on what he found there.

All of this is clear in Luke's birth stories. He follows Matthew's lead, but amends freely. The genealogy, so dominant in Matthew's gospel, is less imposing in Luke. There is no need in Luke's church to prove anything to the hostile Jewish authorities, least of all a lineage from David. So, as we saw in chapter 3, Luke creates a different, and much more accessible version of this genealogy. He extends the lineage of Jesus, taking it far beyond David all the way back to Adam and thence to God. That way, no one in the entire world is excluded, for anyone who so wishes can claim to be connected to Adam and to God.

What emerges most clearly in Luke's gospel is the voice of a poet, and this is manifest in his use of the Hebrew Scriptures.. Time and again he refers back to and echoes some of the most beautiful passages of poetry in the scriptures. Understanding how Luke does this is essential in understanding his birth stories. It is evident from the style and language of his writings that Luke was a highly educated Greek, steeped in Hellenistic traditions.[8] Like every other educated person of his time, Luke would have read the Hebrew Scriptures in the well-known Greek translation of the time. Unlike Matthew he would not have known the original Hebrew.

Matthew, on the other hand, knew the scriptures in two languages. As a trained Jewish teacher he knew the Hebrew text, and he sometimes quotes the scriptures from the original Hebrew. He also knew Greek and quotes from the Greek translation of the time.[9] Greek was the common language of educated people all around the Mediterranean, and the Hebrew Scriptures had been available in Greek for at least two centuries, reputedly ever since Ptolemy Philadelphus one of the Greek rulers of Egypt, had enabled the scriptures to be translated for his library at Alexandria.

This translation or collection of translations is known as the Septuagint, because it was supposed to have been made for Ptolemy, by seventy-two elders of the tribes of Israel. By this translation, more than by any other means, the spread of the scriptures was assured throughout the subsequent empires of the ancient world. In requesting that the translation be made, Ptolemy was making a magnanimous political gesture, showing goodwill to his subject people, the Jews. He was also ensuring, though he could not have realized it, the form in which the Hebrew Scriptures would eventually pass into Christian hands. Josephus records in detail how the translation into Greek began with a letter from Ptolemy to the high priest of the Jewish people:

King Ptolemy to Eleazar the high priest, sendeth greeting.
There are many Jews who now dwell in my kingdom,

---

8 See *Caird* (1963), p. 15.
9 For an example of Matthew quoting from the Greek, see chapter 5, pp. 49-53, the discussion of Isaiah 7:14; for his quoting of the Hebrew see chapter 7, pp. 92-93; the discussion of Hosea 11:1.

whom the Persians, when they were in power, carried captives. These were honoured by my father...and when I had taken the government, I treated all men with humanity, and especially those that are thy fellow citizens, of whom I have set free above a hundred thousand that were slaves...and as I am desirous to do what will be grateful to these, and to all the other Jews in the habitable earth, I have determined to procure an interpretation of your law, and to have it translated out of Hebrew into Greek, and to be deposited in my library. Thou wilt therefore do well to choose out and send to me men of a good character, who are now elders in age, and six in number out of every tribe. These, by their age, must be skillful in the laws, and of abilities to make an accurate interpretation of them; and when this is finished, I shall think that I have done a work glorious to myself.

Antiquities 12.2.5.[10]

Although Josephus's colourful version of how this translation came to be made is disputed by some scholars, this 'work glorious' of Ptolemy's was, after many years, successfully completed. The translation remains in use today as one of the oldest and most authoritative early texts of the scriptures.

By the time Matthew and Luke were writing, the use of the Hebrew Scriptures had been regulated and systematized by Jewish custom for centuries, during which time the body of the scriptures had been slowly growing. These scriptures were handled with reverence, even with awe, by Jewish congregations, and they were read every sabbath in the synagogue. In these scriptural readings the voices of the patriarchs and the prophets were heard, and the voice of God was revealed in their words. Here, in the scriptures, was where truth was to be found, and if any subject was in doubt, a diligent search of scripture was sure to reveal the truth of the matter. Because all truth was certain to be there, all that was needed was the ability to discover and to recognize it within the scriptures.

Matthew, the trained synagogue teacher, was born and bred in this system of reverent searching of scriptures. Luke, the sophisti-

10 *The Works of Flavius Josephus*, p. 247.

cated and erudite Greek leader of a church somewhere in Greece or Asia Minor, was strongly influenced by this attitude to scripture. In their birth stories, both gospel writers turn to the Hebrew Scriptures for help. They tell what they believe to be the truth about Jesus in a dense and complex framework of scriptural references. They mine the Hebrew Scriptures for detail, for colour and for affirmation of what they want to convey.

In the genealogies we saw how the recitation of great names gives access to a wealth of stories from the scriptures, and how these names and stories provide an aristocratic lineage for Jesus. Before moving on to see how Matthew and Luke use the scriptures in other ways, it is essential to look once more at this lineage of Jesus, and in particular to see where the lineage leads, to Mary and to Joseph.

V

The Parents

According to both Matthew and Luke, Mary is the mother of Jesus and at the time of his birth she is a virgin.

The explanation given is that Jesus is somehow conceived by the Holy Spirit, directly from God. Both gospels introduce Joseph of the house of David as the husband of Mary and the legal father of Jesus. Each gospel has stories to tell about these parents of Jesus. In Matthew's account Joseph has doubts about marrying Mary, doubts that are resolved by the intervention of an angel. Luke tells about Mary; her doubts, her eventual acceptance of her role, and her joy. Despite these best efforts of Matthew and Luke, the stories just do not say enough. They leave us wanting to know more.

This desire to know more about Mary and Joseph is at least in part a simple curiosity about the physical details of how Jesus came to be born. For many of us, the assertion of Mary's virginity defies belief. It is incredible. None the less this virginity of Mary has assumed great importance in some forms of Christianity, probably far greater than the gospel writers could have envisaged. To many Christians today Mary's virginity is an essential component of the religion by which they live, while to other equally sincere Christians the question is either unimportant, or a nonsense that makes their religion a laughing-stock. Meanwhile people outside or on the fringes of the Christian religion wonder if the whole issue can possibly be worth so much attention and anxiety.

It would be rash to pretend to decide such an issue here. The paternity of Jesus and the virginity of Mary have been debated for the best part of two thousand years and the debate looks set to continue now that so many Christians are coinciding with those of non-Christians. With this debate in mind it is valuable to look again, very carefully, at the gospel stories. It is also valuable to look beyond them, to see how the stories may have been influenced by the language and literature of their time. This reveals a great deal about the stories of Mary and Joseph, about how these stories were written, and about some of the problems inherent within them. The importance of reaching an absolute conclusion about the parentage of Jesus is debatable. The importance of trying to understand as much as possible about the material involved, is not.

> The Lord will give you a sign in any case:
>   It is this: the young woman is with child
>   and will give birth to a son
>   whom she will call Immanuel.
>
> *Isaiah 7:14*

Probably more than any other passage in the Bible, this passage from the book of Isaiah has a lot to answer for. It is quoted by Matthew in his birth story, but before seeing how Matthew uses Isaiah 7:14, it is worth seeing the passage in its original context. Isaiah was active from about 740 BCE to 698 BCE. He was a prophet, a seer and a political adviser to a succession of kings of Judah, and he had a habit of delivering sonorous and dramatic speeches to these kings and their people. In Isaiah 7:14 he is addressing one King Ahaz, who fears an imminent attack from a coalition of his neighbours, and Ahaz is terrified to the point that his heart and 'his people's hearts shook like forest trees shaking in the wind'. Isaiah tries to reassure Ahaz that the threat will soon pass. He does this by saying that a

young woman who is already pregnant will give birth to a son, and
before the son has grown up all will be well:

> On curds and honey will he feed
> until he knows how to refuse the bad
> and choose the good.
> Before the child knows how to refuse the bad and choose
> the good, the lands whose two kings are frightening you
> will be deserted.

Isaiah 7:15-16

In Isaiah 7:14, Isaiah is quoted as saying that the young woman is
with child and will give birth to a son'. The original political context
of this statement is long lost and it has become significant for other
reasons altogether, reasons that would probably astonish Isaiah.
This passage has presented a thorny problem to biblical translators
for hundreds of years. The extent of this problem becomes clear
when various translations are compared. The above quotation is
from the New Jerusalem Bible. What follows is from the Revised
Standard Version:

> Behold, a young woman shall conceive and bear a son and
> shall call his name Emmanuel.

Isaiah 7:14 [RSV]

The Revised Standard Version of the Bible appeared in 1952. It
is based on a late nineteenth-century translation called the Revised
Version, which was the first major translation of the Bible into
English for nearly three hundred years. It revised the renowned
King James version of 1611. In the last fifty years there has been an
outpouring of new translations in English, including the Revised
Standard Version, the New English Bible, Good News for Modern
Man, the New American Bible, the New International Version,
two versions of the Jerusalem Bible, and the Revised English Bible.
In most of these translations Isaiah 7:14 appears with the words
young woman' or young girl'. In itself, this is not particularly
startling or interesting. These twentieth-century translators are
obviously agreed about the word they are translating. Yet all

Christian Bibles also provide a different version of this passage from Isaiah. This different version of Isaiah seven-fourteen appears much later in the Bible, in the New Testament, when Matthew quotes the passage:

> Now all this took place to fulfil what the Lord had spoken through the prophet:
>
> *Look! the virgin is with child and will give birth to a son whom they will call Immanuel.*
>
>

Matthew 1:23
>

That is from the New Jerusalem Bible. Now here is the Revised Standard Version of the same passage from Matthew.

> All this took place to fulfil what the Lord had spoken by the prophet:
> "*Behold, a virgin shall conceive and bear a son, and his name shall be called Emmanuel.*"
>
>

Matthew 1:23 [RSV]
>

And here is how the passage appears in the New English Bible:

> All this happened in order to fulfil what the Lord declared through the prophet: '*The virgin will conceive and bear a son, and he shall be called Emmanuel,*'
>
>

Matthew 1:23 [NEB]
>

When Matthew quotes Isaiah 7:14, the word 'virgin' appears in the same modern translations that use the words 'young woman' or 'young girl', when they translate the passage directly from the book of Isaiah in the Hebrew Scriptures. What is happening in these modern Bibles is that the translators are simply revealing what Matthew himself has done. They have no choice here, because when Matthew cites Isaiah, 'virgin' is exactly the word he uses. The only problem is that the word 'virgin' does not appear in Isaiah at all. The original prophecy quite categorically uses the term 'young woman'. More than two millennia of translation difficulties lie behind all this.

Matthew was not making up the word 'virgin'. He was quoting the Septuagint, that Greek translation of the Hebrew Scriptures made under Ptolemy Philadelpheus in Alexandria some two hundred years before Jesus was born. In the Septuagint, the Hebrew word *almah* which means 'young girl' or 'young woman' was translated into the Greek word 'parthenos' which means 'virgin'[1]. Matthew quotes from the Greek version when he is quoting Isaiah. This was no accident on Matthew's part. He almost certainly quoted from the Greek Septuagint deliberately. He knew the scriptures in Hebrew as well as in Greek, but chose to quote the Greek 'virgin' over the Hebrew 'young woman'.

Matthew's quotation of a mistranslation has given rise to endless confused debate. In the English language this confusion is exacerbated by the King James Bible. Unlike the modern translations cited above, the King James Bible resoundingly translates Isaiah 7:14 like this:

> Therefore the Lord himself shall give you a sign; Behold, a virgin shall conceive, and bear a son, and shall call his name Immanuel.
> *Isaiah 7:14* [*AV*]

The King James translators probably could see very clearly how the Hebrew 'young woman' had been transformed into the Greek word 'virgin' in the Septuagint. They were excellent scholars and were working from the best documents available, but they were not prepared to challenge this translation. In some ways this is understandable, because a case can be argued for the Hebrew word 'almah' or 'young woman' sometimes implying 'virgin', and this could possibly explain the King James translation. But this argument fails to satisfy most modern translators. There is, after all, another Hebrew term 'bethulah', that actually means 'virgin'.

Although the King James translators created an English version of the Bible that is a work of extraordinary beauty and great erudition, they were, in their translation of Isaiah 7:14, playing safe.

---

1 For the ambiguities surrounding the notion of virginity in both Hebrew and Greek see page 62 below.

They were not prepared to indicate that Matthew was quoting a mistranslation. Instead they compounded the whole problem, adding their own authority to the mistranslation by including it in their own text of Isaiah. Their translation has remained the most influential ever to be published in English, and because the King James Bible is so widely read, the version of Isaiah 7:14 which reads 'a virgin shall conceive' is still widely accepted. Some modern Bibles continue to repeat this reading, in the face of all evidence. The New International Version contains the reading 'the virgin will be with child'. The New American Bible says the virgin shall be with child'. According to Raymond Brown, this reading in the New American Bible was 'imposed on reluctant Catholic translators by a decision of the American bishops'.[2] ·

In 1952 when the Revised Standard Version of the Bible came to the attention of a certain American fundamentalist preacher he was so outraged that the King James reading of 'virgin' had been replaced with 'young woman' that he publicly burned the offending pages and declared that the translation was 'the master stroke of Satan', and 'a scheme of the modernists to make the Lord Jesus Christ the son of a bad woman'.[3] This was followed by other protests.

Such Christian rejection of the original reading of Isaiah 7:14 has a long history. In the classic second-century work by Justin Martyr, *The Dialogue with Trypho*, the author tries to convert a Jew to Christianity. In doing so he maintains that Isaiah 7:14 should be understood refer to a 'virgin', not a 'young woman'. Yet a generation or so before the time of Justin Martyr a Greek translation of the Hebrew Scriptures had been made by a scholar called Aquila and in the face of the established Septuagint tradition he had changed 'virgin' to 'young woman' as it is in the original Hebrew. Aquila's translation was not at all well received by the church, even though some eminent early Christian scholars, including Origen, strongly recommended it.[4] This entire debate has not altered very much over the centuries.

2 *Brown* (1979) p. 146, n. 37.
3 *New York Times*, December 1, 1952.
4 See *Eusebius*, 1981, pp. 212, 256; see *Justin Martyr*, 1930, p. 86; and *Carrington*, 1957, pp. 427, 429 and 438–440.

Throughout his gospel Matthew quotes many passages from the Hebrew Scriptures and uses these in the stories he tells about Jesus. In quoting Isaiah 7:14 he gives himself a particularly hard task by deliberately choosing the translation of the prophecy that is the least easy to believe. Just why Matthew quotes this Greek version of Isaiah complete with the word 'virgin' has given rise to many interesting but completely unverifiable theories. Some of these assert that Matthew knew Mary was a virgin through various lost and untraceable written sources, or from an oral tradition that came directly from Jesus's family. That being the case, he would naturally favour the version of Isaiah's prophecy that included the word 'virgin', for this would support what he already knew to be true. But none of these hypothetical sources can be checked and their very existence is problematic. There is also a possibility that the original translation of the Hebrew young woman' to the Greek 'virgin' was not a scholarly mistake by the translators of the Septuagint, but rather something that they did on purpose, to reflect an expectation which had arisen in their own time. If for whatever reason they expected that a great deliverer of the Jewish people would be miraculously born of a virgin, then all they were doing was updating Isaiah's ancient text to match the mood of the Graeco-Judaic world two centuries before Jesus.[5]

Although Isaiah 7:14 does not mention a virgin conceiving, the general notion of improbable or even miraculous births was certainly nothing new. It was in the air of the ancient world. In many religions and mythologies the conceptions of great men were often achieved with minimal human will or effort. The gods of antiquity in Greece and Rome were very keen to mate with mortals. Zeus, or Jupiter, was forever inflicting his will on some hapless female, descending in showers of gold or in the form of a bull or a swan or whatever seemed to take his fancy. This type of congress often led to the births of great heroes like Perseus, the son of Danae, who was overcome by the renowned shower of gold.

In Plutarch's *Lives* written in the late first century BCE, the births of many famous people involve prodigies and miracles.

5 For a detailed discussion of the problems of translation associated with Isaiah 7:14 see *Vermes* (1973), pp. 217-20 and *Brown* (1979), pp. 143-53. The best modern biblical translations will also provide notes about this difficulty.

Alexander the Great is a particularly dramatic example of this. According to Plutarch, the night before the marriage of his parents, before any sexual contact had occurred, the womb of Alexander's mother was struck by a thunderbolt. So Alexander the Great was not really the son of Philip of Macedon as one might expect, he was instead the son of one of the gods.[6]

Virginity is often honoured in the stories and poems of the ancient world. The chaste Diana, goddess of the hunt, is a particularly good example of how virginity could be sacred, a sign of being set apart and special. Virgil, writing around the year 40 BCE, describes in his Fourth Eclogue an unnamed virgin and a divine child to whom the world will do homage:

> Now the last age of Cumae's Sibyl has come;
> The great succession of centuries is born afresh.
> Now too returns the Virgin; Saturn's rule returns;
> A new begetting now descends from heaven's height.
> O chaste Lucina, look blessing on the boy
> Whose birth will end the iron race at last and raise
> A golden through the world: now your Apollo rules.[7]

Although it cannot be proved that these influences from the pagan world had any impact on Matthew or on Luke, it is probable that they were aware of them. The concept of sacred virginity was so much part of the fabric of the literary and cultural environment of the time, that it would have been hard to avoid.

So far in this chapter we have referred more to Matthew than to Luke. This is because Matthew is the one who so purposefully cites the 'virgin shall conceive' passage from Isaiah. Luke does not mention the passage at all. Like Matthew, he asserts that when Mary learns she is to have a baby she is a virgin. 'But how can this come about, since I have no knowledge of man?' says Mary to the angel in Luke's gospel, and the angel assures her that nothing is impossible to God. At this stage Luke has mentioned twice that Mary is a virgin,

6 Plutarch, *The Lives of the Noble Grecians and Romans*, n.d., p. 801; see also *The Birth Narratives* (1987), p. 5, the discussion with Ed Sanders.
7 Eclogue IV, Virgil p. 57.

but in the rest of his birth story, in fact in the rest of his entire gospel, he never returns to the subject of her virginity.

In Matthew's gospel, as in Luke's, the subject of Mary's virginity is not mentioned anywhere but in the birth narratives. However, it is Matthew's gospel that gives rise to a further debate about Mary's virginity, whether or not she remained a virgin following the birth of Jesus. Matthew tells of the angel appearing to Joseph and assuring him that the pregnant Mary is virtuous, that 'she has conceived what is in her by the Holy Spirit'. Then, according to the translators of the New Jerusalem Bible, 'Joseph took his wife to his home; he had not had intercourse with her when she gave birth to a son; and he named him Jesus.' This is verse 25 of Matthew's first chapter and it opens out a heated dispute concerning both translation and interpretation.

At first glance this passage seems clear enough, stating that before the birth Joseph and Mary had no sexual contact. For some Christians, though, the issue at stake here is not what happened before the birth, but what happened next. There is a persistent Christian tradition, particularly in the Catholic church, that Mary remained a virgin even after the birth of Jesus, a contention that developed out of religious debates of the second and third centuries. This 'perpetual' virginity is hard to substantiate from the biblical text. In some translations it is possible to assume that after the birth, Joseph and Mary went on to have normal sexual relations. In other translations it is possible to assume that after the birth there was no sexual contact. The fact that some gospel passages go on to speak of the brothers of Jesus raises a few problems for anyone who favours the latter interpretation, but several explanations for this are available, including the theory that Joseph must have been married before. What has happened over the years is that Christians tend to favour the translation best suited to their existing beliefs.

The attention paid to this question is a good indication of just how intrigued Christians can be by the story of the virginity of Mary. Very early in the development of Christianity, complex and extraordinary stories began to be told emphasizing Mary's virginity and purity. Some of these stories became enormously important for some Christians, and many of them have developed a considerable authority which has very little to do with what is written in the gospels. They are later Christian preoccupations which have gained their authority through the weight of church tradition. The gospels of Matthew and Luke give surprisingly little information about Mary. Even in Luke's gospel, which so strongly favours her, she disappears from the scene after the stories of Jesus's childhood. The other two gospels hardly refer to Mary at all, and nowhere else in the entire New Testament is her virginity so much as mentioned. Mark refers to Jesus as 'the son of Mary', and Paul says only that Jesus was 'born of woman'.[8]

This lack of information is frustrating because Mary's story is so compelling that more details have always been sought. Over the centuries countless storytellers have happily obliged. Elaborate, optional versions of stories about Mary and Joseph and the birth of Jesus are easy to find, ranging from medieval mystery plays to Hollywood films. Every Christmas carol provides yet another unexpected and sometimes frankly ludicrous detail; everything from that tiresome little drummer boy, to the 'Away in a manger' little Lord Jesus who laid down his sweet head and never cried, to the Huron Carol composed by French missionairies to Canada, which features wandering Indian hunters paying homage to the child Jesus who is wrapped in a 'ragged robe of rabbit's skin' while the mighty Gitchi Manitou benevolently looks on. At the still centre of all these wild flights of fancy are Mary and Joseph, their mystery intact.

The earliest and the most influential of all these fanciful reconstructions can be found in stories that appear in a collection of writings usually known as the Apocryphal New Testament. These stories were composed in the second and third centuries and at first they were thought to carry considerable authority, but later they fell out of favour. The official list of books of the New Testament was formed gradually and by the fifth and sixth centuries it was becoming clear that these apocryphal writings would not be included. Even so some of these writings exerted a strong influence which can still be felt. In the nativity scene the best-known apocryphal contribution is the presence of the ox and ass, looming over the manger. These creatures are certainly not mentioned in the gospels, but they are referred to in the Apocryphal New Testament

8 Mark 6:3; Galatians 4:4-5.

in a text called the Protevangelium of James. This is full of wonderfully detailed stories about the birth of Jesus.

The unknown author of this apocryphal book starts by concentrating largely on Mary, and describes at great length her birth and her early years. According to this account Mary is herself a miraculously conceived child, and she is raised in the temple and fed by doves. When she reaches twelve years of age, the priests fear that she will 'pollute the temple', so they decide to find her a husband. The high priest chooses Joseph for this honour:

> Joseph answered him: 'I already have sons and am old, but she is a girl. I fear lest I should become a laughing-stock to the children of Israel.'9

When Mary becomes miraculously pregnant, Joseph is outraged: 'Who has deceived me? Who has done this evil in my house and defiled her?' he cries, and then he turns on Mary:

> 'You who are cared for by God, why have you done this and forgotten the Lord your God? Why have you humiliated your soul, you who were brought up in the Holy of Holies and received food from the hand of an angel?' But she wept bitterly, saying: 'I am pure, and know not a man.'

After being severely questioned by the priests at the temple and subjected to a number of truth tests, Mary and Joseph are left alone and by that time Joseph has found that he has to go to Bethlehem to register for the census. He seats Mary on a donkey, and off they go.

> And they came half the way, and Mary said to him: 'Joseph, take me down from the ass, for the child within me presses me, to come forth.' And he took her down there and said to her: 'Where shall I take you and hide your shame? For the place is desert.' And he found a cave there and brought her into it, and left her in the care of his sons and went out to seek for a Hebrew midwife in the region of Bethlehem.

9 This and subsequent quotations from the Protevangelium of James, NTA, pp. 370 ff.

As Joseph searches for a midwife he is astonished to observe that all of nature is standing still in anticipation of the wonderful birth.

> Now I, Joseph, was walking, and yet I did not walk, and I looked up to the air and saw the air in amazement. And I looked up at the vault of heaven, and saw it standing still, and the birds of the heaven motionless.

Joseph finds a midwife, and takes her back to the cave. A bright cloud comes over the cave and a dazzling light.

A short time afterwards that light withdrew until the child appeared, and it went and took the breast of its mother Mary.

The midwife then rushes out of the cave and meets her fellow midwife, called Salome.

> And she said to her: 'Salome, Salome, I have a new sight to tell you; a virgin has brought forth, a thing which her nature does not allow.' And Salome said: 'As the Lord my God lives, unless I put forward my finger and test her condition, I will not believe that a virgin has brought forth.' And the midwife went in and said to Mary: 'Make yourself ready, for there is no small contention concerning you.'

When Salome stretches forth her hand to test Mary's virginity, her arm is instantly consumed by fire. She repents her doubts, and her arm is healed when she touches the infant Jesus.

The Protevangelium of James is a fascinating piece of writing, full of action and colour. Its preoccupation with Mary's purity indicates the growing concern about this in the second century. Joseph is given a strong personality and there is an equally strong supporting cast of characters. The settings are memorable. This text has led many an artist to portray the nativity of Jesus inside a cave. The description of Mary seated on a donkey is another enduring image emerge from this story, along with the idea that all nature stood still for the birth of Jesus. The presence of the midwives and Joseph's sons at the birth has had less popular appeal, although in the National Gallery in London there is a small, very old painting by one Guisto de Menabuoi, dated 1387, which shows two midwives present at the nativity, with the elderly Joseph asleep in the foreground, paying no attention whatsoever to the proceedings in the cave behind him.

Joseph has never been the focus of the same amount of curiosity as Mary, and interest in him has certainly not inspired any comparable religious fervour. His fame is much more limited. A few Christmas carols have been written in his honour, and from the very beginning he has been the butt of countless ribald jokes and characterized as the original cuckold, but for the most part he just appears as an ever-faithful presence, always in the background. Yet, as we saw in the genealogies, the direct line of descent from David and from the great patriarchs of Israel is carefully designed so that it leads directly to Joseph. The whole purpose of those long lists of names, laden with historical significance, is to prove Joseph's credentials, presumably as the father of Jesus. If he had no part in fathering Jesus, the genealogies do not seem to make any sense.

In chapter 3 we mentioned the legal argument; Matthew presents Joseph as the legal father of Jesus. This argument maintains that by his marriage to Mary and his acceptance of her child, Joseph legally passes on the line of David to Jesus. However, a number of scholars are far from satisfied with this legalistic approach, and there is some textual evidence that supports another point of view altogether. Different versions are available of this passage from Matthew's genealogy:

> . . . and Jacob fathered Joseph the husband of Mary; of her was born Jesus who is called Christ.
>
> *Matthew 1:16*

This version is taken from the New Jerusalem Bible. It is a translation based on a reading found in the best Greek manuscripts of Matthew's gospels. The verbs here are passive, rather than active: Jesus 'was born' or 'was begotten' of Mary, and Joseph presumably took no action in the process. Usually in genealogies, the fathers are credited with an active verb: they 'beget' or at least 'father' their sons. In two other versions of Matthew 1:16, the wording is subtly different from the above reading, and Joseph appears to take a more active role. In these alternative readings he can arguably be seen as the natural father of Jesus. This first one comes from an early Greek manuscript and it reads:

> ...Jacob was the father of Joseph, to whom the betrothed virgin Mary bore Jesus, called the Christ.[10]

In this version Joseph is not called the husband of Mary; she is called a betrothed virgin; and she bears Jesus to Joseph. This seems to move a bit closer to the usual form of childbearing. The other variation of this passage is from an early manuscript which is not Greek but Semitic. It is the ancient Syriac text found in a monastery on Mount Sinai, already quoted in chapter 3. It reads:

> ... Jacob begot Joseph. Joseph, to whom was betrothed Mary, the virgin, begot Jesus who is called the Messiah.[11]

Removing the reference to Mary in the last phrase, this leaves the bald statement, 'Joseph...begot Jesus...' It is not surprising that these variant readings of Matthew 1:16 have caused considerable debate among scholars. The readings can be taken to mean, or at least to imply, that Joseph was Jesus's natural father. Close analysis of these readings has produced no certain conclusions, but a couple of clear questions emerge. Everyone concerned would like to know which version is the most authoritative, and who wrote it. The difficulty is that many manuscript copyists were involved. Matthew himself was long dead by the time any surviving copy of his gospel was made. The copyists could well have changed Matthew 1:16 to suit their own beliefs about Jesus, or they may have wished to render a clear text ambiguous. As for which text is the most authoritative, if the weight of tradition is anything to go by, most biblical translators favour the first one cited above, that 'Jacob fathered Joseph, the husband of Mary: of her was born Jesus who is called the Christ.' But Geza Vermes puts the case for the old Syriac reading of 'Joseph...begot Jesus' and, in biblical notes and commentaries, many scholars feel obliged to deal with both sides of the argument.

10 Quoted in both *Vermes* (1973) pp. 216-17, and in *Brown* (1979), p. 61-64; for a detailed discussion of this debate see these two references; compare chapter 3, p. 29.
11 Quoted in and discussed *Vermes* (1973), pp. 215-17.

Whether Matthew intended Joseph to be introduced as the legal father or as the natural father, the final verse of his genealogy is unusual. In all three of the possible readings, the wording is puzzling. The established form of biblical genealogy is simply not used when introducing Jesus. In the usual pattern, a genealogist would ignore Mary, and state straightforwardly that Joseph begot, or fathered Jesus. It is strange to mention a woman at all; even more strange to identify a man as the husband of a woman; downright bizarre to stress the virginity of a betrothed wife. Yet in the various readings of Matthew 1:16 one or even all of these strange turns of phrase come up. Perhaps this is entirely due to the copyists and it is a tale of early textual corruption which will never be solved. Perhaps it all goes back to Matthew himself, working out of a well-established tradition of genealogies which he consciously and purposefully changed in order to announce a birth of special significance to him and to his followers. Exactly what he wrote in the original version of 1:16 and whether any one of the three versions above is near to the original is uncertain. What is certain is that this announcement, as we have received it, is phrased in an unusual way.

Whether or not Joseph was Jesus's natural father, and whether or not Mary was a virgin at the time of the birth are questions that have been scrutinized endlessly. Debates theological, biological and psychological have raged around these questions, usually succeeding only in confirming the prejudices of everyone concerned. It might be more helpful to ask what 'virginity' really meant in the language and culture of the first century. Geza Vermes describes how, in both Greek and Hebrew, the concept of virginity was much less precise than it is now in English. Greek inscriptions on Jewish tombs in the catacombs of Rome have been found which refer to wives of many years as 'virgin' wives, most likely meaning that the marriage was the first and only one. In Hebrew the term bethulah was the usual word for 'virgin', but this word could mean different things. It could refer to a woman or a girl who had never had sexual relations, but it could just as easily refer to a young girl who was married, and therefore no longer *virgo intacta*, but unable to conceive because she had not yet reached puberty. According to an early rabbinic source, a virgin is: 'Whosoever has never seen blood even though she is married.'[12]

By itself, this understanding of the word 'virgin' proves very little, but it does show how impossible it is to satisfy curiosity about Mary's virginity, when the whole concept of virginity is so ambiguous. Time and again this curiosity is frustrated. Key words and passages telling the story of Jesus's parents have been mistranslated, misquoted, and perhaps deliberately misinterpreted for centuries. Even when we try to sort out all the confusion, we cannot force these words and phrases to confirm or deny the events leading up to the birth of Jesus.

What we can do is to look beyond Matthew's and Luke's stories. Both gospel writers tell their stories against a rich backdrop of other stories. The very names of Mary and Joseph are resonant of important figures in the Hebrew Scriptures. Joseph of old was the dreamer of extraordinary dreams who became great in the land of Egypt. And the name Mary in its Hebrew form is Miriam. Miriam was the prophetess who danced as she led the people of Israel out of Egypt over the Red Sea. It is against this broad picture of stories and personalities from the Hebrew Scriptures that the birth narratives of Matthew and Luke are best understood. The precise factual details about Mary and Joseph are lost, if ever they were known, and no amount of anxious burrowing is likely to reveal them. More can be learned about their stories by broadening the perspective; by looking into the gospels and then further to what lies beyond them. This leads into the looking-glass world of the Hebrew Scriptures.

12 *Vermes* (1973), p. 218.

VI

Annunciations

The birth narratives of Matthew and Luke reflect stories from the Hebrew Scriptures, consistently and repeatedly. Sometimes these reflections are very clear, sometimes they are a bit obscure, sometimes they are diffuse and puzzling. In trying to understand all this, we have sometimes been reminded of Lewis Carroll's Alice in her looking-glass world. At one point Alice finds a book she cannot understand until finally she realizes how it is written: 'Why it's a looking-glass book, of course! And if I hold it up to a glass, the words will all go the right way again.'

In the next few chapters we will try to "hold up a glass" to the birth stories of Matthew and Luke, to try to understand how they were written and what they contain. We will do this by looking at the main connections between the gospel stories and stories from the Hebrew Scriptures. This process may seem a bit slow, because it involves meandering through a lot of ancient stories which are rich and strange, but in taking the time to look at all these stories an unmistakable pattern emerges.

We start with the annunciation. The way Luke tells the story everything really gets under way when an angel comes to visit.

In the sixth month the angel Gabriel was sent by God to a town in Galilee called Nazareth, to a virgin betrothed to a man named Joseph, of the House of David; and the virgin's name was Mary. He went in and said to her, 'Rejoice, you who enjoy God's favour! The Lord is with you.' She was deeply disturbed by these words and asked herself what this greeting could mean, but the angel said to her, 'Mary, do not be afraid; you have won God's favour. Look! You are to conceive in your womb and bear a son, and you must name him Jesus. He will be great and will be called Son of the Most High. The Lord God will give him the throne of his ancestor David; he will rule over the House of Jacob for ever and his reign will have no end.' Mary said to the angel, 'But how can this come about, since I have no knowledge of man?' The angel answered, 'The Holy Spirit will come upon you, and the power of the Most High will cover you with its shadow. And so the child will be holy and will be called Son of God. And I tell you this too; your cousin Elizabeth also, in her old age, has conceived a son, and she whom people called barren is now in her sixth month, *for nothing is impossible to God.*' Mary said, 'You see before you the Lord's servant, let it happen to me as you have said.' And the angel left her.

Luke 1:26-38

This annunciation, this angelic announcement to Mary is much celebrated in early Italian painting and often appears in Christmas cards. The scene is very familiar. An angel, wearing white and usually bearing a lily, appears to Mary who is often clad in blue and is seated or kneeling in a cloister or an enclosed garden. A dove hovers somewhere in the background emitting a ray of light in Mary's general direction. The dove and the lily and the enclosed garden do not appear in Luke's gospel, but rather, like the ox and the ass in the crèche scene, they have become permanently attached to the annunciation.

This annunciation comes out of a very powerful scriptural tradition. It has unmistakable affinities with announcements of other great births in apparently impossible circumstances. The other earlier proclamations are described in the scriptures in stories that may be long and a bit rambling, but that are usually very beautiful. The impact of these stories builds up as they are read or heard one after another as part of a coherent tradition going back to the earliest stories of all, to the book of Genesis, and the company of Abraham.

Abraham is credited with a life full of visions of the divine. In some of these visions Abraham is promised many descendants through his senior wife Sarah, whom he loves more than all the others, but despite these encouraging visions, Sarah is unable to have children. We have already described one of Abraham's visions in chapter 2. Another tradition in the book of Genesis tells the same story differently:

> Yahweh appeared to him at the Oak of Mamre while he was sitting by the entrance of the tent during the hottest part of the day. He looked up, and there he saw three men standing near him. As soon as he saw them he ran from the entrance of the tent to greet them, and bowed to the ground. 'My lord,' he said, 'if I find favour with you, please do not pass your servant by. Let me have a little water brought, and you can wash your feet and have a rest under the tree. Let me fetch a little bread and you can refresh yourselves before going further, now that you have come in your servant's direction.' They replied, 'Do as you say.' Abraham hurried to the tent and said to Sarah, 'Quick, knead three measures of best flour and make loaves.' Then, running to the herd, Abraham took a fine and tender calf and gave it to the servant, who hurried to prepare it. Then taking curds, milk and the calf which had been prepared, he laid all before them, and they ate while he remained standing near them under the tree.
>
> 'Where is your wife Sarah?' they asked him. 'She is in the tent,' he replied. Then his guest said, 'I shall come back to you next year, and then your wife Sarah will have a son.' Sarah was listening at the entrance of the tent behind him. Now Abraham and Sarah were old, well on in years, and Sarah had ceased to have her monthly periods. So Sarah laughed to herself, thinking, 'Now that I am past the age of

childbearing, and my husband is an old man, is pleasure to come my way again?' But Yahweh asked Abraham, 'Why did Sarah laugh and say, "Am I really going to have a child now that I am old?" Nothing is impossible for Yahweh. I shall come back to you at the same time next year and Sarah will have a son.' Sarah said, 'I did not laugh,' lying because she was afraid. But he replied, 'Oh yes, you did.'

Genesis 18:1-15

At first, Abraham did not know that the visitors he was entertaining were divine visitors. In many such visitations described in the Hebrew Scriptures the figure of the divine is not recognized at first. This is a pattern so often repeated that it gives rise to a comment in the book called Hebrews in the New Testament, saying that strangers must always be made welcome, 'for by doing this, some people have entertained angels without knowing it'.[1]

This story of Abraham sitting under the tree, and the three angels coming, and Sarah laughing in disbelief at what they say is the earliest of many stories following the same theme. Barren women frequently receive supernatural help in bearing children, and great men issue from these unlikely conceptions. To be barren was considered the worst kind of humiliation for a woman, so to bear a remarkable, god-given child after years of childlessness was a triumph and a vindication. Many of the patriarchs and the prophets in the scriptures owe their very existence to some kind of divine help enabling their mothers to become pregnant.

The early generations of Hebrew patriarchs all needed special assistance in order to procreate, according to the scriptural records. Sarah's son Isaac, so miraculously conceived by his elderly parents, grows up to marry Rebekah and they also have reproductive problems:

This is the story of Isaac son of Abraham.

Abraham fathered Isaac. Isaac was forty years old when he married Rebekah the daughter of Bethuel the Aramaean of Paddan-Aram, and sister of Laban the Aramaean. Isaac prayed to Yahweh on behalf of his wife, for

1 Hebrews 13:2.

she was barren. Yahweh heard his prayer, and his wife
Rebekah conceived. But the children inside her struggled
so much that she said, 'If this is the way of it, why go on
living?' So she went to consult Yahweh, and Yahweh said
to her:

There are two nations in your womb,
your issue will be two rival peoples.
One nation will have the mastery of the other,
and the elder will serve the younger.

When the time came for her confinement, there were
indeed twins in her womb. The first to be born was red,
altogether like a hairy cloak; so they named him Esau. Then
his brother was born, with his hand grasping Esau's heel; so
they named him Jacob. Isaac was sixty years old at the time
of their birth. When the boys grew up Esau became a
skilled hunter, a man of the open country. Jacob on the
other hand was a quiet man, staying at home among the
tents. Isaac preferred Esau, for he had a taste for wild game;
but Rebekah preferred Jacob.

Genesis 25:19-28

The family jinx continues because Isaac's heir Jacob marries
Rachel and they have no offspring, even though Jacob has many
other children by his other wives. One of these other wives is
Rachel's sister Leah. Rachel grows more and more desperate as Leah
has more and more children:

Rachel, seeing that she herself gave Jacob no children,
became jealous of her sister. And she said to Jacob, 'Give me
children, or I shall die!' This made Jacob angry with
Rachel, and he retorted, 'Am I in the position of God, who
has denied you motherhood?' So she said, 'Here is my
slave-girl Bilhah. Sleep with her and let her give birth on
my knees; through her, then, I too shall have children!' So
she gave him her slave-girl Bilhah as concubine. Jacob slept
with her, and Bilhah conceived and gave birth to a son by
Jacob. Then Rachel said, 'God has done me justice; yes, he
has heard my prayer and given me a son.' Accordingly she
named him Dan. Again Rachel's slave-girl Bilhah con-

ceived and gave birth to a second son by Jacob. Then Rachel said, 'I have fought a fateful battle with my sister, and I have won!'

Genesis 30:1-8

Unluckily for Rachel, the competition with Leah is far from over. Leah also provides Jacob with a slave-girl who bears him two more sons, and then Leah herself, although she has four sons already and is past childbearing, manages to produce yet another two sons for Jacob, not to mention a daughter. After all of Leah's good luck it is finally Rachel's turn.

Then God remembered Rachel; he heard her and opened her womb. She conceived and gave birth to a son, and said, 'God has taken away my disgrace!' She named him Joseph, saying, 'May Yahweh add another son for me!'

Genesis 30:22-24

In the Hebrew Scriptures it is not just the wives of the early patriarchs who have trouble conceiving. The problem recurs repeatedly and of all the stories in the scriptures the one with the strongest affinities to Luke's story of Mary appears in the book of Samuel. It tells of Hannah, who was wife to one Elkanah. Hannah is heartbroken because Elkanah's other wife has many sons and daughters.

. . . her rival would taunt and provoke her, because Yahweh had made her womb barren. And this went on year after year; every time they went up to the temple of Yahweh she used to taunt her. On that day she wept and would not eat anything; so her husband Elkanah said, 'Hannah, why are you crying? Why are you not eating anything? Why are you so sad? Am I not more to you than ten sons?'

When they had finished eating in the room, Hannah got up and stood before Yahweh. Eli the priest was sitting on his seat by the doorpost of the temple of Yahweh. In the bitterness of her soul she prayed to Yahweh with many tears, and she made this vow. 'Yahweh Sabaoth! Should you condescend to notice the humiliation of your servant and keep her in mind instead of disregarding your servant, and give her a boy, I will give him to Yahweh for the whole of his life and no razor shall ever touch his head.'

While she went on praying to Yahweh, Eli was watching her mouth, for Hannah was speaking under her breath; her lips were moving but her voice could not be heard, and Eli thought that she was drunk. Eli said, 'How much longer are you going to stay drunk? Get rid of your wine.' 'No, my lord,' Hannah replied, 'I am a woman in great trouble; I have not been drinking wine or strong drink — I am pouring out my soul before Yahweh. Do not take your servant for a worthless woman; all this time I have been speaking from the depth of my grief and my resentment.' Eli then replied, 'Go in peace, and may the God of Israel grant what you have asked of him.' To which she said, 'May your servant find favour in your sight.' With that, the woman went away; she began eating and was dejected no longer.

They got up early in the morning and, after worshipping Yahweh, set out and went home to Ramah. Elkanah lay with his wife Hannah, and Yahweh remembered her. Hannah conceived and, in due course, gave birth to a son, whom she named Samuel, 'since', she said, 'I asked Yahweh for him.'

1 Samuel 1:1-21

Samuel is the boy who serves in the shrine with Eli the priest and hears the voice of God. His story has already been quoted in chapter 3. Samuel grows up to become a great seer, and a prophet of Yahweh and he eventually is guided to choose David as the king of Israel. His mother Hannah and Mary the mother of Jesus have a great deal in common. Both praise God with the same song,[2] and both believe their sons are specially chosen to lead the people of Israel.

The story of Mary and Joseph differs from all these ancient prophetic and patriarchal stories. The circumstances are not the same, for Mary is described as a virgin rather than as a barren wife. However, a similar process of divine intervention leads to a

2 See chapter 8, pp. 97-102 for a discussion of the songs of Mary and Hannah.

similarly unexpected conception. Matthew and Luke each tell of a divine figure appearing to announce the forthcoming birth. In Luke's gospel this is in the scene of the annunciation to Mary. In Matthew's gospel the proclamation about Jesus comes in a dream to Joseph.

> This is how Jesus Christ came to be born. His mother Mary was betrothed to Joseph: but before they came to live together she was found to be with child through the Holy Spirit. Her husband Joseph, being an upright man and wanting to spare her disgrace, decided to divorce her informally. He had made up his mind to do this when suddenly the angel of the Lord appeared to him in a dream and said, 'Joseph son of David, do not be afraid to take Mary home as your wife, because she has conceived what is in her by the Holy Spirit. She will give birth to a son and you must name him Jesus, because he is the one who is to save his people from their sins.' Now all this took place to fulfil what the Lord had spoken through the prophet:
>
> > *Look! the virgin is with child and will give birth to a son whom they will call Immanuel.*
>
> a name which means 'God-is-with-us'. When Joseph woke up he did what the angel of the Lord had told him to do: he took his wife to his home; he had not had intercourse with her when she gave birth to a son; and he named him Jesus.
>
> *Matthew 1:18-25*

Although the term 'annunciation' is usually associated with Mary and the angel Gabriel, this announcement to Joseph follows a related pattern. Joseph's angel explains that a miraculous conception has occurred, resolves all doubts, and promises future greatness. In the annunciation to Mary, the angel Gabriel gives a similar explanation, but there is a difference in tone between the two scenes. In the annunciation to Mary, Luke characteristically includes far more poetic detail than Matthew allows in the angelic appearance to Joseph.

Luke is at his best in writing of the annunciation to Mary, not only in how he tells an enduring poetic story, full of intricate allusions to scripture, but in how he introduces that story. Luke does not limit himself to only one annunciation in his gospel. He has two. His gospel opens with the story of the miraculous conception of John the Baptist, and an angelic announcement about the coming child. This directly precedes the annunciation to Mary, but often it receives no more than a cursory reading because it is overshadowed by the better known story that follows. But just as it is a mistake to disregard Matthew's long genealogy, which is the opening gambit in his gospel, so is it a mistake to overlook this opening section of Luke's gospel. Each opening passage is there for a reason. Luke begins with this story:

> In the days of King Herod of Judaea there lived a priest called Zechariah who belonged to the Abijah section of the priesthood, and he had a wife, Elizabeth by name, who was a descendant of Aaron. Both were upright in the sight of God and impeccably carried out all the commandments and observances of the Lord. But they were childless: Elizabeth was barren and they were both advanced in years.
>
> Now it happened that it was the turn of his section to serve, and he was exercising his priestly office before God when it fell to him by lot, as the priestly custom was, to enter the Lord's sanctuary and burn incense there. And at the hour of incense all the people were outside, praying.
>
> Then there appeared to him the angel of the Lord, standing on the right of the altar of incense. The sight disturbed Zechariah and he was overcome with fear. But the angel said to him, 'Zechariah, do not be afraid, for your prayer has been heard. Your wife Elizabeth is to bear you a son and you shall name him John. He will be your joy and delight and many will rejoice at his birth, for he will be great in the sight of the Lord; he must drink no wine, no strong drink; even from his mother's womb he will be filled with the Holy Spirit and he will bring back many of the Israelites to the Lord their God. With the spirit and power of Elijah, he will go before him *to reconcile fathers to their children* and the disobedient to the good sense of the upright, preparing for the Lord a people fit for him.' Zechariah said

to the angel, '*How can I know this:* I am an old man and my wife is getting on in years.' The angel replied. 'I am Gabriel, who stands in God's presence, and I have been sent to speak to you and bring you this good news. Look! Since you did not believe my words, which will come true at their appointed time, you will be silenced and have no power of speech until this has happened.' Meanwhile the people were waiting for Zechariah and were surprised that he stayed in the sanctuary so long. When he came out he could not speak to them, and they realized he had seen a vision in the sanctuary. But he could only make signs to them, and remained dumb.

When his time of service came to an end he returned home. Some time later his wife Elizabeth conceived and for five months she kept to herself, saying, 'The Lord has done this for me, now that it has pleased him to take away the humiliation I suffered in public.'

Luke 1:5-25

This story sounds familiar, bringing to mind the birth of Samuel to Hannah, and how he is dedicated to God from birth. It also recalls a story we have not yet mentioned of how Samson, of Samson and Delilah fame, was born.

There was a man of Zorah of the tribe of Dan, called Manoah. His wife was barren; she had borne no children. The Angel of Yahweh appeared to this woman and said to her, You are barren and have had no child, but you are going to conceive and give birth to a son. From now on, take great care. Drink no wine or fermented liquor, and eat nothing unclean. For you are going to conceive and give birth to a son. No razor is to touch his head, for the boy is to be God's nazirite from his mother's womb; and he will start rescuing Israel from the power of the Philistines.'

Judges 13:2-5

The nazirites were a group of what can best be described as special holy men; they were judges, seers or prophets who held a privileged place in Israelite society. Samson is one of the earliest nazirites mentioned in the scriptures. The great prophet Elijah is another, and centuries later John the Baptist follows in the same tradition.[3]

Luke's story of the angelic announcement to Zechariah echoes many stories from the scriptures. The promise of a special child recalls the stories of Samuel and Samson, those specially dedicated and miraculously conceived children who went on to lead their people. Zechariah's disbelief calls to mind the disbelief of Sarah when she was told she would conceive. Elizabeth's humiliation in being barren recalls the plight of Rachel, and that of Hannah. This announcement to Zechariah, with all its layers of scriptural references, sets the stage for Luke's story of the angel Gabriel going to visit Mary to make another announcement that follows in the same tradition, but which is, according to Luke, even more important.

The importance of the annunciation to Mary is emphasized in a very evocative and telling passage when the angel says:

> 'The Holy Spirit will come upon you, and the power of the Most High will cover you with its shadow . . .'
>
> *Luke 1:35*

This symbol of the shadow of the power of the Most High is very ancient. It is often referred to in the Hebrew Scriptures, usually as a means of trying to express the inexpressible holiness of Yahweh. The bright shadow or the dazzling cloud shields the godhead from mortal gaze; it is his dwelling place; it is the glory of the most high deity, and it is how this deity reveals himself to his favoured people. The cloud is often bright and always awesome. It can take the form of fire or even smoke. In the book of Exodus it is in the cloud on Mount Sinai that Moses comes face to face with his god:

> Cloud covered the mountain. The glory of Yahweh rested on Mount Sinai and the cloud covered it for six days. On the seventh day Yahweh called to Moses from inside the cloud. To the watching Israelites, the glory of Yahweh looked like a devouring fire on the mountain top, Moses went right into the cloud and went on up the mountain. Moses stayed on the mountain for forty days and forty nights.
>
> *Exodus 24:16-18*

3 See chapter 8, p. 97; chapter 9, p. 128.

Later, in the story of the exodus from Egypt, another cloud appears to the people of Israel who are following Moses out of slavery towards the promised land:

> The cloud then covered the Tent of Meeting and the glory of Yahweh filled the Dwelling. Moses could not enter the Tent of Meeting, since the cloud stayed over it and the glory of Yahweh filled the Dwelling.
>   At every stage of their journey, whenever the cloud rose from the Dwelling, the Israelites would resume their march. If the cloud did not rise, they would not resume their march until the day it did rise. For Yahweh's cloud stayed over the Dwelling during the daytime and there was fire inside the cloud at night, for the whole House of Israel to see, at every stage of their journey.
>
> *Exodus 40:34-38*

Much later when the Kingdom of Israel was established and Solomon was king, the temple was being built in Jerusalem, and the awesome cloud was still a force to be reckoned with.

> Now when the priests came out of the Holy Place, the cloud filled the Temple of Yahweh, and because of the cloud the priests could not stay and perform their duties. For the glory of Yahweh filled the Temple of Yahweh.
>   Then Solomon said:
> Yahweh has chosen to dwell in thick cloud.
> I have built you a princely dwelling,
> a residence for you forever.
>
> *1 Kings 8:10-13*

When Luke writes of the power of the Most High overshadowing Mary he is drawing on this ancient tradition. To be under the shadow of the Most High means being protected and guided by the cloud of Yahweh. It is a sign of being singled out by God. The Israelite people are so favoured as they leave Egypt, and Moses is so favoured on Mount Sinai. Centuries later the cloud of glory comes to dwell in the Holy of Holies in Solomon's temple. In many other scattered references in the scriptures, when Yahweh or his divine messenger appears, he arrives or departs in a cloud and the tradition is carried through to New Testament descriptions of the appearances of Jesus after his death.

Given this tradition, the idea that Mary should be overshadowed by the power of the Most High makes perfect sense in Luke's gospel. In the sacred shadow she is protected by and answerable to the Most High. She has found favour with God, as the angel says, but there is even more to it than that. After all, many other women in the scriptures find favour with God and miraculously conceive. But because in his annunciation scene Luke stresses that Mary is under the shadow of the Most High, she is set apart and particularly blessed.

VII

Stars and Dreams

One of the favourite symbols of the Christmas-card industry is a star, usually an abnormally large star, twinkling over a wide variety of nativity scenes. This star appears only in Matthew's gospel, closely followed by the wise men from the east:

> After Jesus had been born at Bethlehem in Judaea during the reign of King Herod, suddenly some wise men came to Jerusalem from the east asking, 'Where is the infant king of the Jews? We saw his star as it rose and have come to do him homage.' When King Herod heard this he was perturbed, and so was the whole of Jerusalem.
>
> *Matthew 2:1-3*

The movement of the stars and planets has always been observed with awe and many belief systems have been based on interpretations of celestial activity. The regularity and reliability of this activity never fails to amaze, so any unusual movements of heavenly bodies have always caused interest and excitement.

The science of astronomy is probably the oldest and one of the best documented of all the sciences and certainly in Matthew's time knowledge of the stars was profound. By 150 CE Ptolemy, the famous astronomer in Egypt, was preparing a geocentric model of the universe and this still works today as a basis for accurate navigation of ships at sea. Ptolemy was working from centuries of Babylonian and Greek observations as well as from his own. In another part of the world, at more or less the same time, the Chinese were also developing a sophisticated knowledge of the skies. Yet despite the impressive early history of astronomy and its equally impressive current history, all attempts to identify the famous 'star in the east' of Matthew's birth story have failed. This is certainly not through any lack of effort.

There are several astronomical theories about this star and these have met with varying degrees of enthusiasm over the years. The first is that this was a new star, a 'supernova'. On a very distant, almost invisible star an explosion occurs and for a short while the light of that explosion — the supernova — shines brightly in the sky. The trouble with this theory is that it is purely speculative because there is no pattern of supernovae that can be traced back in time. There is however a pattern for comets and extensive calculations have been made to try to determine if the star could have been a comet; Halley's comet for preference. But Halley's comet would have appeared around the year 12 BCE according to ancient Chinese records, so the timing is not right. Then there is the possibility that the star was not a star at all but a conjunction of planets, and although Jupiter and Saturn obliged in the early part of the first century, once again the timing cannot be made to fit with Matthew's gospel. Finally there is the notion that the star that led the wise men to Jesus was a unique and miraculous phenomenon, for which there is no explanation at all. This is a contention that can be neither proved nor disproved. Not everyone finds it helpful.[1]

It is probably more helpful to see the story of the star against the general background of Matthew's time instead of struggling to identify it in astronomical terms. Given this background there is

1 For a more detailed discussion of the star theories, see *Brown*, (1979), pp. 171-5.

nothing at all strange about the story of a star rising to proclaim a great event, for this happens frequently in the literature of the ancient world. Special stars could be portents of wonderful promise, or portents of doom. In the *Aeneid*, Virgil tells how Aeneas is guided by a star on his travels to the site of the future city of Rome.[2]

In his history of the calamitous fall of Jerusalem, Josephus complains that the people

> disregarded and disbelieved the unmistakable portents that foreshadowed the coming desolation, and, as though thunderstruck, blind, senseless, paid no heed to the clear warnings of God. It was like this when a star that looked like a sword stood over the city and a comet that continued for a whole year.[3]

Special stars were widely believed to shine forth when great men were born and when they died. At such times, extraordinary celestial portents were only to be expected. Suetonius, writing early in the second century, mentions several portents that accompanied the birth of Augustus Caesar. One of these, which he does not actually describe, caused great consternation amongst the ruling classes:

> a public portent warned the Roman people some months before Augustus's birth that Nature was making ready to provide them with a king; and this caused the Senate such consternation that they issued a decree which forbade the rearing of any male child for a whole year. However, a group of senators whose wives were expectant prevented the decree from being filed at the Treasury and thus becoming law — for each of them hoped that the prophesied King would be his own son.[4]

2 See *Virgil*, (1956), book III, line 694, p. 71.
3 *Josephus*, (1982), book VI, chapter 5, verse 3, p. 426.
4 *Suetonius*, (1957), pp. 100-1.

Suetonius also describes how the Emperor Nero reacted, or over-reacted, to the appearance of a heavenly portent:

> A comet, popularly supposed to herald the death of some person of outstanding importance, appeared several nights running and greatly disturbed him. His astrologer Balbillus observed that monarchs usually avoided portents of this kind by executing their most prominent subjects and thus directing the wrath of heaven elsewhere; so Nero resolved on a wholesale massacre of the nobility.[5]

It was characteristic of Nero to indulge in the occasional wholesale massacre, but this one is noteworthy because it was a direct response to the appearance of a comet. This was evidently a portent of great power.

Matthew's star fits into this pattern. It is the most publicized of a whole galaxy of important stars in the literature of the ancient world. In Matthew's story, the magi greet this star with awe and wonder while Herod hears of it with suspicion and fear. At one and the same time this star is a portent of wonder and a portent of fear, depending entirely on the point of view of the observer. Interpreting Matthew's star is a complex undertaking for not only is it characteristic of the literature of its time, it also carries coded information from the Hebrew Scriptures, recalling other stories of other stars significant in the history of Israel.

One scriptural star closely related to Matthew's is found in an ancient oracle delivered by the man whose donkey is at least as famous as he is. It appears in the story of Balaam the soothsayer. This story takes us back to approximately 1200 BCE, a time roughly contemporary with the conquest of Canaan by the nomadic tribes of Israel, and the story was recorded in something like its present form two or three hundred years later, perhaps around 900 BCE. Even though he is not an Israelite, Balaam is inspired by Yahweh the god of Israel to speak out in favour of the Israelites. This puts Balaam in a difficult position because he has been asked for an oracle by Balak, King of Moab, a region threatened by the incursions of the Israelites. He knows that if he follows Yahweh's instructions Balak will not

5 Ibid., pp. 229.

like what he has to say, because Balaam has no good oracles for Moab. Understandably, Balaam tries to avoid going to see Balak, and when he finally gives in and undertakes the journey, the angel of Yahweh bars his way. Balaam's donkey sees the angel and very sensibly balks, refusing to cross the angel's path. Balaam doesn't see the angel so he beats the donkey and then the donkey is miraculously gifted with speech so he protests loudly. The angel joins the ensuing discussion, and Balaam at last sees and hears the angel. An agreement is struck that Balaam will continue on his journey to go and visit King Balak and that he will say only what Yahweh tells him to say, even if Balak objects. So Balaam carries on to Moab and declaims this oracle:

> The prophecy of Balaam son of Beor,
> the prophecy of the man with far-seeing eyes,
> the prophecy of one who hears the words of God,
> of one who knows the knowledge of the Most High.
> He sees what Shaddai makes him see,
> receives the divine answer, and his eyes are opened.
> I see him — but not in the present.
> I perceive him — but not close at hand:
> a star is emerging from Jacob,
> a sceptre is rising from Israel,
> to strike the brow of Moab,
> the skulls of all the children of Seth.
> Edom too will be a conquered land,
> Seir too will be a conquered land,
> when Israel exerts his strength,
> when Jacob tramples on his enemies
> and destroys the last survivors of Ar.
>
> *Numbers 24:15-20*

This eloquence is not welcome. The star rising from Israel to 'strike the brow' of Moab is a very poetic concept, but it fails to win the heart of the king of Moab. No wonder the donkey balked. But that is another story.

The point of quoting this ancient oracle is the star that will rise from Jacob, meaning from Israel. Later generations understood this star of Balaam's to symbolize a powerful new leader for Israel. In

Matthew's gospel the star rises to mark the birth of a child believed to be just such a powerful new leader. Matthew emphasizes how both the child and the star have risen 'out of Jacob', in more than one sense. The star rests over Bethlehem in the province of Judaea, in the land of Jacob. And in his genealogy Matthew says, 'Matthan fathered Jacob, and Jacob fathered Joseph the husband of Mary', naming one Jacob as the father of Joseph. Because Joseph is responsible for the newborn child it all fits and so in genealogical as well as geographical terms Matthew ensures that the star rises out of Jacob.

There are strong undercurrents here of another Jacob and another Joseph because the patriarchal Jacob, who was none other than Israel himself, also fathered a Joseph, incidentally by miraculous conception through his apparently barren wife Rachel. That earlier Joseph has a great deal in common with Matthew's Joseph. Both Josephs are dreamers of dreams and both are influenced by stars. Joseph of old is one of the greatest of all biblical dreamers, and one of his dreams as a teenager is reported like this:

> Now Joseph had a dream, and he repeated it to his brothers, who then hated him more than ever. 'Listen', he said, 'to the dream I had. We were binding sheaves in the field, when my sheaf suddenly rose and stood upright, and then your sheaves gathered round and bowed to my sheaf.' 'So you want to be king over us,' his brothers retorted, 'you want to lord it over us?' And they hated him even more on account of his dreams and of what he said. He had another dream which he recounted to his brothers. 'Look, I have had another dream,' he said. 'There were the sun, the moon and eleven stars, bowing down to me.' He told his father and brothers, and his father scolded him. 'A fine dream to have!' he said to him. 'Are all of us then, myself, your mother and your brothers, to come and bow to the ground before you?'
>
> *Genesis 37:5-10*

This dream of stars doing obeisance is a prophetic dream for the young Joseph, although it does not win him any friends at the time.

His brothers become thoroughly exasperated by his dreams of greatness:

> 'Here comes that dreamer,' they said to one another. 'Come on, let us kill him now and throw him down one of the storage-wells; we can say that some wild animal has devoured him. Then we shall see what becomes of his dreams.'
>
> *Genesis 37:19-20*

Joseph is accordingly thrown down the well, although he is not immediately killed. Later the brothers decide to get rid of him in another way. They pull him out of the well, they smear his coat of many colours with blood; they tell their father Jacob that Joseph is dead, and they sell him to slave-dealers who in turn sell him to an Egyptian. As a Hebrew slave in Egypt Joseph faces a bleak future, but much against the odds he does well for himself, serving a wealthy master. But as he grows older trouble arises. Because Joseph is 'well built and handsome', his master's wife attempts to seduce him and in striving manfully to protect his virtue, Joseph ends up in gaol. There his luck returns. He makes friends with two other gaoled slaves who are from the pharaoh's household. They are unhappy and puzzled by dreams they have had and Joseph interprets their dreams for them with uncanny accuracy. Later, one of the slaves hears that the pharaoh is troubled by his dreams and he recommends Joseph as an interpreter:

> Pharaoh told Joseph, 'In my dream there I was, standing on the bank of the Nile. And there were seven cows, fat and sleek, coming up out of the Nile, and they began to feed among the rushes. And then seven other cows came up, behind them starved, very wretched and lean; I have never seen such poor cows in all Egypt. The lean and wretched cows ate up the first seven fat cows. But when they had eaten them up, it was impossible to tell they had eaten them, for they looked as wretched as ever. Then I woke up. And then again in my dream, there, growing on one stalk, were seven ears of grain, beautifully ripe; but then sprout-

ing up behind them came seven ears of grain, withered, meagre and scorched by the east wind. Then the shrivelled ears of grain swallowed the seven ripe ears of grain. I have told the magicians, but no one has given me the answer.'

Genesis 41:17-24

Joseph interprets this dream to mean that famine will descend and he warns the pharaoh to be prepared. For this wise counsel he is promoted to the highest rank in the civil service:

'Since God has given you knowledge of all this, there can be no one as intelligent and wise as you. You shall be my chancellor, and all my people shall respect your orders; only this throne shall set me above you.'

Genesis 41:39-40

Thanks to his skilled knowledge of dreams the first Joseph is established in Egypt very satisfactorily, and Egypt is saved from famine. Later his brothers have to appeal to him for food:

Thus the sons of Israel were among the other people who came to get supplies, there being famine in Canaan. It was Joseph, as the man in authority over the country, who allocated the rations to the entire population. So Joseph's brothers went and bowed down before him, their faces touching the ground. As soon as Joseph saw his brothers he recognised them. But he did not make himself known to them, and he spoke harshly to them. 'Where have you come from?' he asked. 'From Canaan to get food,' they replied.

Genesis 42:5-7

So Joseph's prophetic dream comes true, and his brothers bow before him, doing him obeisance. His star has risen above theirs. Thanks to him, the Israelite brothers bring their father from Canaan to Egypt where everyone prospers, at least for a while. The biblical chronology becomes a bit fuzzy at this point, but conventional wisdom maintains that the Israelites lived more or less contentedly in Egypt for the next two to four centuries before there was serious trouble:

> Then Joseph died, and his brothers, and all that generation. But the Israelites were fruitful and prolific; they became so numerous and powerful that eventually the whole land was full of them. Then there came to power in Egypt a new king who had never heard of Joseph. 'Look,' he said to his people, 'the Israelites are now more numerous and stronger than we are. We must take precautions to stop them from increasing any further, or if war should break out, they might join the ranks of our enemies. They might take arms against us and then escape from the country.' Accordingly they put taskmasters over the Israelites to wear them down by forced labour.
>
> *Exodus 1:7-11*

Thus Joseph's triumph in Egypt gave way to enslavement and oppression for the Israelites, something even Joseph never dreamed of.

In Matthew's gospel the later Joseph's dreams are just as powerful and prophetic as the dreams of the Joseph of old. There are four such dreams. In the first the angel reassures Matthew's Joseph and tells him to take Mary as his wife. The other dreams are full of specific geographical instructions. In the second dream Joseph is told to flee danger and take Mary and the child to Egypt, in the third he is told to return to the land of Israel, and in the fourth Nazareth is specified as his destination. Although the Joseph in Matthew's gospel does not dream of stars like the Joseph of old, it is because of the star his dreams are necessary. The star brings the wise men and their presence in the country activates Herod:

> ...some wise men came to Jerusalem from the east asking, 'Where is the infant king of the Jews? We saw his star as it rose and have come to do him homage.' When King Herod heard this he was perturbed, and so was the whole of Jerusalem. He called together all the chief priests and the scribes of the people, and enquired of them where the Christ was to be born. They told him, 'At Bethlehem in

Judaea, for this is what the prophet wrote:
And you, Bethlehem, in the land of Judah,
you are by no means the *least among the leaders of Judah*
for you will come a leader
who will *shepherd* my people Israel.'

Matthew 2:2-6

Herod does not like what he hears. The idea of a new leader emerging for the Israelite people arouses his murderous interest. This is Herod the Great who died in the year 4 BCE. He had a long life and wielded great power, but power was his only by courtesy of the Roman Empire. He was the ruler of the puppet kingdom of Judaea, which however powerful remained in the control of Rome, much to the bitter anger of the local people. Not surprisingly, as the representative of a colonizing force, Herod was unpopular with the Jewish people he ruled even though he was half Jewish himself. The other half of his lineage was Idumean and this made him tribally and racially unacceptable to the Jews. An Idumaean was an Edomite, or a descendent of Esau. In the patriarchal line Esau was a son of Isaac and the twin brother of Jacob/Israel. It is Esau who sells his birthright as the first-born son for what the King James Bible terms 'bread and pottage of lentiles', now translated less graphically as 'lentil stew':

> Once, when Jacob was cooking a stew, Esau returned from the countryside exhausted. Esau said to Jacob, 'Give me a mouthful of that red stuff there; I am exhausted' — hence the name given to him, Edom. Jacob said, 'First, give me your birthright in exchange.' Esau said, 'Here I am, at death's door; what use is a birthright to me?' Then Jacob said, 'First give me your oath'; he gave him his oath and sold his birthright to Jacob. Then Jacob gave him some bread and lentil stew; he ate, drank, got up and went away. That was all Esau cared about his birthright.

Genesis 25:29-34

These transactions emerge in stories from the pre-history of the tribes of Israel, but Judaic dislike of Edom and vice versa remained strong in Matthew's time. Naturally Herod the Edomite emerges as the villain of Matthew's birth narrative. At best he is not to be trusted, at worst he is the hated and bloodthirsty tyrant who comes from a rival tribe. It is worth emphasizing here that anything related to Herod, including the wise men, the dreams and the flight into Egypt, is found only in Matthew's gospel. Matthew and his congregation would have been well versed in the historical and racial innuendo attached to Herod's name, but such subtleties would have meant little to Luke and his distant Greek congregation. In Matthew's gospel, these ancient subtleties are very important:

> . . . Herod summoned the wise men to see him privately. He asked them the exact date on which the star had appeared and sent them on to Bethlehem with the words, 'Go and find out all about the child, and when you have found him, let me know, so that I too may go and do him homage.' Having listened to what the king had to say, they set out. And suddenly the star they had seen rising went forward and halted over the place where the child was. The sight of the star filled them with delight, and going into the house they saw the child with his mother Mary, and falling to their knees they did him homage. Then, opening their treasures, they offered him gifts of gold and frankincense and myrrh. But they were given a warning in a dream not to go back to Herod, and returned to their own country by a different way. After they had left, suddenly the angel of the Lord appeared to Joseph in a dream and said, 'Get up, take the child and his mother with you, and escape into Egypt, and stay there until I tell you, because Herod intends to search for the child and to do away with him.' So Joseph got up and, taking the child and his mother with him, left that night for Egypt, where he stayed until Herod was dead. This was to fulfil what the Lord had spoken through the Prophet:
>
> *I called my son out of Egypt.*
>
> *Matthew 2:7-15*

Matthew's Joseph goes to Egypt because of a dream about danger. The way Matthew tells the story, Herod becomes very suspicious about the new 'infant king of the Jews', and he takes drastic action.

> Herod was furious on realizing that he had been fooled by the wise men, and in Bethlehem and its surrounding district he had all the male children killed who were two years old or less, reckoning by the date he had been careful to ask the wise men.
>
> *Matthew 2:16*

There is a strong precedent for this story. The book of Exodus also tells how Israelite baby boys are killed by a ruthless king. The pharaoh of Egypt is the villain of the piece:

> The king of Egypt then spoke to the Hebrew mid-wives, one of whom was called Shiphrah, and the other Puah. 'When you attend Hebrew women in childbirth,' he said, 'look at the two stones. If it is a boy, kill him; if a girl, let her live.' But the midwives were God-fearing women and did not obey the orders of the king of Egypt, but allowed the boys to live. So the king of Egypt summoned the midwives and said to them, 'What do you mean by allowing the boys to live?' The midwives said to Pharaoh, 'Hebrew women are not like Egyptian women, they are hardy and give birth before the midwife can get to them.' For this, God was good to the midwives, and the people went on increasing and growing more powerful; and since the midwives feared God, he gave them families of their own.
>
> Pharaoh then gave all his people this command: 'Throw every new-born boy into the river, but let all the girls live.'
>
> *Exodus 1:15-22*

The pharaoh and Herod are presented as two of a kind. Whether or not there is any historical basis for Matthew's story of the 'massacre of the innocents' is hard to tell. No outside documents offer any support for this tale, but it is plausible for many reasons. It is just the sort of story an Israelite would have told about a despised Edomite puppet king. It also fits in with what is known of Herod who was renowned for his cruelty. Without any apparent qualms, he disposed of two of his own sons and their mother when they became troublesome, so murdering a small number of children in the small town of Bethlehem would not have bothered him unduly. The scriptural precedents for this story are also strong, and there are many different strands. A parallel is set up between Herod and the pharaoh; Bethlehem is emphasized as the birthplace; and Egypt becomes a place of escape for Matthew's Joseph just as it was for the earlier Joseph. The story of Joseph and Mary and Jesus, the 'new Israel', fleeing the wrath of Herod recalls another story from the scriptures about how Jacob/Israel had to flee from a murderous foe:

> Esau hated Jacob because of the blessing his father had given him, and Esau said to himself, 'The time to mourn for my father will soon be here. Then I shall kill my brother Jacob.' When the words of Esau, her elder son, were repeated to Rebekah, she sent for her younger son Jacob and said to him, 'Look, your brother Esau means to take revenge and kill you. Now, son, listen to me; go at once and take refuge with my brother Laban in Haran. Stay with him a while, until your brother's fury cools, until your brother's anger is diverted from you and he forgets what you have done to him. Then I will send someone to bring you back. I do not want to lose you both on one day!'
>
> *Genesis 27:41-45*

So Esau the Edomite vowed to kill his brother and Jacob fled. The wrath of Herod, the killing of the babies in Bethlehem and the flight into Egypt are connected to many different stories in the Hebrew Scriptures, but probably the strongest connection of all is to the story of Moses. Just as the infant Jesus escapes from Herod, Moses escapes the pharaoh's plot to kill all the Israelite boy babies in Egypt. His mother's ingenuity saves him:

> She conceived and gave birth to a son and, seeing what a fine child he was, she kept him hidden for three months.

> When she could hide him no longer she got a papyrus basket
> for him; coating it with bitumen and pitch, she put the child
> inside and laid it among the reeds at the River's edge. His
> sister took up position some distance away to see what
> would happen to him.
>
> *Exodus 2:2-4*

What happens next in the book of Exodus is that the pharaoh's
sister finds the child. She picks him up basket and all, and raises him.
All is well until Moses is grown up, when he kills an Egyptian for
beating one of his fellow Israelites. At that point the pharaoh, true to
form, decides it is time to put Moses to death. Moses flees to the land
of Midian somewhere on the Sinai Peninsula, and 'sat down by a
well', contemplating his exile. In due course he meets Jethro, the
priest of Midian, marries his daughter, and settles down. Meanwhile, back in Egypt, things go from bad to worse for the Israelites:

> During this long period the king of Egypt died. The
> Israelites, groaning in their slavery, cried out for help and
> from the depths of their slavery their cry came up to God.
> God heard their groaning; God remembered his covenant
> with Abraham, Isaac and Jacob. God saw the Israelites and
> took note . . .
>
> *Exodus 2:23-25*

One day while Moses is tending the flock 'the angel of Yahweh
appeared to him in a flame blazing from the middle of a bush'. After
some initial discussion, Yahweh tells Moses what to do:

> Yahweh then said, 'I have indeed seen the misery of my
> people in Egypt, I have heard them crying for help on
> account of their taskmasters. Yes, I am well aware of their
> sufferings. And I have come down to rescue them from the
> clutches of the Egyptians and bring them up out of that
> country, to a country rich and broad, to a country flowing
> with milk and honey, to the home of the Canaanites, the
> Hittites, the Amorites, the Perizzites, the Hivites and the
> Jebusites. Yes indeed, the Israelites' cry for help has
> reached me, and I have also seen the cruel way in which the

Egyptians are oppressing them. So now I am sending you to Pharaoh, for you to bring my people the Israelites out of Egypt.' Moses said to God, 'Who am I to go to Pharaoh and bring the Israelites out of Egypt?' 'I shall be with you,' God said, 'and this is the sign by which you will know that I was the one who sent you. After you have led the people out of Egypt, you will worship God on this mountain.'

Exodus 3:7-12

Before saving his people Moses must return to Egypt. His journey there is startlingly similar to Matthew's description of how Joseph leaves Egypt with Mary and the child Jesus to return to Israel. The instructions received by Moses and by Joseph are almost identical:

After Herod's death, suddenly the angel of the Lord appeared in a dream to Joseph in Egypt and said, 'Get up, take the child and his mother with you and go back to the land of Israel, for those who wanted to kill the child are dead.' So Joseph got up and, taking the child and his mother with him, went back to the land of Israel.

Matthew 2:19-21

Yahweh said to Moses in Midian, 'Go, return to Egypt, for all those who wanted to kill you are dead.' So Moses took his wife and his son and, putting them on a donkey, started back for Egypt;

Exodus 4:19-20

Note the donkey. This image, so beloved of Christmas-cards, of a donkey carrying a mother and child, is featured in the story of Moses. The donkey also appears in the Protevangelium of James in the New Testament Apocrypha, which we have already mentioned in chapter 5. The donkey is, regrettably, entirely absent from Matthew's gospel story, despite all the insistence of Christmas-cards to the contrary.

Returning to the story of Moses, once back in Egypt he goes to the pharaoh with the ringing demand of 'Let my people go', and after much ado he leads the Israelites on their exodus from Egypt. They go across the Red Sea, led by the cloud of Yahweh by day and the pillar of fire by night. *En route* Moses meets Yahweh in the cloud on Mount Sinai and following that encounter he returns from the mountain bearing the ten commandments inscribed on tablets of stone.

Matthew and his largely Jewish congregation were keenly aware of the tradition of how God called Moses and the enslaved Israelites out of Egypt to another land. Moses was and still is seen as the great liberator of his people. Matthew portrays the child Jesus as another liberator, the long-awaited leader, 'the one who is to save his people from their sins'. This comparison of Jesus and Moses is never explicit. It is achieved by skilful scriptural allusions, and parallel stories, and it is unmistakable even though Matthew does not quote the Moses story directly. In other places in his birth story Matthew does cite scriptural passages word for word:

> So Joseph got up and, taking the child and his mother with him, left that night for Egypt, where he stayed until Herod was dead. This was to fulfil what the Lord had spoken through the prophet:
> *I called my son out of Egypt.*
>
> *Matthew 2:14-15*

The prophet quoted here is Hosea who was active around the year 750 BCE. What Hosea actually says in the Hebrew Scriptures is:

> When Israel was a child I loved him,
> and I called my son out of Egypt.
>
> *Hosea 11:1*

Matthew quotes this passage directly from the Hebrew Scriptures, not using the Greek Septuagint as he does earlier in his gospel when he quotes from the book of Isaiah.[6] The Septuagint version of Hosea 11:1 reads 'Out of Egypt have I summoned his children', a translation which would have been more difficult to fit into Matthew's

---

6 See chapter 5 and the discussion of Isaiah 7:14, pp. 49-54.

story of how Jesus, 'the new Israel', is called back to his own land. Matthew chose the version best suited to his purposes.[7]

The words of the prophet Hosea and many stories of ancient Israel are echoed in how Matthew tells of Joseph moving his family to and from Egypt. These movements are dictated entirely by dreams: a dream takes him to Egypt, and a dream brings him back:

> After Herod's death, suddenly the angel of the Lord appeared in a dream to Joseph in Egypt and said, 'Get up, take the child and his mother with you and go back to the land of Israel, for those who wanted to kill the child are dead.' So Joseph got up and, taking the child and his mother with him, went back to the land of Israel. But when he learned that Archelaus had succeeded his father Herod as ruler of Judaea he was afraid to go there, and being warned in a dream he withdrew to the region of Galilee. There he settled in a town called Nazareth.
>
> *Matthew 2:19-23*

This passage covers Joseph's third dream, which takes him back to Israel, and the fourth which leads him to Nazareth. Thanks to his final dream, Joseph does not go back to Judaea, where the town of Bethlehem is situated, but to Nazareth in Galilee. As usual in Matthew's gospel, there is a sound political reason for this. When Herod had died in the year 4 BCE two of his sons, Archelaus and Antipas, had split his territory between them, and so Judaea and Galilee now came under two different jurisdictions. Archelaus carried on the family tradition of cruel tyranny in Judaea, but Antipas was a more tranquil leader, so Galilee was the better place to be. Instead of returning to Bethlehem in Judaea, Matthew has Joseph take the family to Nazareth in Galilee.

In recounting Joseph's dreams and the movements occasioned by these dreams, Matthew's allusions to the scriptures are very involved, and many-layered. He recalls the Joseph of old who led

---

7 For a discussion of this citation, see *Brown*, (1979), pp. 220-221; for further discussion of Matthew's citations of prophecy, see chapter 9 below, pp. 126-130.

the Israelites into Egypt, and he recalls Moses who delivered them. His story is rich with reminders of former journeys into and out of Egypt; former leaders of Israel and Egypt; former stars and former dreams. Matthew draws all these strands together effortlessly, almost invisibly, to create his own story.

Songs

Nothing highlights the difference between Matthew and Luke more clearly than the songs. Matthew has none; his is not a lyric voice. It is Luke who has the voice of a poet. In the first two chapters of his gospel, in the stories of the birth of Jesus, Luke provides three songs, or to be more accurate three poems which have been used as lyrics for songs almost ever since they were written. Evidence for the popularity of these lyrics is easy to find. All three have been put to music and are sung regularly in meeting houses and in great cathedrals, in recording studios and in monastery chapels all over the world. All three are used by individuals in their own meditations. All three are read as part of Christian church services. By any standard, poetic or religious, these three sets of lyrics are among the greatest songs of praise and blessing ever written. And that is not all, for within his birth narrative Luke has two more recitations of praise in the shape of a chorus and a mantra. These are shorter than the songs and probably even more famous.

According to Luke, as soon as Mary receives the message from the angel about her miraculous pregnancy she leaves home and goes to stay with her older cousin Elizabeth who by then is six months into her own miraculous pregnancy:

> Mary set out at that time and went as quickly as she could into the hill country to a town in Judah. She went into Zechariah's house and greeted Elizabeth. Now it happened that as soon as Elizabeth heard Mary's greeting, the child leapt in her womb and Elizabeth was filled with the Holy Spirit. She gave a loud cry and said, 'Of all women you are the most blessed, and blessed is the fruit of your womb. Why should I be honoured with a visit from the mother of my Lord? Look, the moment your greeting reached my ears, the child in my womb leapt for joy. Yes, blessed is she who believed that the promise made her by the Lord would be fulfilled.'
>
> *Luke 1:39-45*

That passage contains the mantra that is told on the rosary beads of hundreds of millions of people. In its most familiar English form it reads: 'Blessed art thou amongst women and blessed is the fruit of thy womb Jesus.'

Luke describes the meeting of Elizabeth and Mary as an occasion of pure joy. Both women unexpectedly find themselves bearing children they know have been conceived for a divine purpose: children who already have been dedicated to or claimed by God. What the two women are experiencing, according to Luke, is the culmination of a long tradition in which miraculously conceived children were dedicated to serve God. This returns us to the book of Judges with its story of the wife of Manoah[1], who could not conceive. The angel of Yahweh comes with the astonishing news that she is to bear a son who is to be a nazirite of God. She then tells her husband what has happened:

> '. . . A man of God has just come to me, who looked like the Angel of God, so majestic was he. I did not ask him where he came from, and he did not tell me his name. But he said to me, "You are going to conceive and will give birth to a son. From now on, drink no wine or fermented liquor, and eat

---

1 See chapter 6, p. 73.

nothing unclean. For the boy is to be God's nazirite from his mother's womb to his dying day."'"

Judges 13:6-7

It is unusual to hear of a child being dedicated to God in this way so long ago. This record refers us to a period some twelve centuries before the time of Jesus when, among all the tribal religions of the Middle and Near East, dedicating a child to the deity normally meant human sacrifice. But the tribes of the children of Israel were different, for as the record in Genesis shows Abraham had been told to spare Isaac, and after that animal sacrifice gradually replaced human sacrifice in the Hebrew tradition.[2]

When the story of Manoah's wife was told, dedicating a child to God through service to the deity was a new idea. About two hundred years later a similar dedication is recounted in the scriptures and this time the dedication is made by Hannah. She is the barren woman found praying in the temple by Eli the priest when she is so distressed and so fervent in her prayers that Eli thinks she is drunk. Hannah vows that if Yahweh gives her a child she will give the child to his service. As the story goes, 'Yahweh remembered her, Hannah conceived and, in due course, gave birth to a son...' This son is Samuel, the seer, the man of God. After he is weaned she presents him to Yahweh at the shrine and then she delivers a long prayer, often called the song of Hannah:

> Hannah then prayed as follows:
> My heart exults in Yahweh,
> in my God is my strength lifted up,
> my mouth derides my foes,
> for I rejoice in your deliverance.
>
> There is no Holy One like Yahweh,
> (indeed, there is none but you)
> no Rock like our God.
>
> Do not keep talking so proudly.
> let no arrogance come from your mouth.

2 See chapter 3, p. 22.

for Yahweh is a wise God.
his to weigh up deeds.

The bow of the mighty has been broken
but those who were tottering are now braced with
    strength.
The full fed are hiring themselves out for bread
but the hungry need labour no more;
the barren woman bears sevenfold
but the mother of many is left desolate.

Yahweh gives death and life.
brings down to Sheol and draws up:
Yahweh makes poor and rich,
he humbles and also exalts.

He raises the poor from the dust.
he lifts the needy from the dunghill
to give them a place with princes,
to assign them a seat of honour;
for to Yahweh belong the pillars of the earth,
on these he has poised the world.

He safeguards the steps of his faithful
but the wicked vanish in darkness
(for human strength can win no victories).
Yahweh, his enemies are shattered,
the Most High thunders in the heavens.

Yahweh judges the ends of the earth,
he endows his king with power,
he raises up the strength of his Anointed.

1 Samuel 2:1-10

Such is Hannah's fervent prayer. Now back to Luke's gospel.
After reporting the joyous meeting between Mary and Elizabeth,
Luke then writes his first great song. This is the most famous of the
three songs in the gospel and it is usually called the Magnificat. It is

important to remember here that Luke was an educated Greek and that he was working within an established tradition of Greek historical writing. Whenever good Greek historians reported memorable events they were always careful to include what the protagonists had to say. The result is that Greek histories are full of the most wonderful speeches because great people at great moments in their lives were always credited with great speeches, whatever the circumstances. As Professor Ed Sanders has pointed out, a Greek historian would not hesitate to attribute such speeches to his main characters even though he had little or no access to what that character actually said. An important part of an historian's role was to supply speeches that were appropriate and fitting to the character and the circumstances.[3]

Thucydides provides good examples of this in his account of the Peloponnesian War, written some four hundred years before the time of Jesus. His history is full of speeches and he explains his reporting technique very clearly:

In this history I have made use of set speeches some of which were delivered just before and others during the war. I have found it difficult to remember the precise words used in the speeches which I listened to myself and my various informants have experienced the same difficulty; so my method has been, while keeping as closely as possible to the general sense of the words that were actually used, to make the speakers say, what, in my opinion, was called for by each situation.[4]

The role of a Greek historian, according to Ed Sanders, was to attribute to the chief characters of his history well-expressed, sound and appropriate sentiments, and to have the insight to know what these sentiments would have been. Luke, the Greek historian, credits Mary with one of the finest speeches or songs of all time. This is what he knows she would have uttered at such a time in her life, for

3 *The Birth Narratives* (1987), p. 11.
4 *Thucydides* (1954), book I, p. 24.

he had strong precedents to work from. The roots of Mary's[5] song go
all the way to Hannah:

> And Mary said:
>> My soul proclaims the greatness of the Lord
>> and my spirit *rejoices in God my Saviour*;
>> because *he has looked upon the humiliation of his servant.*
>> Yes, from now onwards all generations will call me
>>> blessed,
>> for the Almighty has done great things for me.
>> *Holy is his name,*
>> *and his faithful love extends age after age to those who*
>>> *fear him.*
>> He has used the power of his arm,
>> he has routed the arrogant of heart.
>> *He has pulled down princes* from their thrones and *raised*
>>> *high the lowly.*
>> *He has filled the starving with good things*, sent the rich
>>> away empty.
>> *He has come to the help of Israel his servant, mindful of*
>>> *his faithful love*
>> — according to the promise he made to our ancestors —
>>> his mercy to Abraham and to his descendants for ever.
>>>> *Luke 1:46-55*

Now look at the prayer of Hannah and the song of Mary together. All of Mary's song is here with the more obvious parts of
Hannah's alongside:

Hannah	*Mary*
My heart exults in Yahweh,	My soul proclaims the greatness of the Lord
in my God is my strength lifted up,	and my spirit *rejoices in God my Saviour*;

5 It is usual to call this Mary's song, but there is some doubt as to whether Luke did
attribute it to Mary. See NJB footnote p. 1689.

my mouth derides my foes,
for I rejoice in your
  deliverance.

There is no Holy One like
  Yahweh,
(indeed, there is none but
  you)
no Rock like Our God.

. . .

The bow of the mighty has
  been broken
. . .

The full fed are hiring
  themselves out for bread
but the hungry need labour
  no more;
. . .
He raises the poor from the
  dust,

he lifts the needy from the
dunghill
to give them a place with
  princes,
. . .
He safeguards the steps of his
faithful . . .
. . .
he endows his king with
  power,

because *he has looked*
  upon the humiliation
  of his servant.
Yes, from now onwards
  all generations will
  call me blessed,
for the Almighty has
  done great things for
  me.

Holy is his name,
and his faithful love
  extends age after age
  to those who fear
  him.
He has used the power
  of his arm,
He has routed the
  arrogant of heart.
He has pulled down
  princes from their
  thrones and *raised*
  high the lowly
He has filled the
  starving with good
  things, sent the rich
  away empty.
He has come to the help
  of Israel his servant,
  mindful of his faithful
  love

— according to the
  promise he made to
  our ancestors —
of his mercy to
  Abraham and to

<table>
<tr><td>he raises up the strength of
his Anointed.</td><td>his descendents for
ever.</td></tr>
<tr><td style="text-align:center">Samuel 2:1-10</td><td style="text-align:right">Luke 1:46-55</td></tr>
</table>

These striking parallels between the songs of Mary and Hannah are not the only scriptural echoes in the Magnificat. Luke had many other precedents to draw on. In table I, pp. 184-91, there are no fewer than forty-two scriptural references listed for Mary's song. Trying to sort them out is rather like being a tourist alone on a first visit to Rome, or Paris or London; there is so much to see that guidance of some kind is essential, even in deciding where to start. Such guidance is by nature highly selective. The same applies with any guidance through these scriptural passages related to Mary's song. Table I points out many scriptural connections, but because it takes time and some determination to work through any such table, we are listing a few of the major scriptural connections and echoes here.

1) The voices of both Rachel and Leah are heard again in Mary's song. These are the sisters who were wives of JacobIsrael, who try to outdo each other bearing children. Two rival sisters as rival wives in a polygamous family gives rise to serious competition, leading to a succession of humiliations as well as periods of great happiness. Their story is told in the book of Genesis. At one point in the childbearing competition when things are going well, Leah declares: 'What blessedness! Women will call me blessed!', and when Rachel's turn finally comes she says 'God has taken away my disgrace!' In Mary's song the circumstances are different but the echo is clear, as Mary declares that God has '...looked upon the humiliation of his servant. Yes, from now onwards all generations will call me blessed, for the Almighty has done great things for me.'

2) Near the end of the song, Luke has Mary refer to how God has 'come to the help of Israel his servant, mindful of his faithful love (according to the promise he made to our ancestors) of his mercy to Abraham and to his descendants for ever'. These promises start with Abraham in the book of Genesis, when Abraham is promised many descendants and a new land. The promises continue, still mostly in

Genesis, in favour of the immediate children of Abraham and then are extended to Jacob and Joseph and their descendants. Several centuries later the prophet Isaiah receives and amplifies these earlier promises; and Mary's song resonates with many passages from the book of Isaiah.

> But you, Israel, my servant
> Jacob whom I have chosen,
> descendant of Abraham my friend,
> whom I have taken to myself, from the remotest parts of the
>   earth
> and summoned from countries far away,
> to whom I have said, 'You are my servant,
> I have chosen you, I have not rejected you,'
> do not be afraid, for I am with you;
> do not be alarmed, for I am your God.
> I give you strength, truly I help you,
> truly I hold you firm with my saving right hand.
> Look, all those who rage against you
> will be put to shame and humiliated;
> those who picked quarrels with you
> will be reduced to nothing and will perish.
>
> *Isaiah 41 : 8-11*

In the same spirit, at the beginning of chapter 42 of Isaiah, the Lord speaks: 'Here is my servant whom I uphold, my chosen one in whom my soul delights. I have sent my spirit upon him, he will bring fair judgement to the nations.' This language is very similar to the language in Mary's song. Further on, at the beginning of chapter 49 there is another related passage:

> Coasts and islands, listen to me,
> pay attention, distant peoples.
> Yahweh called me when I was in the womb,
> before my birth he had pronounced my name.
> He made my mouth like a sharp sword,
> he hid me in the shadow of his hand.
> He made me into a sharpened arrow

and concealed me in his quiver.
He said to me, 'Israel, you are my servant,
through whom I shall manifest my glory.

Isaiah 49:1-3

Here again is the chosen child, dedicated from the womb to the service of God. These passages are from the second part of the book of Isaiah and were written some five hundred years before the time of Jesus. They not only echo the stories of how JacobIsrael becomes the servant of God and is promised great things, they also recall stories of how Samson and Samuel were especially chosen. Luke had all of these stories as well as Isaiah's elaborations to refer to in composing Mary's song. The influences are clear; there is the chosen servant, the dedicated child, the song of praise to a mighty God, and so the story builds, layer upon layer.

3) In the New Jerusalem Bible the words 'faithful love' appear in Mary's song. This comes from a short Hebrew word *hesed*, a word appearing often in the Hebrew Scriptures. Its appears significantly in the book of the prophet Hosea who lived in the northern kingdom of Israel around 750 BCE. Hosea had married a prostitute called Gomer and they had three children, but Gomer was not faithful to Hosea and the marriage became a series of disasters. In chapter 2 of the book of Hosea there is an outburst of bitter anger and recrimination:

To court, take your mother to court!
For she is no longer my wife
nor am I her husband.
She must either remove her whoring ways from her face
and her adulteries from between her breasts.
or I shall strip her and expose her
naked as the day she was born;
I shall make her as bare as the desert,
I shall make her as dry as arid country,
and let her die of thirst. .

Hosea 2:2-4

After a lot of such wild rhetoric, Hosea calms down and begins to see a parallel between his marriage and the agreement between Yahweh and the Hebrew people. He sees how Yahweh overlooks the failures of his people, always treating them with 'hesed', or 'faithful love'. He applies this to himself and his wife:

> I shall betroth you to myself for ever,
> I shall betroth you in uprightness and justice,
> and faithful love and tenderness.
> Yes, I shall betroth you to myself in loyalty
> and in the knowledge of Yahweh.
>
> *Hosea 19-20*

Having sorted that out, Hosea records the approval of Yahweh:

> Yahweh said to me, 'Go again, love a woman who loves another man, an adulteress, and love her as Yahweh loves the Israelites although they turn to other gods and love raisin cakes.'
>
> *Hosea 3:1*

This concept of 'faithful love' is central to Mary's song. It emerges from a period of religious change in the Hebrew Scriptures. The perception of the deity was changing, and the wrathful tribal god of Mount Sinai was giving way to the idea of a universal deity, one more inclined to understand and to forgive the vagaries of humankind. In Christian thinking this more accessible deity, the god of a faithful love, has been very important. For many Christians Mary herself stands as a symbol for this kind of faithful love and this is at least in part due to the way Luke portrays Mary in her Magnificat. In the face of all difficulties and improbabilities she is seen to accept her role in the divine scheme, and this is expressed in her song of praise.

After this song Luke continues his story, telling how Mary stays with Elizabeth for three months before returning home. Attention is then focused on the birth of John the Baptist.

The time came for Elizabeth to have her child, and she gave
birth to a son; and when her neighbours and relations heard
that the Lord had lavished on her his faithful love, they
shared her joy.

Luke 1:57-58

On the prescribed eighth day John is circumcised. The only trouble
is that everyone wants to call the child Zechariah after his father.
The old man had been struck dumb several months earlier for
disbelieving the angel who told him Elizabeth was pregnant, and he
cannot speak to protest. Protest he must, because the angel had
commanded him to call the child John. So Zechariah writes 'His
name is John' on a writing tablet, and miraculously his speech is
restored. Once he starts speaking Zechariah does not want to stop
and he delivers an extraordinary oracle, which is Luke's second
song. This is known as the Benedictus:

> His father Zechariah was filled with the Holy Spirit and
> spoke this prophecy:
> *Blessed be the Lord, the God of Israel,*
> for he has visited his people, *he has set them free,*
> and he has established for us a saving power
> in the House of his servant David,
> just as he proclaimed,
> by the mouth of his holy prophets from ancient times,
> that he would save us from our enemies
> and *from the hands of* all *those who hate us,*
> and show *faithful love to our ancestors,*
> and so *keep in mind his* holy covenant.
> This was the oath he swore
> to our father Abraham,
> that he would grant us, free from fear,
> to be delivered from the hands of our enemies,
> to serve him in holiness and uprightness
> in his presence, all our days.
> And you, little child,
> you shall be called Prophet of the Most High,
> for you will go before the Lord

> *to prepare a way for him,*
> to give his people knowledge of salvation
> through the forgiveness of their sins,
> because of the faithful love of our God
> in which the rising Sun has come from on high to visit us,
> to give light to *those who live*
> *in darkness and the shadow dark as death,*
> and to guide our feet
> into *the way of peace.*

Luke 1:67-79

With Zechariah's song, as with Mary's, there is a model in the Hebrew Scriptures. More accurately, there are a great many models. Here again, as with Mary's song, Table I comes in useful. It lists a number of references for Zechariahs song in the Hebrew Scriptures and there are many more which are not listed.

These scriptural roots are less obvious than those for Mary's song, but they are just as strong. They start with a poem that appears twice in the Hebrew Scriptures. One appearance is in Psalm 18, and the other is in the twenty-second chapter of the second book of Samuel. Both of these are thanksgivings of King David who is praising Yahweh for delivering him from violence. The two versions of the poem are almost identical until the very end when the version in Samuel continues with a few extra verses called the 'last words of David'. These last words alter the tone of the preceding poem, because David here is shown to be an old man, signing off and relinquishing his hold on life with a hymn of thanks. In the same way, in the Benedictus, Zechariah is shown to be an old man giving thanks and signing off, while he blesses God for protecting the people of Israel. Here are two of the many points of resemblance between David's poem and Zechariah's song:

1) Both Psalm 18 and the book of Samuel contain the following passage:

> He reached down from on high, snatched me up,
> pulled me from the watery depths,
> rescued me from my mighty foe,

from my enemies who were stronger than I
They assailed me on my day of disaster
but Yahweh was there to support me;
he freed me, set me at large.
he rescued me because he loves me.

Psalm 18:16-19
2 Samuel 22:17-20

As he proclaims his song of praise in Luke's gospel, Zechariah similarly thanks God who 'visited his people and set them free', and who had promised he 'would save us from our enemies and from all those who hate us'.

2) Another passage found in both Psalm eighteen and the book of Samuel is as follows:

For this I will praise you, Yahweh, among the nations,
and sing praise to your name
He saves his king, time after time,
displays faithful love for his anointed,
for David and his heirs for ever.

Psalm 18:49-50
2 Samuel 22:50-51

On the same note, Zechariah praises God saying:

. . . that he would save us from our *enemies*, and *from the hand of* all *those who hate us*,
and show *faithful love to our ancestors*,
and so *keep in mind* his holy *covenant*.
This was the oath he swore
to our father Abraham,
that he would grant us, free from fear,
to be delivered from the hands of our enemies,
to serve him in holiness and uprightness
in his presence, all our days.

Luke 1: 70-75

In the next part of the song Zechariah goes on to deliver an oracle over his young child. Here John the Baptist is identified as the one who precedes the Lord. 'And you little child, you shall be called the prophet of the Most High' says Zechariah, 'for you will go before the Lord to prepare a way for him...' This oracle is his answer to the question asked by friends and neighbours who are wondering about the identity of the child John. All four gospel writers have their own ways of establishing the identity of John. Here Luke is drawing on what both Matthew and Mark say in their earlier gospels, and all three of them are quoting almost verbatim for the book of Isaiah:

> A voice cries 'Prepare in the desert
> a way for Yahweh.
> Make a straight highway for our God
> across the wastelands.
> Let every valley be filled in,
> every mountain and hill be levelled,
> every cliff become a plateau,
> every escarpment a plain;
> then the glory of Yahweh will be revealed
> and all humanity will see it together,
>   for the mouth of Yahweh has spoken.'
>
> *Isaiah 40:3-5*

Zechariah ends his song speaking of the coming Lord for whom his son John will prepare the way. In doing so, he uses the metaphor of a 'rising sun' which will cast light on those who live in darkness. This is a very familiar figure of speech throughout the book of Isaiah:

> The people who walk in darkness have seen a great light;
> on the inhabitants of a country in shadow dark as death light
> has blazed forth.
>
> *Isaiah 9:1*

> I have made you a covenant of the people
> and light to the nations,
> to open the eyes of the blind,
> to free captives from prison,
> and those who live in darkness from the dungeon.
>
> *Isaiah 42:6-7*

In Luke's gospel the story goes on from Zechariah's song and the briefly mentioned boyhood of John the Baptist to the birth of Jesus. Luke maintains there is a census, ordered by Quirinius, which forces Joseph to go back to his home city of Bethlehem to register. As discussed in chapter 1[6], Luke makes a mistake in naming Quirinius as governor at the time of Jesus's birth. Luke has to move Joseph and Mary to Bethlehem because the new leader of Israel is expected to be born there. Once Mary and Joseph reach Bethlehem, Luke goes on to explain that there is no accommodation to be found and so when the child is born he is placed in a manger. Luke does not say that the birth takes place in a stable, although for centuries this has been inferred from his reference to a manger. Equally, the presence of the ox and ass have been inferred from the reference to a manger. Another argument in favour of the ox and ass is that in first century Palestine it was not unusual for ordinary people to share their housing with domestic animals. However, this is all speculation for Luke does not mention animals at all, nor does he really specify the location of the birth. The word he uses to describe the location is ambiguous. It is *katalyma*, a Greek word, which in this context can be taken to mean a 'home', a 'room', or 'lodgings'. It is the same word that appears later in his gospel to describe the location of the last supper, and in that context is usually translated as an 'upper room' or even 'guest room'.[7] However, no linguistic uncertainties about the word *katalyma* are likely to dislodge the idea of Jesus being born in a stable. For better or worse, this has become one of the most popular images of the nativity, in company with the ox and the ass, the flight into Egypt on a donkey, and the blond angel bearing lilies to Mary wearing blue.

After Luke's description of the birth the scene shifts to the shepherds out in the countryside at night, and this is the setting for Luke's famous angelic chorus:

> In the countryside close by there were shepherds out in the
> fields keeping guard over their sheep during the watches of
> the night. An angel of the Lord stood over them and the
> glory of the Lord shone round them. They were terrified,

6 See chapter 1, pp. 7-8; chapter 10, pp. 135-137.
7 *Brown* (1979), pp. 399-401. For the translation 'guest room' see NIV.

but the angel said, 'Do not be afraid. Look, I bring you news of great joy, a joy to be shared by the whole people. Today in the town of David a Saviour has been born to you; he is Christ the Lord. And here is a sign for you: you will find a baby wrapped in swaddling clothes and lying in a manger.' And all at once with the angel there was a great throng of the hosts of heaven, praising God with the words:
> Glory to God in the highest heaven,
> and on earth peace for those he favours.

Luke 2:8-14

This chorus of angels has a distinguished background. This awesome 'glory of the Lord' shining around them is a reminder of the bright cloud of Yahweh, and their song recalls powerful music from the first part of the book of Isaiah:

In the year of King Uzziah's death I saw the Lord seated on a high and lofty throne; his train filled the sanctuary. Above him stood seraphs, each one with six wings: two to cover its face, two to cover its feet and two for flying; and they were shouting these words to each other:
> Holy, holy, holy is Yahweh Sabaoth
> His glory fills the whole earth.

The door-posts shook at the sound of their shouting, and the Temple was full of smoke.

Isaiah 6:1-4

This describes a vision of the young Isaiah dating back to about the year 740 BCE, when King Uzziah died. Here the exultant glory of Yahweh is hidden in the temple smoke, and this glory is proclaimed by strange other-worldly creatures, referred to as seraphs. These seraphs were a feature of the first temple Solomon built; they were fantastical statues and along with other fantastical statues called cherubs they flanked the holiest place of the Temple, the place of sacrifice where the smoke originated. Just what the statues of these seraphs looked like no one really knows, but figures of contemporary Assyrian cherubs have survived. They are sphinx-like winged creatures, more like gargoyles than guardian angels. If the seraphs were anything like the cherubs they would have been an awesome presence in the Holy of Holies. Luke describes his chorus of angels as 'a great throng of the hosts of heaven'. The shepherds are terrified.

The last of Luke's lyrics is the song called the Nunc Dimittis and it is attributed to one Simeon:

> Now in Jerusalem there was a man named Simeon. He was an upright and devout man; he looked forward to the restoration of Israel and the Holy Spirit rested on him. It had been revealed to him by the Holy Spirit that he would not see death until he had set eyes on the Christ of the Lord. Prompted by the Spirit he came to the Temple; and when the parents brought in the child Jesus to do for him what the Law required, he took him into his arms and blessed God; and he said:
>> Now, Master, you are letting your servant go in peace
>> as you promised;
>> for my eyes have seen the salvation
>> which you have made ready in the sight of the nations;
>> a light of revelation for the gentiles
>> and a glory for your people Israel.
>
> *Luke 2:25-32*

Just like the other songs, this short poem unlocks a network of scriptural references. Luke is here restating a passage from the second part of the book of Isaiah:

> Yahweh has bared his holy arm
> for all the nations to see,
> and all the ends of the earth
> have seen the salvation of our God.
>
> *Isaiah 52:10*

In the book of Isaiah there are many references to the 'nations'. These nations are generally assumed to mean the territories and kingdoms surrounding what had been the kingdom of Israel under David and Solomon. These were foreign powers, and hostile tribes. Throughout the book of Isaiah both the hope and the confidence are fervently expressed that the former golden age of the kingdom of Israel will be restored, to the wonder and amazement of all these outsiders:

> And now Yahweh has spoken,
> who formed me in the womb to be his servant,
> to bring Jacob back to him
> and to re-unite Israel to him;
> — I shall be honoured in Yahweh's eyes,
> and my God has been my strength.
> He said, 'It is not enough for you to be my servant,
> to restore the tribes of Jacob and bring back the survivors of
>   Israel:
> I shall make you a light to the nations
> so that my salvation may reach the remotest parts of earth.'
>
> *Isaiah 49:5-7*

And in the same spirit:

> I, Yahweh, have called you in saving justice,
> I have grasped you by the hand and shaped you;
> I have made you a covenant of the people
> and light to the nations, . . .
>
> *Isaiah 42:6*

When Luke echoes these passages from Isaiah in Simeon's song, he emphasizes that Jesus is to be 'a light of revelation to the gentiles', as well as a glory to Israel. He speaks of a salvation 'made ready in the sight of the nations'. From Luke's vantage point, writing in Greece or Turkey, it is worth stressing that Jesus has been born for the benefit of outsiders as well as for the benefit of Israel. In Simeon's song he does this by recalling Isaiah's repeated references to 'the nations', and casting an entirely new light on them.

Table I provides detailed scriptural references for all the songs in Luke's birth stories. The table is far from definitive, but it can be very helpful. Glancing through it will give an idea of the strength of scriptural tradition Luke draws on. He turns to the book of Isaiah repeatedly; particularly to the second part of Isaiah which contains some of the finest poetry in the scriptures; he turns to the stories of the patriarchs, and to the psalms. He turns to well-known and beautiful scriptural passages and he uses them in writing his great songs. This technique has proved effective. The songs have endured.

Recognition:
The MAGI

After Jesus had been born at Bethlehem in Judaea
during the reign of King Herod, suddenly some
wise men came to Jerusalem from the east asking
'Where is the infant king of the Jews? We saw his star as it
rose and have come to do him homage.'

Matthew 2:1-2

Now it happened that when the angels had gone from them
into heaven, the shepherds said to one another, 'Let us go to
Bethlehem and see this event which the Lord has made
known to us.'

Luke 2:15

No nativity scene is complete without the wise men and the
shepherds. Often they are pictured together, the regal strangers

with their gifts and the humble herdsmen with their animals, all crowding into a stable to worship the child in the manger. In the gospel stories the scene is not quite so crowded. The wise men are found only in Matthew's gospel, the shepherds only in Luke's. These are not the only characters in the birth stories who recognize the child Jesus and pay homage to him, but they are certainly the best known. In the next two chapters we will be looking at the assorted characters who act as witnesses in the birth stories, all the people who recognize and honour the child Jesus. We begin with the most intriguing of them, and this takes us into Matthew's gospel and into the company of the wise men.

Over the centuries the wise men have become enormously popular figures. In the Christmas-card trade they may be even more popular than Mary and Joseph and the baby Jesus. With his story of these exotic visitors, Matthew for once outdoes Luke. Luke's shepherds have never generated the same amount of interest or captured the imagination in the same way as Matthew's wise men. Yet Matthew does not provide much detail about these wise men. They come from 'the east', he says, but that is all the information he supplies about their origins. He does not give their names, nor does he say how many of them there are. This has given rise to a lot of speculation. In early Christian art there are sometimes two wise men, sometimes three, and sometimes four. The number goes as high as twelve in some medieval lists within the Eastern Christian tradition.[1] But because Matthew says they present three gifts — gold, frankincense, and myrrh — the wise men are usually numbered as three.

Perhaps because so little information is provided about them, these mysterious figures add a special fascination to Matthew's birth story. They carry with them an aura of inspired knowledge, of wealth, and of far exotic lands. Elaborate, highly embellished stories have always been told about the 'three' wise men. They have been called astrologers, seers and soothsayers; they have been transformed into crowned kings dressed in rich garments; they are pictured crossing vast desert lands on their camels with their rich

---

1 For a discussion of the numbers of the wise men see *Brown* (1979), p. 198.

gifts glinting in the starlight. Great paintings often show one black king, one elderly king and one fair young king; representing all races and ages and nations coming to pay homage to Jesus. These kings' have been given many different names. In an early tradition of Eastern Christianity they were called Hormizdah, King of Persia; Yazdegerd, King of Saba; and Perozadh, King of Sheba. They have also been known as Hor, Basanter and Karusdan. In western Christianity the names of Balthasar, Melchior and Gaspar, or Caspar are better known, names that can be traced back to the sixth century.[2]

Matthew does not use the word 'king' for the wise men. He uses 'magi', a term covering a wide range of astrologers, augurers and sages involved with mysterious sciences or magical arts. There were in Matthew's time respected magi who studied and interpreted celestial movements as well as dubious characters dealing in strange portents, foretelling the future and interpreting dreams. When Matthew says that his magi come from 'the east' he could mean Persia, or Babylon, or Arabia. What is important in Matthew's story is that these men are foreigners from outside the Jewish world. They are portrayed as wise gentiles inspired to come from a great distance to honour the child Jesus; presenting gifts, paying homage, and acknowledging him as the infant 'King of the Jews'. This type of recognition and obeisance would not have seemed at all odd in Matthew's day. Strangers had honoured kings of Israel in this way before. In the Hebrew Scriptures, many stories tell of noble foreigners bringing gifts of great value to the rulers of Israel:

> The kings of Sheba and Saba
>   will offer gifts;
> all kings will do him homage,
>   all nations will become his servants.
> . . . (Long may he live; may the gold of Sheba be given him!)
> Prayer will be offered for him constantly,
>   and blessings invoked on him all day.
>
> *Psalm 72:10,11,15*

2 For a discussion of the magi as kings, details of their names, etc., see *Brown* (1979), pp. 197-200.

Passages like this were part of Matthew's background and part of the political and religious history of the Jewish people. Psalm 72 tells of the glory of King David, whose reign was a time of such power and prosperity that many other nations came to pay homage. Matthew's story of the wise men recalls the honours heaped on King David, and on David's son and successor, Solomon. Solomon's glory was even greater than that of David. He reaped the benefit of the achievements of his father who had unified the Hebrew tribes into one kingdom. In Solomon's time the nation flourished and the wealth poured in. The reputation for wealth was assumed to carry with it great wisdom, and reports of the wealth and wisdom of Solomon spread far and wide. They even reached Sheba, that half-mythical land which today is probably the Yemen or Ethiopia.

> The queen of Sheba heard of Solomon's fame and came to test him with difficult questions. She arrived in Jerusalem with a very large retinue, with camels laden with spices and an immense quantity of gold and precious stones. Having reached Solomon, she discussed with him everything that she had in mind, and Solomon had an answer for all her questions; not one of them was too obscure for the king to answer for her. When the queen of Sheba saw how very wise Solomon was, the palace which he had built, the food at his table, the accommodation for his officials, the organization of his staff and the way they were dressed, his cupbearers, and the burnt offerings which he presented in the Temple of Yahweh, it left her breathless...
>
> *1 Kings 10:1-6*

After all this display of wealth the queen of Sheba is totally convinced of the wisdom of Solomon, and she says:

> '... Blessed be Yahweh your God who has shown you his favour by setting you on the throne of Israel! Because of Yahweh's everlasting love for Israel, he has made you king to administer law and justice.' And she presented the king with a hundred and twenty talents of gold and great quantities of spices and precious stones; no such wealth of

spices ever came again as those which the queen of Sheba
gave to King Solomon.

1 Kings 10:9-10

This was the zenith of the power of Israel. Following Solomon's
reign, the Hebrew tribes split into two kingdoms and after a few
generations of continued success for the larger northern kingdom,
their power slowly faded. By Matthew's time the acknowledged
golden age was the age of David and Solomon. Nothing ever
surpassed this time:

> All King Solomon's drinking vessels were of gold, and all
> the plate in the House of the Forest of Lebanon was of pure
> gold; silver was little thought of in Solomon's days, since
> the king had a fleet of Tarshish at sea with Hiram's fleet,
> and once every three years the fleet of Tarshish would
> come back laden with gold and silver, ivory, apes and
> baboons. For riches and for wisdom, King Solomon sur-
> passed all kings on earth, and the whole world consulted
> Solomon to hear the wisdom which God had implanted in
> his heart; and every one would bring a present with him:
> things made of silver, things made of gold, robes, armour,
> spices, horses and mules; and this went on year after year.

1 Kings 10:21-25

These stories of the wonders of King Solomon's time were
compiled over a period of three or four hundred years following the
time of Solomon. From this same period in the writing of the
Hebrew Scriptures, comes a very tender, very beautiful set of love
poems which celebrate the golden age of Israel at the time of
Solomon. The poems appear in the Hebrew Scriptures as the Song
of Solomon, or the Song of Songs, or just the Song. The place of such
love poetry in the scriptures has long been debated. In the first
century the Song was staunchly defended by a leading rabbi named
Akiba. After the fall of Jerusalem in 70 CE, Rabbi Akiba was one of
those responsible for establishing the headquarters and school at
Jamnia which we discussed in chapter 4. In speaking of the Song of
Songs, Rabbi Akiba is reported to have said that 'the whole world is

not worth the day on which the Song was given to Israel. For all the Writings are holy, but the Song of Songs is a holy of the holies.'[3]

The Song of Songs not only celebrates the love of a man and a woman, it also celebrates all the good things of life which were part of this confident and happy time in the history of Israel. The costly gifts the magi present to the infant Jesus in Matthew's gospel bring with them a sense of the blessing of wealth which is so pervasive in the Song of Songs:

> What is this coming up from the desert
> like a column of smoke,
> breathing of myrrh and frankincense
> and every exotic perfume?

Song 3:6

In the first century, the Song was a reminder of a paradise long lost to the people of Israel, of an era that could be recovered only if Israel were to regain status and power. The stories of David and Solomon; their wealth, their wisdom, and the high esteem they enjoyed were also reminders of this vanished glory. In 587 BCE Solomon's temple (founded by Solomon), of such magnifcient repute, was pillaged and destroyed by the Babylonians under King Nebuchadnezzar, and Jerusalem was laid waste. This destruction of Jerusalem led to a reported seventy years of exile in Babylon for many Israelites, and to an acute yearning for a renewal of the glories of the past. This is why so much of the writing in the scriptures looks back to the age of David and Solomon with wonder and with longing.

Most of the second part of the book of Isaiah was written during the Babylonian exile. The writer, often called the second Isaiah, is an unknown poet who spent most if not all of his life in exile in Babylon. His writings became attached to those of the first Isaiah, the prophet and political adviser to kings of Judah, who had lived nearly two centuries earlier in Jerusalem. The writings of the second Isaiah both mourn the time of exile and console the people of Israel with the great hope that their glory will come again:

3 Quoted in the article on the Song of Songs in *A Dictionary of the Bible* (1902), vol. 4, p. 589.

Arise, shine out, for your light has come,
and the glory of Yahweh has risen on you.
Look! though night still covers the earth
and darkness the peoples,
on you Yahweh is rising
and over you his glory can be seen.
The nations will come to your light
and kings to your dawning brightness.
Lift up your eyes and look around:
all are assembling and coming towards you,
your sons coming from far away
and your daughters being carried on the hip.
At this sight you will grow radiant,
your heart will throb and dilate,
since the riches of the sea will flow to you,
the wealth of the nations come to you;
camels in throngs will fill your streets,
the young camels of Midian and Ephah;
everyone in Saba will come,
bringing gold and incense
and proclaiming Yahweh's praises.

Isaiah 60:1-6

Through his reading of the Hebrew Scriptures Matthew would have known this great declaration of hope in the book of Isaiah. He would also have known its background; the fall of Jerusalem, the Babylonian exile, the overpowering sense of loss, and the yearning for renewed power and glory. In Matthew's time this had a very contemporary ring. He was writing his gospel in 70 CE after another catastrophic fall of Jerusalem, when the temple and the city had again been devastated, this time by the Romans. Isaiah's declaration of hope and promise, the stories of the glory of David, and the insistence that the glory would come again all reach a joyful culmination in Matthew's stories of the birth of Jesus. These stories are assertions that the glory of Israel has indeed come again. This can be seen in everything Matthew says of the infant Jesus, and particularly in his story of the magi. In telling of the magi Matthew describes what he believes to be the formal recognition of the new

Israel, and he does so by using recognizable language and images from the scriptures. The gold and frankincense and myrrh presented to Matthew's 'infant King of the Jews' are gifts symbolizing the long-awaited renewal of a wonderful kingdom. Noble envoys from other nations once again are seen to honour Israel, and their gifts are signs of new joy and hope, signs of homage to the new Israel, signs that an age of glory has come again.

As always when examining the scriptural background of the gospel stories, there is more to come. In telling of the magi and their gifts and how they followed the star to find the child Jesus, Matthew is drawing on more than this one strand of well-known stories about the wealth and glory of Israel. His story looks back far beyond the golden age of Israel to a period well before King David had established a united kingdom. Matthew draws on ancient visions and prophecies in the scriptures which held out great hope for the Hebrew people who had escaped from Egypt. Balaam the seer, the man with the recalcitrant donkey was a leading visionary of ancient times. His oracles can be interpreted as foreseeing the glory of David, or the glory of Jesus, or both:

> The prophecy of Balaam son of Beor,
>   the prophecy of the man with far-seeing eyes,
> the prophecy of one who hears the words of God,
> . . . He sees what Shaddai makes him see,
> receives the divine answer, and his eyes are opened.
> I see him — but not in the present.
> I perceive him — but not close at hand:
> a star is emerging from Jacob,
> a sceptre is arising from Israel, . . .
>
> *Numbers 24:15-17*

This passage has already appeared once, in chapter 7, but it is worth repeating Balaam's remarkable oracle about the star rising from Israel. This oracle is a direct influence on Matthew's story of the magi and it is also a good indication of how Matthew folds many layers of scriptural references into his stories. On the face of it, Matthew simply tells an interesting story of noble visitors who come bearing gifts of great worth to a new 'infant king', but in doing so he opens out a wealth of similar stories and references to noble visitors bringing rich gifts. Then in going on to say that these visitors are led by a star, Matthew draws in even more and earlier layers of scripture, including the ancient oracle of Balaam.

Balaam and the wise men have a lot in common. Like Matthew's magi, Balaam is a mysterious figure possessing strange visionary powers. When he declares to the outraged King Balak of Moab that he will not curse the Israelites as requested, the language of Balaam is the language of superstition and the occult, the language of magic and enchantment: 'There is no omen whatever against Jacob,' he says, no augury at all against Israel.' Balaam is acknowledged as a powerful augurer, for when he is sought out by King Balak it is because the king believes that whatever Balaam pronounces will come true:

> Now Balak son of Zippor was king of Moab at the time. He sent messengers to summon Balaam son of Beor, at Pethor on the River, in the territory of the Amawites, saying, 'Look, a people coming from Egypt has overrun the whole countryside; they have halted at my very door. I beg you come and curse this people for me, for they are stronger than I am. We may then be able to defeat them and drive them out of the country. For this I know: anyone you bless is blessed, anyone you curse is accursed.'
>
> *Numbers 22:5-6*

Balaam, like Matthew's magi, comes from a region to the east of Israel. His region is named as 'Pethor on the river, in the territory of the Amawites', which means on the Euphrates river three or four hundred miles upstream from Babylon. Although Balaam is not an Israelite, he espouses the cause of the Israelites despite pressure from a powerful king. In refusing to curse the Israelites, he refuses to help the king who wants to get rid of them. It is the same with the wise men in Matthew's gospel: a king with evil intentions asks foreign seers to help destroy his enemy and the foreigners do not co-operate.

Then Herod summoned the wise men to see him privately. He asked them the exact date on which the star had appeared and sent them on to Bethlehem with the words, 'Go and find out all about the child, and when you have found him, let me know, so that I too may go and do him homage.' Having listened to what the king had to say, they set out. And suddenly the star they had seen rising went forward and halted over the place where the child was. The sight of the star filled them with delight, and going into the house they saw the child with his mother Mary, and falling to their knees they did him homage. Then, opening their treasures, they offered him gifts of gold and frankincense and myrrh. But they were given a warning in a dream not to go back to Herod, and returned to their own country by a different way.

Matthew 2:7-12

The magi here are 'given warning in a dream' to avoid Herod. Once again, the power of dreams is crucial, just as it is with Joseph the husband of Mary and the Joseph of old. In the case of Balaam the seer, no warning dream is described, but divine instructions do reach him. Just like the magi he is told to refuse to co-operate with a hostile king, so when Balak sends for Balaam the seer has been forewarned:

God said to Balaam, 'You are not to go with them. You are not to curse the people, for they are blessed.' In the morning Balaam got up and said to the chiefs sent by Balak, 'Go back to your country, for Yahweh will not let me go with you.' So the chiefs of Moab got up, went back to Balak and said, 'Balaam refuses to come with us.' And again Balak sent chiefs, more numerous and more renowned than the first. They came to Balaam and said, 'A message from Balak son of Zippor, "Now do not refuse to come to me. I will load you with honours and do whatever you say. I beg you come and curse this people for me."' In reply, Balaam said to Balak's envoys, 'Even if Balak gave me his house full of silver and gold, I could not go against the order of Yahweh my God in anything, great or small . . .'

Numbers 22:12-19

Eventually Balaam does go to Moab and delivers his unwelcome oracle. After that, 'Balaam then got up, left and went home.' Similarly the magi in Matthew's gospel 'returned to their own country by a different way'.

As we saw in chapter 7 it is the star that activates the magi and brings them to Bethlehem. Matthew establishes this location very firmly, and in doing so he brings in an explicit scriptural explanation:

> He called together all the chief priests and the scribes of the people, and inquired of them where the Christ was to be born. They told him, 'At Bethlehem in Judaea, for this is what the prophet wrote:
> *And you, Bethlehem,* in the land of Judah,
> you are by no means the *least among the leaders of Judah,*
> for *from you will come a leader*
> who will *shepherd* my people Israel.'
>
> *Matthew 2:4-6*

The prophet Matthew quotes here is Micah, one of the twelve prophets whose short books are grouped together at the end of the Hebrew Scriptures. Micah was writing about eight centuries before Matthew's time when everything was going wrong for Israel. This was the time of the Assyrian conquests when the already splintered kingdom of Israel was in danger of splintering even further. Although Micah's book has been much altered since he wrote it, it still carries his message about the evils perpetrated by the privileged classes of his day, and it still clearly voices his expectation that one day a great ruler will come to clear up all the problems. The passage Matthew quotes from Micah follows a description of the trials of Jerusalem during one of the many times it was under threat. For Matthew, writing a mere decade or so after the devastation of Jerusalem in a later era, the words of Micah carried great weight:

> But you (Bethlehem) Ephrathah,
> the least of the clans of Judah,
> from you will come for me
> a future ruler of Israel

whose origins go back to the distant past,
to the days of old.
Hence Yahweh will abandon them
only until she who is in labour gives birth,
and then those who survive of his race
will be reunited to the Israelites.
He will take his stand and he will shepherd them
with the power of Yahweh,
with the majesty of the name of his God,
and they will be secure, for his greatness will extend
henceforth to the most distant parts of the country.

Micah 5:1-3

Here Micah longs for a ruler of Israel whose 'origins go back to the distant past'; a ruler of stature and authority who would deliver Jerusalem and all of Israel. The passage from the second Isaiah quoted earlier in this chapter voices the same desire from a later era. Both the passage from Isaiah and the one from Micah hope for another David, another glorious and powerful leader, and by Matthew's time they had become part of what looked like a very strong prophetic tradition.

This prophetic tradition can be traced back some thirteen centuries before Matthew's time, to Balaam the seer and his favourable oracles for Israel. Later seers followed, men like Samuel and Nathan, Elijah and Elisha. By the time of the late eighth century many more had appeared, men like Micah and Amos, Hosea and the first Isaiah. There was by then an established tradition of great visionary leaders among the Israelites. The words of such seers or prophets were considered by later generations to be divinely inspired, filled with insight and knowledge about the joys and the griefs that awaited Israel. It is easy enough to see how this came about. The oracles of the earliest seers were known from a mixture of oral and written tradition. Many centuries passed before this material was assembled into the form we now recognize as the first books of the scriptures. During these centuries when the recorded scriptures were taking shape, the glory of the kingdom of Israel came and went and by the time of such prophets as the first Isaiah the sayings of the very early seers such as Balaam were being assembled and interpreted in the full knowledge of a glory that had both come and gone. So when the oracles of Balaam, the 'man with far-seeing eyes', were being honoured as prophetic visions of the future, that 'future' had already occurred in the golden age of David and Solomon, and thus Balaam's foresight was being honoured with the benefit of hindsight. In other words those who read or heard his oracles in later centuries knew what had happened in the intervening years and could interpret Balaam's words in a way that might have surprised Balaam himself. This same process continues throughout the Hebrew Scriptures. Many more prophetic writings were recorded and by the time of Matthew and Luke the tradition of looking back to the oracles and prophecies of the past and relating them to what had already happened was so strong that the writers routinely understood recent events, whether favourable or catastrophic, as fulfilments' of prophecy. Prophetic writings were examined minutely, like a kind of inspired code. Such writings were believed to contain every possible political and religious insight and all that could be known about the unfolding history of the people of Israel.

In his gospel Matthew naturally turns to the prophets and examines their writings and uses their authority to support what he is saying. He is convinced that a great new leader of Israel has been born and he tries to convey this by quoting from these prophets. In his birth stories Matthew declares that no fewer than five selected passages from prophetic writings have been 'fulfilled', and he cites them verbatim. Some of these citations are very puzzling. As we saw in chapter 5, he quotes a disputed version of Isaiah 7:14, and he goes on to quote some other very difficult passages.

When Joseph dreams his final dream, and is instructed to return to Nazareth, Matthew says:

> ... being warned in a dream he withdrew to the region of Galilee. There he settled in a town called Nazareth. In this way the words spoken through the prophets were to be fulfilled:
>
> *He will be called a Nazarene.*
>
> *Matthew 2:22-3*

Much baffled searching of scriptures has resulted from Matthew citing these particular 'words spoken by the prophets'. No one is at all sure what words Matthew is referring to. The most logical explanation for 'He will be called a Nazarene' should of course be geographical, and it is natural to assume that Matthew is quoting a passage from the scriptures referring to Nazareth. Unfortunately there is no prophetic text in the Hebrew Scriptures that even mentions Nazareth. These 'words spoken by the prophets' do not exist. Yet geographically the citation does makes sense, because in all the gospels Jesus is called a Nazarene which seems to mean that he came from Nazareth in Galilee. In this citation Matthew could simply be playing with words. He could be alluding to the term 'nazirite', a word already discussed in chapter 6. Nazirites were special holy men selected to serve the deity. Over the centuries their number had included Samson and Elijah and John the Baptist. Matthew also could be playing on the Hebrew word *neser*, meaning branch or shoot. This word recalls a passage from the book of Isaiah:

> A shoot will spring from the stock of Jesse,
> a new shoot will grow from his roots.
> On him will rest the spirit of Yahweh, . . .
>
> *Isaiah 11 :1*

No matter how this passage is interpreted, Matthew is here asserting the identity of Jesus, be it as a neser of the line of David who was Jesse's son, or as a 'nazirite', or as the teacher from Nazareth. The citation 'He will be called a Nazarene' could be a pun bringing together all these forms of identification. Although no prophet in the Hebrew Scriptures declares anything about Nazarenes, Matthew apparently believes there should be such a prophecy.

Matthew's other citations from the prophets also try to emphasize the identity of Jesus. The citation from Micah quoted earlier in this chapter establishes Bethlehem as the birthplace, and being born there at once links Jesus to the house of David. Another of the citations is also connected to the 'town of David'. When Mary and Joseph depart for Egypt, they escape the killing of the boy babies and they leave behind a grieving Bethlehem:

Then were fulfilled the words spoken through the prophet Jeremiah:

> *A voice is heard in Ramah,*
> *lamenting and weeping bitterly:*
> *it is Rachel weeping for her children,*
> *refusing to be comforted*
> *because they are no more.*

Matthew 2:18

In Ramah poor Rachel is said to be weeping eternally for the children she could not have. Ramah refers to more than one location in the general vicinity of Jerusalem, and this is where Rachel is said to have died at a time when she and Jacob were travelling to Bethlehem. None of these places are more than a few miles apart. There is a strong tradition that Rachel was buried in or near Bethlehem, and her grave there is a place of pilgrimage to this day. Of course Bethlehem was a town of high honour in Israel for reasons other than Rachel's grave. This was where Ruth, the great-grandmother of David, went to live when she left Moab and where she found and was found by Boaz. Bethlehem was where the young David had been raised by his father Jesse before being discovered by the prophet Samuel and chosen as the king of Israel. In emphasizing the connection with Bethlehem, Matthew is again affirming the lineage of Jesus, and again asserting his identity as the promised leader of Israel.

Although Matthew firmly sets the birth of Jesus in Bethlehem with the help of two citations from scriptures, he is equally firm in moving Joseph and Mary and Jesus away from Bethlehem to Egypt. They stay in Egypt for an unspecified length of time 'to fulfil what the Lord had spoken through the prophet', as Matthew says. Here he refers to the prophecy of Hosea already quoted in chapter 7: 'Out of Egypt have I called my son.' This aligns Jesus with Moses. Moses had led the Israelites out of Egypt to freedom, and he had led his people towards a new understanding of their deity through the revelations made to him on Mount Sinai. In Matthew's gospel, Jesus is pro-claimed as an even greater leader than Moses. Matthew presents Jesus as the great liberator of Israel and all people, and as the one who leads all people to a new understanding of the deity.

In citing five prophetic passages in his birth story, Matthew quite evidently sets out to emphasize the identity of Jesus. Some of the passages he quotes seem to have been forced into the story for no immediately obvious reason, but all of them are basic to Matthew's method. He is writing in a tradition that had always looked back to the prophets and to other parts of the scriptures, and that had always understood recent events in the light of what the scriptures said. From the very outset Matthews' gospel is concerned with who Jesus is. It is not surprising that Matthew, who opens his gospel with an immensely long genealogy, also searches the scriptures so diligently for prophetic passages he believes help to identify Jesus.

Matthew's five citations are the most obvious of all his scriptural references. They are cited baldly and with little explanation. Matthew uses other scriptural material in his birth stories with far more artistry. The story of the magi is probably the best-known example of this. It is rooted in an intricate web of scriptural allusion that is never intrusive and never didactic. The star is another example, and Joseph the dreamer is yet another. Layer upon layer, scriptural references come together to create stories in that there is a wealth of allusion that unfolds as the text is read.

Matthew's layers of scriptural references are many and complex, but they can be disentangled and examined one strand at a time. What emerges from that process is how at a very basic level these scriptural references serve one purpose. Direct citations and indirect allusions alike, they all help to identify Jesus and proclaim him as the 'infant king of the Jews'. This process of identification is publicly acknowledged and publicly recognized in Matthew's story when the magi arrive. This is where Matthew's method in his gospel can be seen at its best.

X

Recognition:
Shepherds and Elders

> In the countryside close by there were shepherds
> out in the fields keeping guard over their sheep dur-
> ing the watches of the night. An angel of the Lord
> stood over them and the glory of the Lord shone round
> them. They were terrified, but the angel said, 'Do not be
> afraid. Look, I bring you news of great joy, a joy to be
> shared by the whole people. Today in the town of David a
> Saviour has been born to you; he is Christ the Lord. And
> here is a sign for you: you will find the baby wrapped in
> swaddling clothes and lying in a manger.'
>
> *Luke 2:8-13*

After the pomp and circumstance of Matthew's magi, Luke's
frightened shepherds seem a bit pale by comparison. But Luke
clearly prefers his shepherds to any exotic wise men. His shepherds
are given the honour of being the first to recognize Jesus and the first
to spread the word about him. Luke has no time for magi. Throughout his writings, anyone remotely resembling a magus receives very
bad press from Luke. Practitioners of any kind of mysterious or

magical art are quite unacceptable and on more than one occasion such characters are routed by heroic early Christians like Barnabas and Saul:

> ... at Paphos they came in contact with a Jewish magician and false prophet called Bar-Jesus. He was one of the attendants of the proconsul Sergius Paulus who was an extremely intelligent man. The proconsul summoned Barnabas and Saul and asked to hear the word of God, but Elymas the magician (this is what his name means in Greek) tried to stop them so as to prevent the proconsul's conversion to the faith. Then Saul, whose other name is Paul, filled with the Holy Spirit, looked at him intently and said, 'You utter fraud, you impostor, you son of the devil, you enemy of all uprightness, will you not stop twisting the straight-forward ways of the Lord? Now watch how the hand of the Lord will strike you: you will be blind, and for a time you will not see the sun.' That instant, everything went misty and dark for him, and he groped about to find someone to lead him by the hand. The proconsul, who had watched everything, became a believer, being much struck by what he had learnt about the Lord.
>
> *Acts 13:6-12*

The proconsul might well be struck by what he had learned. The unfortunate magus never stood a chance against Paul, not in an account written by Luke. Elsewhere in the book of Acts, that Luke almost certainly wrote, there are other examples of his dislike of the occult. At one point he describes how several itinerant Jewish exorcists had been trying to cast out an evil spirit in Jesus's name. This use of the name of Jesus by unauthorized magi led to a lot of trouble, and the exorcists were attacked and badly mauled:

> Everybody in Ephesus, both Jews and Greeks, heard about this episode; everyone was filled with awe, and the name of the Lord Jesus came to be held in great honour.
>
> Some believers, too, came forward to admit in detail how they had used spells and a number of them who had

practised magic collected their books and made a bonfire of them in public.

Acts 19:17-19

Given Luke's suspicion of magical arts, it is hardly surprising he does not repeat Matthew's earlier story of the magi and their star. Shepherds suit Luke better. He emphasizes throughout his gospel the virtue of humble and ordinary people, and stresses how they can be faithful followers of Jesus. More than any other gospel writer Luke also stresses the virtue of poverty and the evils of wealth. Of all four gospel writers only Luke has Jesus say to his followers that 'none of you can be my disciple without giving up all that he owns'. The poor and the powerless are always treated with sympathy by Luke. 'When you have a party,' says Jesus in Luke's gospel, 'invite the poor, the crippled, the lame, the blind; then you will be blessed . . .' The other gospels do not have Jesus saying that. Luke's is also the only gospel in which Jesus tells his followers to refuse to take the place of honour at table, and in which Jesus picks up a small child and sets the child beside him saying, 'Anyone who welcomes this little child in my name welcomes me . . .' Luke's most famous parables are all stories of compassion for the unfortunate or undeserving: the good Samaritan and the story of the prodigal son are two of the best examples of such parables and these appear only in Luke's gospel. Luke is also particularly compassionate towards women. He shows a deep sympathy for Mary the mother of Jesus; his is the story of Martha and Mary; it is Luke who tells of Jesus's kindness towards a woman who had a bad reputation, and it is Luke who declares that a number of women, as well as the disciples, were with Jesus as he went about his ministry.[1]

To have shepherds as the first witnesses who recognize Jesus as the Christ, meaning the messiah, reflects Luke's usual sympathy for ordinary people. These shepherds help to make real all the bizarre and extraordinary things Luke has been describing up until that point. They take us away from descriptions of divine annunciations

---

1 The passages from Luke's gospel referred to in this paragraph are, in the order they appear: 14:13-14, 14:8-11, 9:48; parable of the good Samaritan: 10:30-7; parable of the prodigal son: 15:11-32; story of Martha and Mary: 10:38-42; story of the woman of bad reputation: 7:36-52; account of women accompanying Jesus: 8:1-3.

and miraculous conceptions and angel choirs into the world of normal working people who react with awe and with fear to things they do not comprehend. This is perfectly understandable. Hosts of singing angels in a cloud of glory would frighten most normal people. Once the angel host disappears, the shepherds recover from their shock and they are curious:

> Now it happened that when the angels had gone from them into heaven, the shepherds said to one another, 'Let us go to Bethlehem and see this event which the Lord has made known to us.' So they hurried away and found Mary and Joseph, and the baby lying in the manger. When they saw the child they repeated what they had been told about him, and everyone who heard it was astonished at what the shepherds said to them. As for Mary, she treasured all these things and pondered them in her heart. And the shepherds went back glorifying and praising God for all they had heard and seen, just as they had been told.
>
> *Luke 2:15-20*

In reporting favourably about his shepherds, Luke is taking an unusual position, just as he does in favouring women and in speaking well of Samaritans. Shepherds were not overly popular at the time of Jesus, especially in the Jewish world where they were thought to be dubious characters who operated on the shady side of the law. They neglected their religious observances, and they were associated with trespass and dishonest sheep-dealings. The idea of a loving and gentle shepherd doting peacefully on his little lambs in a starlit field is not true to first century Palestine. This has grown largely out of Luke's sympathetic gospel account that owes a lot to his Greek background. In some Greek stories and poetry there was a long-established pastoral tradition maintaining that shepherds were kindly gentle rustics, an idealized form of humanity.[2]

The idea of shepherding a flock and caring for helpless creatures is often used symbolically to characterize Jesus himself. This symbolism has become pervasive in the Christian tradition, and it can be traced back to the Hebrew Scriptures, despite the unsavoury

2 See *Fitzmeyer* (1981), p. 395, and *Caird* (1963), p. 61.

reputation of shepherds in Jesus's time. In the book of the prophet Micah the coming of a new shepherd-like leader is announced:

> . . . then those who survive of his race
> will be reunited to the Israelites.
> He will take his stand and he will shepherd them
> with the power of Yahweh,
> with the majesty of the name of his God,
> and they will be secure, for his greatness will extend
> henceforth to the most distant parts of the country.
>
> *Micah 5:3*

Long before the time of Micah when the prophet Samuel is looking for a king among the sons of Jesse he finds none of them to be suitable. So he asks Jesse 'Are these all the sons you have?' and Jesse replies, 'There is still one left, the youngest; he is looking after the sheep.' David is then called from the herd and Samuel anoints him as the future king of Israel. Both Luke and Matthew are always keen to establish connections between King David and Jesus. The shepherds help Luke to do this because of the implied link with David. The boy David was a shepherd and he tended his flock near Bethlehem, and it was in Bethlehem that Samuel recognized David as the future king of Israel. In Luke's gospel, the shepherds are the first to recognize Jesus, and they are 'in the countryside close by' Bethlehem, the 'town of David'.

This brings us back to Bethlehem and as always the slightest mention of Bethlehem gives rise to a lot of discussion. According to Luke, Mary and Joseph and the baby are there more or less by accident. They are away from their home in Nazareth because of the census ordered by Quirinius, governor of Syria. In chapter 1 we discussed this problematic census, how Luke simply got his dates wrong, and how Jesus was almost certainly born ten years or so before the time of the census. There was a good reason for Luke's mistake. The unpopular census of Quirinius is known to have taken place in the year 7 CE and it caused a lot of trouble, leading in the end to riots and rebellion.

Ten years before that, nearer to the time of the birth of Jesus, there had been other riots when King Herod died and power was split between his two sons. Writing some eighty years later, Luke may simply have muddled up the two sets of riots in trying to establish the date of the birth of Jesus. The real point of all this is that Luke knew there had been a troublesome Roman census earlier in the century, even if he was wrong in connecting it to the date of the birth. He also knew that this census had triggered a rebellion, that is clear in the book of Acts where Luke reports a speech of Gamaliel, the famous Pharisee:

> And then there was Judas the Galilean, at the time of the census, who attracted crowds of supporters; but he was killed too, . . .
>
> *Acts 5:37*

This census of 7 CE was not the only troublesome census in Luke's background. In the Hebrew Scriptures another unpopular census also causes trouble. It is all King David's fault. He calls this census and it is a terrible mistake. He should know better because the book of Exodus indicates that it is up to God, not man, to keep a record of the people.[3] But in the face of this, David goes ahead and orders a census. He soon regrets it:

> . . . afterwards David's heart misgave him for having taken a census of the people. David then said to Yahweh, 'I have committed a grave sin by doing this. But now, Yahweh, I beg you to forgive your servant for this fault, for I have acted very foolishly.'
>
> *2 Samuel 24:10*

Yahweh is not about to forgive David so easily. An epidemic comes upon the people of Israel as a punishment. Seventy thousand people die, and more are about to be destroyed by a vengeful angel, when Yahweh intervenes:

> . . . when the angel stretched his hand towards Jerusalem to destroy it, Yahweh felt sorry about the calamity and said to the angel who was destroying the people, 'Enough now!

---

3 See NJB, p. 429, referring to Exodus 32:32-3 and 30:12.

Hold your hand!' The angel of Yahweh was standing by the
threshing-floor of Araunah the Jebusite. When David saw
the angel who was ravaging the people, he said to Yahweh,
'I was the one who sinned. I was the one who acted
wrongly. But these, the flock, what have they done? Let
your hand lie heavy on me and on my family!'

2 Samuel 24:24-25

In order to propitiate Yahweh, David is instructed to buy this
'threshing-floor of Araunah the Jebusite', where the ravaging angel
stood, and he is told to raise an altar there to Yahweh:

David bought the threshing-floor and the oxen for fifty
shekels of silver. David built an altar to Yahweh and
offered burnt offerings and communion sacrifices. Yahweh then took pity on the country and the plague was lifted
from Israel.

2 Samuel 24:24-25

Clearly, censuses meant trouble, but they could serve useful
purposes. Luke's census takes Mary and Joseph to Bethlehem,
thereby ensuring that Jesus is born in the city of David. And King
David's foolish census determined the location of what became the
great temple of Jerusalem. David's son Solomon carried on the
work that had already begun on the site of the 'threshing-floor of
Araunah the Jebusite' and established the central shrine of Judaism:

Solomon then began building the house of Yahweh in
Jerusalem on Mount Moriah where David his father had
had a vision — on the site that David had prepared — on the
threshing-floor of Ornan[4] the Jebusite. He began building
it on the second day of the second month of the fourth year of
his reign.

2 Chronicles 3:1-3

When homage is paid to the child Jesus in Luke's gospel, Luke
draws in a large cast of characters. More people than the shepherds
at Bethlehem are involved. Their recognition of Jesus is the earliest

4 Ornan is another form of the name Araunah.

recognition, and probably the best known, but more follows in the birth story. The scene moves from Bethlehem to the temple at Jerusalem, in other words, from the city of David to the place of David's vision. Jesus is first taken to the temple at Jerusalem by his parents when he is still very young:

> And when the day came for them to be purified in keeping with the Law of Moses, they took him up to Jerusalem to present him to the Lord — observing what is written in the Law of the Lord: *Every first-born male must be consecrated to the Lord* — and also to offer in sacrifice, in accordance with what is prescribed in the Law of the Lord, *a pair of turtledoves or two young pigeons.*
>
> *Luke 2:22-24*

This account is problematic. To present Jesus at the temple in this way was almost certainly not the normal Jewish practice, even for firstborn sons. However, Luke knew from the Hebrew Scriptures that Hannah had done this, or something very similar, with her miraculously conceived firstborn son Samuel, when she presented him to Eli the priest:

> Elkanah, the husband, went up with all his family to offer the annual sacrifice to Yahweh and to fulfil his vow. However, Hannah did not go up, having said to her husband, 'Not before the child has been weaned. Then I shall bring him and present him before Yahweh and he will stay there for ever.' Elkanah her husband then said to her, 'Do what you think fit; wait until you have weaned him. May Yahweh bring about what he has said.' So the woman stayed behind and nursed her child until she weaned him.
>
> When she had weaned him, she took him up with her, as well as a three-year-old bull, an *ephah* of flour and a skin of wine, and took him into the temple of Yahweh at Shiloh; the child was very young. They sacrificed the bull and led the child to Eli. She said, 'If you please, my lord! As you live, my lord, I am the woman who stood beside you here, praying to Yahweh. This is the child for which I was

praying, and Yahweh has granted me what I asked of him.
Now I make him over to Yahweh for the whole of his life.
He is made over to Yahweh.' They then worshipped
Yahweh there.

1 Samuel 1:21-28

This precedent may go a long way to explain Luke's story of the
presentation of Jesus. And there is another, darker precedent in the
story of Abraham and Isaac:

It happened some time later that God put Abraham to the
test. 'Abraham, Abraham!' he called. 'Here I am,' he
replied. God said, 'Take your son, your only son, your beloved Isaac, and go to the land of Moriah, where you are to
offer him as a burnt offering on one of the mountains which I
shall point out to you.'

Genesis 22:1

The unfortunate Isaac is saved from this sacrificial fate at the last
moment when Yahweh changes his mind and instructs Abraham to
kill a ram instead of Isaac. The place of the planned sacrifice was
popularly believed, in Luke's day to be the hill in Jerusalem on which
the temple stood, the same temple where Jesus is presented by his
parents.[5]

When Jesus is presented at the temple he is welcomed by
Simeon, an old man who is described very much as if he is an elderly
priest, although his identity is unclear. As Simeon holds the child
Jesus he utters the Nunc Dimittis, his song of praise that has already
been discussed in chapter 8. This is not only a song of praise, but
another outstanding moment of recognition:

He was an upright and devout man; he looked forward to
the restoration of Israel and the Holy Spirit rested on him. It
had been revealed to him that he would not see death until
he had set eyes on Christ the Lord. Prompted by the Spirit
he came to the Temple; and when the parents brought in

5 See NJB, p. 41 notes.

the child Jesus to do for him what the Law required, he took
him into his arms and blessed God; and he said:
>   Now, Master, you are letting your servant go in peace as
>   you promised;
>   for my eyes have seen the salvation
>   which you have made ready in the sight of the nations;
>   a light of revelation for the gentiles
>   and glory for your people Israel.
>
> *Luke 2:29-32*

Like the shepherds Simeon recognizes the greatness of Jesus,
and pays homage to him. Simeon's recognition brings a new element
to Luke's stories of recognition and homage because for the first
time gentiles are mentioned. Simeon sees the salvation Jesus offers as
a salvation not only for Israel, but for all people. At the same time,
Simeon's words recall a famous landmark of reconciliation within
the Hebrew Scriptures when Jacob/Israel is reunited with his son
Joseph in Egypt:

> Israel said to Joseph, 'Now I can die, now that I have seen
> you in person and seen you still alive.'
>
> *Genesis 46:30*

Following his song of praise and recognition, Simeon goes on to
deliver a puzzling and rather ominous oracle to Jesus's parents:

> Simeon blessed them and said to Mary his mother, 'Look,
> he is destined for the fall and for the rise of many in Israel,
> destined to be a sign that is opposed — and a sword will
> pierce your soul too — so that the secret thoughts of many
> may be laid bare.'
>
> *Luke 2:34-35*

This is the first shadow to cross Luke's otherwise joyous birth
story. It looks ahead to the fate of Jesus and in doing so it recalls other
passages from the scriptures, from the book of Isaiah in particular:

'... Yahweh Sabaoth is the one you will proclaim holy,
him you will dread, him you will fear.
He will be a sanctuary, a stumbling-stone,
a rock to trip up the two Houses of Israel;
a snare and a trap for the inhabitants of Jerusalem,
over which many of them will stumble, fall and be broken,
be ensnared and made captive.
Bind up the testimony, seal the instruction
in the heart of my disciples.'
My trust is in Yahweh who hides his face from the House of
    Jacob;
I put my hope in him.

                                                         Isaiah 8:13-17

Simeon is speaking to Mary when he delivers his chilling oracle, and
he indicates that she will know the sadness of Jesus's death. Several
passages of grief and mourning from the scriptures are echoed here,
particularly from the book of Zechariah:

> ... over the House of David and the inhabitants of Jerusa-
> lem I shall pour out a spirit of grace and prayer, and they
> will look to me. They will mourn for the one whom they
> have pierced as though for an only child, and weep for him
> as people weep for a first-born child.
>
>   *Zechariah 12:10*

The words of Simeon to Mary about the sword that will pierce
her heart also recall Psalm 22, a song of despair and abandonment
that is quoted in the gospels of Mark and Matthew at the time of the
crucifixion. This psalm begins with the cry, 'My God, my God, why
have you forsaken me?', and halfway through the psalm a sword is
mentioned:

> A pack of dogs surrounds me,
> a gang of villains is closing in on me
> as if to hack off my hands and my feet.
> I can count every one of my bones,
> while they look on and gloat;

> they divide my garments among them and cast lots for my
>   clothing.
> Yahweh, do not hold aloof!
> My strength, come quickly to my help,
> rescue my soul from the sword,
>   the one life I have from the grasp of the dog!
>
> *Psalm 22:20*

After Simeon's oracle, the atmosphere lightens in Luke's gospel
with the introduction of Anna the prophetess. She is also in the
temple, and she also recognizes and pays homage to Jesus:

> There was a prophetess, too, Anna the daughter of Pha-
> nuel, of the tribe of Asher. She was well on in years. Her
> days of girlhood over, she had been married for seven years
> before becoming a widow. She was now eighty-four years
> old and never left the Temple, serving God night and day
> with fasting and prayer. She came up just at that moment
> and began to praise God; and she spoke of the child to all
> who looked forward to the deliverance of Jerusalem.
>
> *Luke 2:36-38*

This story of Anna brings together many of Luke's most attractive
qualities as a storyteller. He moves away from the shadow of sorrow
that Simeon's oracle has cast on the birth story, and tells of an old
lady of holy persuasion who lives in the temple and who is delighted
to recognize Jesus as a future leader. She has nothing negative to say,
and her testimony lifts the whole narrative. Yet this is the testimony
of a woman who has no particular status. She is of the tribe of Asher,
a lineage of little significance. Asher was the least of the sons of
Jacob and his family was one of the least of the twelve tribes of Israel,
sometimes referred to as a handmaid tribe. There were four such
handmaid tribes, whose origins went back to the four sons born to
Jacob by the slave girls of Rachel and Leah. When Moses blesses the
sons of Israel, Asher is the last one mentioned:

> Most blessed of the sons let Asher be!
> Let him be the most privileged of his brothers

and let him bathe his feet in oil!
Be your bolts of iron and of bronze
and your security as lasting as your days!

Deuteronomy 33:24-25

Asher may not have been a prominent and famous tribe of Israel, but it was blessed with good fortune. Leah rejoices wholeheartedly when her slave girl gives birth to Asher, for she herself is then past the age of childbearing. 'What blessedness!' Leah cries when Asher is born, 'Women will call me blessed!', a line that Luke echoes in Mary's song of praise who says 'from now onwards all generations will call me blessed'. In this way, having foretold Mary's sorrow in Simeon's oracle, Luke gently eases the blow by bringing in Anna of the tribe of Asher, and a reminder of Mary's joy. This story of how the prophetess of the fortunate tribe of Asher happily recognizes Jesus is a subtle masterpiece.

Unlike Matthew's gospel, that gives no details of the childhood of Jesus, Luke's birth story carries on into Jesus's early years. After hearing from Anna, Mary and Joseph go home and in the space of two or three lines, twelve years pass:

When they had done everything the Law of the Lord required, they went back to Galilee, to their own town of Nazareth. And as the child grew to maturity, he was filled with wisdom; and God's favour was with him. Every year his parents used to go to Jerusalem for the feast of the Passover. When he was twelve years old, they went up for the feast as usual. When the days of the feast were over and they set off home, the boy Jesus stayed behind in Jerusalem without his parents knowing it. They assumed he was somewhere in the party, and it was only after a day's journey that they went to look for him among their relations and acquaintances. When they failed to find him they went back to Jerusalem looking for him everywhere.

It happened that, three days later, they found him in the Temple, sitting among the teachers, listening to them, and asking them questions; and all those who heard him were astounded at his intelligence and his replies. They were overcome when they saw him, and his mother said to him, 'My child, why have you done this to us? See how worried your father and I have been, looking for you.' He replied, 'Why were you looking for me? Did you not know that I must be in my Father's house?' But they did not understand what he meant.

Luke 2:16-20

This story of the boy Jesus in the temple has given rise to a lot of speculation about the childhood of Jesus. Theories abound, none of them at all satisfactory, about what is termed the 'hidden life' in Nazareth when Jesus is growing up. In the New Testament Apocrypha, a book called 'The Infancy Story of Thomas' attempts to fill in many of the gaps. The unknown writer Thomas takes up Luke's story of the child Jesus in the temple and embellishes it freely. At one point the child Jesus who has had no schooling is taken into a school:

And he went boldly into the school and found a book lying on the reading-desk and took it, but did not read the letters in it, but opened his mouth and spoke by the Holy Spirit and taught the law to those that stood by. And a large crowd assembled and stood there listening to him, wondering at the grace of his teaching and the readiness of his words, that although an infant he made such utterances.[6]

Later, this account repeats Luke's story almost word for word about the young Jesus teaching in the temple, and at the end of the story there is an addition:

. . . his mother Mary came near and said to him: 'Why have you done this to us, child? Behold, we have sought you sorrowing.' Jesus said to them: 'Why do you seek me? Do you not know that I must be in my Father's house?' But the scribes and Pharisees said: 'Are you the mother of this child?' And she said: 'I am.' And they said to her: 'Blessed are you among women, because the Lord has blessed the

6 NTA, The Infancy Story of Thomas, p. 397.

fruit of your womb. For such glory and such excellence and wisdom we have never seen nor heard.'[7]

The embellishments made in the gospel of Thomas always lead to some form of recognition when the child Jesus is regarded with awe and wonder. In the story of Jesus in the temple it is as if the writer feels that Luke's original version is not forceful enough in making the teachers of the temple appreciate the true identity of Jesus. Time and again, recognition is emphasized. The whole idea of telling these highly coloured stories about the childhood of Jesus is to point out just who this child really is.

The story of Jesus in the temple also serves as another reminder of the child Samuel in the temple. Samuel was left in the temple for his entire childhood:

> Samuel was in Yahweh's service, a child wearing a linen loincloth. His mother used to make him a little coat which she brought him each year when she came up with her husband to offer the yearly sacrifice. Eli would bless Elkanah and his wife and say, 'May Yahweh grant you an heir by this woman in exchange for the one that she has made over to Yahweh,' and they would go home.
>
> *1 Samuel 2:18-20*

The connections between the story of Samuel and the story of Jesus are most apparent in the close parallels between Hannah and Mary. Neither of these women should have been able to conceive, they both know that their miraculously conceived sons are dedicated to God from the womb, they each praise God with similar songs, and they each find their child in the temple. Hannah then carries on and has several other children, and disappears from the story of her son Samuel:

> Meanwhile, the child Samuel went on growing in stature and in favour both with Yahweh and with people.
>
> *1 Samuel 2:26*

---

7 NTA, The Infancy Story of Thomas, p. 399.

In Luke's gospel Mary also fades from the story after the visit to the temple in Jerusalem. But throughout the birth story, Mary is stage centre. From her song near the beginning to the very end of the stories of Jesus's childhood, Mary's attitude towards her son provides the tone of wonder that is the essence of Luke's birth narrative, and that is repeated each time the child Jesus is greeted and recognized:

His mother stored up all these things in her heart. And Jesus increased in wisdom, in stature, and in favour with God and with people.

Luke 2:52

XI

Recognition:
The Text

In the Preface the story was told of how the idea for this book can be traced back to a Christmas dinner a few years ago, and to a question about the magi and where they come from. 'They come marching right out of the Old Testament, didn't you know?' was the answer to that question. In the past few chapters we have seen many other elements of the birth stories coming marching right out of the Old Testament, or the Hebrew Scriptures, including the angelic appearances, the stars, the songs, the dreams, the magi and all the other witnesses. What we have done so far is to try to reveal as many as possible of these scriptural sources and to show what Matthew and Luke do with them; how they adapt some of them for use in their stories, allude to some of them indirectly, and repeat others verbatim.

Seeing how Matthew and Luke use the scriptures leads inevitably to questions about what they really are doing in their birth stories. It looks as if they read the scriptures and then proceeded to create their stories about Jesus's birth from a patchwork of scriptural references, with little or no concern for presenting the basic facts. Because of this scarcity of what today would be called hard facts, or verifiable evidence, the birth stories are sometimes dismissed rather scornfully as little more than fanciful religious legends. This attitude brings out a defensive reaction in many people and a dogged insistence that the gospels do indeed present reliable factual reports about the birth of Jesus. According to this argument, the birth stories are unquestionably factual and any resemblance to stories in the Hebrew Scriptures is miraculous and coincidental. Thus Mary coincidentally sings the same song Hannah sang ten centuries earlier, the magi coincidentally bring Jesus the same gifts noble visitors brought to David and to Solomon, and the angel chorus coincidentally resembles the seraphs in the book of Isaiah.

Whether the birth stories are believed to be a string of miraculous coincidences or dismissed out of hand as fanciful legends, such emphatic conclusions about these stories run the risk of merely reflecting prejudices. To dismiss these stories loftily or to believe every word fervently may seem to represent two very different points of view, but such conclusions have a lot in common. They both represent easy options because they are tidy and absolute. They both give the text minimal consideration. It is worth asking if such absolute conclusions are appropriate, or even possible, given the nature of the available evidence. The birth stories are closely connected to a vast number of scriptural passages, and to reach any understanding of these connections requires perceptive reading and systematic analysis. It also requires discussion and investigation. Through all this a world of text comes alive, a world in which story is built on story, theme on theme, and character on character. In trying to understand what Matthew and Luke really are doing in their birth stories, it helps to see how their writing forms part of a much larger pattern. Similar writing techniques are used throughout the Hebrew Scriptures. Stories are often told and retold in the scriptures; similar themes and personalities and circumstances often appear and reappear. In this chapter we want to look at some examples of these patterns of storytelling within the Hebrew scriptures, and then see how Matthew and Luke continue this pattern.

The technique of powerful, repetitive storytelling begins as far back as one cares to go in the Hebrew Scriptures. Take the crossing of the Red Sea when the Israelites came out of Egypt led by Moses:

> Then Moses stretched out his hand over the sea, and Yahweh drove the sea back with a strong easterly wind all night and made the sea into dry land. The waters were divided and the Israelites went on dry ground right through the sea, with walls of water to right and left of them.
>
> *Exodus 14:21-22*

That account of the exodus from Egypt represents a very ancient story which was repeated over many centuries. The exodus itself probably took place around the year 1300 BCE, and stories of the exodus began to be written down around 850 BCE. These stories were finally gathered into a book about the exodus around 650 BCE.

The biblical book of Joshua was being compiled about the same time or a bit later, and in Joshua a similar story is told of the crossing of the river Jordan:

> As soon as the bearers of the ark reached the Jordan and the feet of the priests carrying the ark touched the waters — the Jordan is in spate throughout the harvest season — the upper waters stood still and formed a single mass over a great distance, at Adam, the town near Zarethan, while those flowing down to the Sea of the Arabah, the Salt Sea, were completely separated. The people crossed opposite Jericho. The priests carrying the ark of the covenant of Yahweh stood firm on dry ground in mid-Jordan, while all Israel crossed on dry ground, . . .
>
> *Joshua 3:14-17*

The Jordan River again parts to allow a dryshod crossing in the second book of Kings, which was probably compiled shortly after the book of Joshua. The two prophets Elijah and Elisha are spared a wetting here:

Fifty of the brotherhood of prophets followed them, halting some distance away as the two of them stood beside the Jordan. Elijah took his cloak, rolled it up and struck the water; and the water divided to left and right, and the two of them crossed over dry-sod.

2 Kings 2:7-8

Later, Elisha performs the same feat, and once again the Jordan River parts:

Now as they walked on, talking as they went, a chariot of fire appeared and horses of fire coming between the two of them; and Elijah went up to heaven in the whirlwind. Elisha saw it, and shouted, 'My father! My father! Chariot of Israel and its chargers!' Then he lost sight of him, and taking hold of his own clothes he tore them in half. He picked up Elijah's cloak which had fallen, and went back and stood on the bank of the Jordan.

He took Elijah's cloak and struck the water. 'Where is Yahweh, the God of Elijah?' he cried. As he struck the water it divided to right and left, and Elisha crossed over. The brotherhood of prophets saw him in the distance, and said, 'The spirit of Elijah has come to rest on Elisha; . . .'

2 Kings 2:11-16

All of the above passages tell vivid stories. The central theme of the waters parting is used over and over as an indication of divine favour towards whoever is involved. The more times the theme is repeated, the more powerful the images become, because they build on and add to an existing story tradition. This is only one example of how the writers of the Hebrew Scriptures are inclined to recycle a good story. Another memorable example of this comes when Moses meets his god on Mount Sinai. There are several descriptions of this encounter in the Hebrew Scriptures. One of these descriptions has already been quoted in chapter 8, telling how cloud covers the mountain and how Moses is then called into this sacred cloud by

Yahweh. The following passage is another version of the same story, from another part of the book of Exodus. Exodus, like the book of Genesis and most of the other early scriptures, combines many different storytelling traditions, and often the same story is told in two or three forms within the space of a few pages. These different versions of the same story result from the different religious and political interests of the various tribes of Israel. As they went their own ways and settled in different parts of Palestine, they told and recorded their own versions of ancient stories. This explains why place names change from one story to another, and why the name of the deity can vary. The Hebrew Scriptures refer to the deity as Yahweh, Elohim, Shaddai, and there are many other names. Bethlehem is called Ephratah, Jamnia can be Jabneh or Jabneel, and Mount Sinai is sometimes called Horeb:

> Now at daybreak two days later, there were peals of thunder and flashes of lightning, dense cloud on the mountain and a very loud trumpet blast; and, in the camp, all the people trembled. Then Moses led the people out of the camp to meet God; and they took their stand at the bottom of the mountain. Mount Sinai was entirely wrapped in smoke, because Yahweh had descended on it in the form of fire. The smoke rose like smoke from a furnace and the whole mountain shook violently. Louder and louder grew the trumpeting. Moses spoke, and God answered him in the thunder. Yahweh descended on Mount Sinai, on the top of the mountain, and Yahweh called Moses to the top of the mountain; and Moses went up.
>
> *Exodus 19:16-20*

All of this about Moses meeting his god on the mountain follows long descriptions of how he leads the children of Israel out of Egypt. The Israelites are not easy travelling companions. They complain about Moses, and about their hunger and thirst. God intervenes and provides manna and water for them, but the complaints continue and Moses is near despair. This despair in the desert, the provision of food and water, and the encounter with the deity on a fiery mountain all reappear in a later story. This time the protagonist is the prophet Elijah and his story is found in the book of Kings:

> He himself went on into the desert, a day's journey, and sitting under a furze bush wished he were dead. 'Yahweh,' he said, 'I have had enough. Take my life; I am no better than my ancestors.' Then he lay down and went to sleep. Then all of a sudden an angel touched him and said, 'Get up and eat.' He looked round, and there at his head was a scone baked on hot stones, and a jar of water. He ate and drank and then lay down again. But the angel of Yahweh came back a second time and touched him and said, 'Get up and eat, or the journey will be too long for you.' So he got up and ate and drank, and strengthened by that food he walked for forty days and forty nights until he reached Horeb, God's mountain. There he went into a cave and spent the night there. Then the word of Yahweh came to him saying, 'What are you doing here, Elijah?' He replied, 'I am full of jealous zeal for Yahweh Sabaoth, because the Israelites have abandoned your covenant, have torn down your altars and put your prophets to the sword. I am the only one left, and now they want to kill me.' Then he was told, 'Go out and stand on the mountain before Yahweh.' For at that moment Yahweh was going by. A mighty hurricane split the mountains and shattered the rocks before Yahweh. But Yahweh was not in the hurricane. And after the hurricane, an earthquake. But Yahweh was not in the earthquake. And after the earthquake, fire. But Yahweh was not in the fire. And after the fire, a light murmuring sound. And when Elijah heard this, he covered his face with his cloak and went out and stood at the entrance of the cave.
>
> *1 Kings 19:4-13*

It is not only outstanding events like divine revelations on fiery mountains and the parting of seas and rivers that are told and retold within the scriptures. Some of the clearest examples of this technique are found in what are usually known as the history books of the

Hebrew Scriptures, particularly in the books of Samuel and Kings and Chronicles. The writers of Chronicles radically revise and almost entirely retell stories from the second book of Samuel and the two books of Kings, providing a great deal of extra detail and colour.

For a straightforward example of how the Chroniclers work, look again at the story of King David's census, already mentioned in chapter 10. David took a grave political risk in ordering this census, for it was a very unpopular act. There are two different accounts of the undertaking. The earlier of the two is from the book of Samuel and it maintains that Yahweh was angry with Israel, so he incited David to take the census. In the later revision, the Chroniclers say that 'Satan took his stand against Israel and incited David to take a census of Israel'[1]. The Chroniclers here have changed the text from the source in the book of Samuel. 'Yahweh' becomes 'Satan', giving a strikingly different tone to the whole story. This is because the book of Chronicles is a revisionist history in which nothing bad could be said about the great King David. If David is tempted to a foolish act like taking a census, it must be an evil force that leads him to such an act, not the god of his people. The earlier writers in the book of Samuel were much closer to the events described and took a less idealized and more practical view of their kings. In their time they were still ruled by kings in the line of David and it seemed to them quite feasible that a king could be tested by Yahweh and fail the test by making a foolish mistake. Times had radically changed when the Chroniclers were writing three or four hundred years later. In these intervening years, the kingdom of Israel and the city of Jerusalem had been conquered by Nebuchadnezzar. Israel's élite had been deported to Babylon and its royal family rendered powerless. Some of the exiles had then returned and rebuilt the temple and part of the city, and they had established a rather dull hierarchy of ruling priests in place of their kings. The writers of Chronicles looked back with awe to the golden age of David and Solomon. They were scandalized by the idea that Yahweh could be responsible for urging David to carry out such an impious act as a census. Such was the pressure of a changed political situation and the

1 1 Chronicles 21:2 and 2 Samuel 24:1-4.

changed religious climate that went with it, and such was its effect on a text.

Another example of this partisan approach of the Chroniclers is their treatment of the story of Bathsheba. According to the earlier account in the book of Kings, the great King David commits adultery with the wife of another man:

> At the turn of the year, at the time when kings go campaigning, David sent Joab and with him his guards and all Israel. They massacred the Ammonites and laid seige to Rabbah-of-the-Ammonites. David, however, remained in Jerusalem.
>
> It happened towards evening when David had got up from resting and was strolling on the palace roof, that from the roof he saw a woman bathing; the woman was very beautiful.
>
> *2 Samuel 11:1-2*

The corresponding passage in Chronicles goes like this:

> At the turn of the year, at the time when kings go campaigning, Joab led out the troops and, having ravaged the Ammonites' territory, proceeded to lay seige to Rabbah. David, however, remained in Jerusalem. Joab reduced Rabbah and dismantled it. David took the crown off Milcom's head and found that it weighed a talent of gold, and in it was set a precious stone which went on David's head instead.
>
> *1 Chronicles 20:1-2*

After the second sentence of this extract, ending 'remained in Jerusalem', the source report in the book of Kings, written centuries before the time of the Chroniclers, has the whole Bathsheba story, telling how she becomes pregnant and how David contrives the death of her ill-fated husband Uriah the Hittite. The Chroniclers left all that out, presumably on the grounds that it is not seemly to relate such a tale about the great and good king David.

The Chroniclers freely reconstructed the history provided by the writers of the books of Samuel and Kings, and this technique provides many entertaining examples of revisionist storytelling.

But the Chroniclers had a problem. They never knew when to stop, and often were quite carried away trying to rehabilitate remarkably tedious personalities who may not have deserved such attention in the first place. One of the best examples of this comes in the story of one Abijah, also known as Abijam. Abijah was an undistinguished king of Judah who reigned from 913 to 911 BCE. The earlier account of his reign appears in Kings, which was compiled nearly three centuries after Abijah's reign. The second account is in Chronicles, written as much as six centuries after his reign. The record in Kings consists of eight terse and not very favourable verses, probably about what Abijah's reign was worth. The account in Chronicles covers his reign in glorious Technicolor, improving the tone of the eight verses in Kings. The Chroniclers pull in extra material from many other places in the scriptures, creating a text which is a very obvious patchwork.[2]

It may seem a far cry from the chronicles of a lacklustre king of Judah who reigned for a mere two years to the gospel stories of the birth of Jesus, but there is a distinct continuity of method between the writers of the Hebrew Scriptures and the writers of the gospels. Both were working within a tradition that turned to older sources repeatedly for information, ideas, and allusions; a tradition that freely amended, and quoted and enlarged on these sources. The writers of the gospels were part of this established system of using old texts to create new texts. There is a clue planted about this system in a statement in Chronicles at the end of the story of Abijah:

> The rest of the history of Abijah, his conduct and his sayings, are recorded in the *midrash* of the prophet Iddo.
>
> *2 Chronicles 13:22*

Similarly, after another story in Chronicles involving a different cast of characters, the concluding statement reads:

> These were the conspirators: Zabad son of Shimeath the Ammonite and Jehozabad son of Shimrith the Moabite. As regards his sons, the heavy tribute imposed on him, and the

2 See Table II for a detailed look at how the story of Abijah was composed from several sources.

restoration of the Temple of God, this is recorded in the
Midrash on the Book of Kings . . .

2 Chronicles 24:26-7 [JB][3]

These two passages bring in the word midrash. This word does
not appear in all translations, in fact most translators have tried to
avoid it. In place of the word midrash the words 'commentary',
'annals', 'annotations', 'story' and 'history' appear in various Bibles.
This seems to be a sensible move on the part of the translators, for
midrash is neither a friendly nor a familiar term. Given the choice
most people would much prefer a word like 'story'. But midrash can
be a helpful term, although it requires a certain amount of patience
to determine what the word really means. Experts seem to enjoy
arguing about midrash. Originally it was an esoteric Jewish concept, associated mostly with rabbinic writings of the middle ages.
Within the last twenty years it has become a fashionable term
amongst biblical scholars, both Jewish and Christian. The more the
term is used, the less agreement there is about its meaning. Midrash
can mean a type of sermon or study, a form of storytelling, and a style
of interpretation; it can mean all of the above, and it can also mean a
body of literature incorporating some or all of the above. Barry
Holtz is a Jewish scholar who defines midrash in this way:

> It is helpful to think of Midrash in two different, but
> related, ways: first, Midrash (deriving from the Hebrew
> root 'to search out') is the process of interpreting. The
> object of interpretation is the Bible or, on occasion, other
> sacred texts; second, Midrash refers to the corpus of work
> that has collected these interpretations . . .[4]

Barry Holtz stresses that in reinterpreting and retelling vital
passages from the scriptures the process of midrash uncovers what is
already there. The rabbis trained in this tradition believed that all
wisdom and all truth could be found in the Hebrew Scriptures, and
so they searched for what they believed to be the truth from the most

3 See the original Jerusalem Bible for this translation.
4 Holtz (1984), p. 178.

authoritative and dependable source they knew, and then they restated this truth in new terms.

For many of us, it takes a while for this concept of midrash to sink in. It can seem very strange, this method of examination and reexamination, interpretation and reinterpretation of a set of old texts in a search for revelations that are certain to be there. Few of us are accustomed to the idea that ancient texts can be so eternally relevant, let alone that they contain the ultimate means of expressing our current perceptions. Certainly we have not been encouraged to think that Matthew and Luke were relying on the powerful authority of the scriptures to provide what they needed in writing their gospels. But they were.

The idea of midrash comes as a shock to many Christians. The Church has never encouraged its flock to understand the Jewish traditions of storytelling that permeate the Bible. Little attention is paid to how stories within the Hebrew Scriptures are told and retold. The similar stories about the parting of the Red Sea and the River Jordan are seldom analysed together; the way Elijah in the desert resembles Moses in the desert is rarely discussed from the pulpit; the skilled rewriting of different sources in the books of Chronicles raises hardly any interest at all. Thus the basic pattern of the scriptures is ignored, and they are treated as disparate stories rather than as closely interconnected texts. As for how the gospel writers refer to and use the scriptures, this is all too often regarded as window dressing for stories about Jesus, rather than as the profound and essential source without which the gospel writers could not have begun to write about Jesus. The Christian Church has chosen to overlook the obvious about its own sacred literature: that the roots of this literature are profoundly Judaic, and that everything we are told about Jesus, the whole New Testament, can best be understood as a Christian midrash on the Hebrew Scriptures[5]. The gospel writers were working within a storytelling tradition which led them to search the scriptures for what they believed and expected would be there. In the scriptures they found what they

5 This point is made by Lloyd Gaston, Professor of the New Testament at the Vancouver School of Theology, in his presidential address at the Canadian School of Biblical Studies in 1987, which was published in the Society's bulletin (vol. 47) of that year.

interpreted as proof about the identity of Jesus, and validation for their belief in him. They then took what they found in the scriptures and retold it in a new form, to emphasize that Jesus was the realization of all the promises and expectations of the scriptures.

The Christian tradition stems so directly out of the Jewish tradition that all Christian assertions about the identity of Jesus make little sense without an understanding of their roots in the Hebrew Scriptures. That is why, if we want to understand what Matthew and Luke really are doing, it is important to connect their gospels to the scriptures that informed and inspired them. That is why the birth stories, with all their emphasis on identity and recognition, are so enriched when they are seen in the context of the Hebrew scriptures. That is why glib conclusions about the nature of these complex stories are so patently inadequate.

Discovery

Everything that has appeared so far in this book cries out to be checked against a copy of the Bible. For some two hundred pages we have been making connections and showing similarities between biblical passages, but there is no reason to rely solely on our analysis. It would be much better, and much more interesting, for every reader to discover such biblical connections for himself or herself. The only problem might be knowing where to begin to look in the Bible.

So far we have put forward a great deal of what we understand to be source material for the birth stories of Matthew and Luke, but we have not said anything about how to locate these sources in the scriptures. Admittedly, this can be a daunting task for anyone who is completely unfamiliar with the Bible. The Bible is a long book, full of bizarre and baffling accounts of wanderings and begettings; visions and wars; poetry and prophecy. It is a textual jungle, and finding your bearings can be a nightmare. As for making connections between various sections of the Bible, that can seem altogether too much like hard work. But it is something anyone can do.

The first step is picking up the Bible itself, an act that for many people means overcoming some very basic prejudices. The aura of sanctity that surrounds this book is more than enough to repel most potential readers. The fact that it lurks on so many bookshelves, dusty and unread, in some antiquated and incomprehensible edition, is another reason to avoid it. Quite often such editions are in tiny print, on impossibly thin paper; the cover of the book is limp imitation leather, and the pages are edged with fading gold. This is not a book many of us would choose to be seen reading on the bus. And even if all objections are overcome and the Bible is opened, the problems are only just beginning. The title page, more often than not with someone else's name on it, is probably half torn out and it is followed by a peculiar ceremonial preface:

> To the Most High and Mighty Prince James, by the grace of God, King of Great Britain, France, and Ireland, Defender of the Faith, etc., the Translators of the Bible wish Grace, Mercy, and Peace, through Jesus Christ our Lord.

This unpromising start heralds the well-known King James Bible, often called the Authorized Version, or AV. This is the edition beloved of most family bookshelves, many churches, and countless hotel rooms. The chances are strong that any AV Bible picked up at random has no notes, and no cross-referencing. If it has notes they are probably in such small print that they are virtually unreadable, and they may well be hopelessly out of date, so no real guidance is provided through the biblical jungle. A reading of the first chapter of Matthew, for example, will reveal forty-two generations of unpronounceable names and the extremely unlikely story of the pregnancy of Mary, complete with a quotation from an unnamed prophet. When the baby is born the mysterious wise men from the east appear following their star, and more unnamed prophets are quoted. As it continues the story becomes more and more far-fetched, and the further it goes the more guidance is needed.

If, against the odds, the Bible picked up at random has notes and a cross-referencing system the reading will be easier. In Matthew's gospel, the first prophet quoted will be shown to be Isaiah, and if the system is a good one the star in the east will be cross-referenced to Balaam's oracle about a star in the book of Numbers. If the system is very good the forty-two generations (really forty-one) of strange names at the beginning of the gospel will all be explained, and characters like Tamar will be connected back to the remarkable story in Genesis 38. However, this is hoping for a lot from a Bible picked up at random. Most Bibles do not bother to explain very much at all.

If any reader really wants to look into the Bible and search out connections, the single most useful suggestion we can make is to use a good modern translation with a comprehensive and up-to-date reference system. This suggestion often gives rise to howls of protest. How can anyone put aside grandmother's King James Bible with that overpoweringly beautiful language in favour of a less poetic modern translation? How indeed. It is perfectly true that the poetry of the King James Bible has never been equalled, but it might be worth asking how many of us fully comprehend that language of Jacobean England. The Bible is a complex enough text to understand without being cloaked in language nearly four hundred years old. If you have been accustomed to the King James Bible it can be a great revelation to turn to a modern translation that enables you to read the words instead of intoning them.

There are a great number of modern translations available, all of which, like the King James Bible, have both merits and weaknesses. We have been using the New Jerusalem Bible throughout this book because it is clear and it has good notes. It also has the virtue of having been published recently. Other helpful translations are the New English Bible, and the Revised Standard Version, and then there are translations like the Good News Bible, the New International, the New American, the Revised English Bible and countless others. It can be extremely interesting to have two or three different translations on hand and to check them one against the other. If nothing else, this helps to show how biblical translation is a human process that changes over time, and is always open to new forms of expression.

A very basic test of any modern translation is to look at Isaiah 7:14. This is the prophecy that 'a young woman shall conceive', discussed at length in chapter 5[1]. This is one of the most famous, or infamous, points of translation in the entire Bible. The passage should read 'young woman' rather than 'virgin'. If it does read 'virgin' this might be acceptable on the understanding that it expresses a sincerely held bias, but there should at least be a footnote explaining the debate about 'young woman' and 'virgin'. Anything less indicates that bias is outbidding scholarly honesty.

Apart from obtaining one or two modern translations, preferably with notes and cross-references, there are other biblical tools that can be helpful in the process of checking and connecting scriptural passages. One of the more venerable and interesting is Cruden's *Concordance*. This complete guide to all the words, phrases and names in the King James Bible, was compiled in the eighteenth century. It is still in print and is only now being superseded by computerized concordances. Alexander Cruden MA (1701-1770) was born and educated in Aberdeen but spent most of his life in or near London. He is said to have been unbalanced mentally, and it is not clear whether compiling the concordance brought on the madness or whether Cruden was half mad in the first place to take on such an immense task. He laboured on the concordance for much of his life. It is an awesomely thorough work.

There are countless other biblical reference books that can be employed, and they are extremely variable. Concordances, dictionaries and encyclopaedias of the Bible proliferate. Biblical commentaries of every hue and persuasion are published regularly, everything from one volume editions for the whole Bible to multi-volumed tomes for one solitary gospel. Some of these reference books are excellent scholarly searches; some are blatant religious propaganda. Like all books of reference they need to be assessed coolly.[2]

One reliable standby among reference books is called the Hastings Dictionary of the Bible, after James Hastings DD, who

1 See pp. 49-56.

2 To check the thoroughness and the bias of biblical reference books we suggest looking up the following biblical passages: Isaiah 7:14; Matthew 1:16 (discussed here, pp. 60-63; Matthew 1:25 pp. 56-71). It is also interesting to note how various books deal with Mary's song (Luke 1:45-56); the virginal conception (Matthew 1: 18-25; Luke 1:26-38); Luke's dating of Jesus' birth (Luke 2:1); and the story of the star and the magi (Matthew 2:1-12). All of these can also be checked in the present book, and can be found in the Index of Biblical references.

edited the first five-volume edition at the beginning of this century. There have been numerous new editions since 1900, many of them shortened to one volume. This dictionary is widely available and usually manages to avoid taking a partisan line; each edition has been academically excellent for its time and almost ponderously reliable.

The point of turning to modern translations with good notes, and having good reference books on hand, is to try to discover and to understand the patterns within the Bible. Checking one translation against another, and cross-referencing names and places is a good way to begin to see how similar stories and themes are repeated throughout the Bible, how similar characters emerge from time to time, how one text can be rooted in another. Searching out the connections within the Bible in this way does not need to be a solemn and weighty undertaking. It can be like tracing the lines of a family tree, with branches going off in every direction, and with folk memories and lively stories attached to every branch. And just like any family tree, the tradition that connects many of these biblical stories to one another is an oral rather than a written tradition. Tracing the origins of biblical stories through books and written sources is a modern phenomenon. Few of us today can claim to have strong folk memories of the scriptures, so we cannot readily make connections from story to story without turning to written sources for help, but in times past the oral tradition was paramount. Before the days of widespread printing and literacy, people did not read the scriptures, they heard them, and they usually heard them in groups.

In the very distant past, oral transmission was the only way of passing on any kind of story. The stories that found their way into the earliest scriptures were initially passed down orally; from family to family, and from group to group. By about the tenth century BCE a few of the earlier parts of the Hebrew Scriptures were being written down. This early recording process continued until by about 600 BCE a substantial amount of scriptural text had been recorded. These records were kept on highly treasured scrolls, and a system gradually evolved of using these scrolls to aid the memories of those who knew the oral tradition. In turn this developed into a system of reading aloud from the scrolls to assembled groups of people. This way of proclaiming the holy writings tended to gain strength at crucial times when the religion felt itself to be under threat, when there was a perceived need to emphasize and repeat the traditions and the laws and the stories out of which the religion had grown. There is a strong argument for believing that systematic reading of the scriptures began to be formalized around the time of the Babylonian exile. In the year 587 BCE the Babylonians, led by King Nebuchadnezzar, destroyed Jerusalem and the temple. This meant humiliation, exile and an enduring sense of lost glory for the defeated Jewish people. According to the book of Chronicles, this was all their own fault:

> . . . all the leaders of Judah, the priests and the people too, added infidelity to infidelity, copying all the shameful practices of the nations and defiling the Temple of Yahweh which he himself had consecrated in Jerusalem. Yahweh, God of their ancestors, continuously sent them word through his messengers because he felt sorry for his people and his dwelling, but they ridiculed the messengers of God, they despised his words, they laughed at his prophets, until Yahweh's wrath with his people became so fierce that there was no further remedy. So against them he summoned the king of the Chaldaeans and he put their young men to the sword within the very building of their Temple, not sparing young man or girl, or the old and infirm; he put them all at his mercy. All the things belonging to the Temple of God, whether large or small, the treasures of the Temple of Yahweh, the treasures of the king and his officials, everything he took to Babylon. He burned down the temple of God, demolished the walls of Jerusalem, burned all its palaces to the ground and destroyed everything of value in it. And those who had escaped the sword he deported to Babylon, where they were enslaved by him and his descendants until the rise of the kingdom of Persia — to fulfil Yahweh's prophecy through Jeremiah: *Until the country has paid off its Sabbaths, it will lie fallow for all the days of its desolation — until the seventy years are complete.*[3]

> *2 Chronicles 36:14-21*

3 For other accounts of this same destruction of Jerusalem, see 2 Kings 25:1-12, and Jeremiah 39:1-14.

This meant the end of sacrificial offerings at the great temple of Solomon, built on the site of the 'threshing-floor of Araunah' where King David had had his vision of an avenging angel. For the four and a half centuries since the time of David, sacrifices had been made on this site every day. With the temple and the holy city destroyed and the elite of the people deported, the religion of Israel should have come to an ignominious end. It did nothing of the kind, because the scribes of Israel had begun to assemble a religious resource that the world had never seen before, a resource that gave their religion a remarkable staying power. This was the scriptures, recorded on scrolls. By the time of the Babylonian exile most of the Torah (the books of Genesis, Exodus, Leviticus, Numbers and Deuteronomy) had been written down by the scribes of Jerusalem, some of the earlier prophetic writings had also been recorded, and there was the beginning of a collection of great lyrics now called psalms. There were many copies of the scrolls containing all these writings and these scrolls made the religion portable.[4]

Although there is no surviving record of the scrolls being taken to Babylon at the time of the exile following the destruction of Jerusalem, there are strong indications that these writings were carefully preserved and studied, and that more writings were added during the Babylonian exile. Throughout their exile the Jews yearned to return to Jerusalem. The ancient grief of their exile is well known:

By the rivers of Babylon
we sat and wept
at the memory of Zion.
On the poplars there
we had hung up our harps.
For there our gaolers had asked us
to sing them a song,
our captors to make merry,
'Sing us one of the songs of Zion.'
How could we sing a song of Yahweh
on alien soil?

4 For an incidental account of the working lives of the scribes responsible for these scrolls, see Jeremiah 36.

If I forget you, Jerusalem,
may my right hand wither . . . .

Psalm 137:1-5

Many great writings of the Hebrew Scriptures emerged from the years of exile in Babylon, including a number of psalms, the writings of the second Isaiah, and most of the book of the prophet Ezekiel. The dominant theme of many of these writings is a yearning to return to Jerusalem. But there was more to the time of exile than these great expressions of grief. Because they were unable to slaughter animals as offerings at their holy temple, the religious practices of the Jews changed. Their meetings began to be centred on their sacred writings. In reading the Torah aloud when they met together in groups they were beginning to develop what has become the dominant public expression of religion for a very large proportion of the population of the world. In reading aloud from their sacred writings, they were developing a religion of the book, and they took this practice back to Jerusalem.

In the book of Nehemiah that was compiled by the same group of scribes who compiled both books of Chronicles, there is a description of an early public reading of the 'Book of the Law of Moses' from the newly rebuilt walls of Jerusalem. This public reading sounds uncannily like a modern revivalist meeting:

In the square in front of the Water Gate, in the presence of the men and women, and of those old enough to understand, he read from the book from dawn till noon; all the people listened attentively to the Book of the Law.

The scribe Ezra stood on a wooden dais erected for the purpose; beside him stood, on his right, Mattithiah, Shema, Anaiah, Uriah, Hilkiah and Maaseiah; on his left, Pedaiah, Mishael, Malchijah, Hashum, Hashbaddanah, Zechariah, and Meshullam. In full view of all the people — since he stood higher than them all — Ezra opened the book; and when he opened it, all the people stood up. Then Ezra blessed Yahweh, the great God, and all the people raised their hands and answered, 'Amen! Amen!'; then they bowed down and, face to the ground, prostrated themselves before Yahweh. And Jeshua, Bani, Sherebiah, Jamin, Akkub, Shabbethai, Hodiah, Maaseiah, Kelita, Azariah, Jozabab, Hanan, Pelaiah, who were Levites, explained the Law to the people, while the people all kept their places. Ezra read from the book of the Law of God, translating and giving the sense; so the reading was understood.

Then His Excellency Nehemiah and the priest-scribe Ezra and the Levites who were instructing the people said to all the people. 'Today is sacred to Yahweh your God. Do not be mournful, do not weep.' For the people were all in tears as they listened to the words of the Law.

Nehemiah 8:1-9

Because this description of the scribe Ezra reading from the 'Book of the Law of Moses' was compiled in its present form by the Chroniclers who were so skilled at creating highly inventive histories, it should probably be received with some caution. Yet, as an indication of a tradition of the importance of the written record of the scriptures, this account is very telling. It probably does reflect, at least to some extent, the practice the Jews developed while in Babylon, and this practice has not only endured, it has spread. Now at Jewish synagogues there are regular readings from the Torah. In Christian churches there are regular readings from the Bible. In Muslim mosques there are regular readings from the Koran. Both Christians and Muslims inherited this practice from the Jews. This is a religion of the book based on but transcending the written word, ensuring that the stories of the sacred writings are passed on orally, as well as in a literary form.

This kind of public reading gives rise automatically to one of the best methods of making connections between parts of the scriptures. When the scriptures are regularly read aloud to groups, a collective memory forms. One person can turn to the others and say, 'That story reminds me of . . .', making a connection that may not have occurred to the rest of the people there. The resources of any group can be pooled for the reading and understanding of any book, and with a book as long and complex as the Bible this is particularly true.

There is little doubt that both the Hebrew Scriptures and the Christian writings of the New Testament have consistently been read aloud to groups of people. There is some doubt about exactly what this means in practice, and how the practice may have affected the writing of the texts. The possibilities are many. Certain parts of the New Testament may have been written in a specific way because they were designed to be read aloud in a specific situation; perhaps in a particular synagogue or church, to a particular group of people, at a certain time of year, or even in conjunction with specific passages from the Hebrew Scriptures. In this way the connections between the gospels and the scriptures could be heard, as well as read. An oral folk memory could then develop, linking together all the passages that were read at the same time. However, because very little is known about how readings were organized in the synagogues of the first century or in the early church, the full consequences of this theory have yet to be worked out. Some scholars feel that although it is an attractive idea, there is not enough information to support it. Others have laboured long and hard to try to provide the necessary support, but as yet there is no consensus of opinion.[5]

So far in this chapter we have discussed many ways and means of discovering interconnections between biblical passages. Whether these connections are revealed by the pooling of folk memories and through oral traditions; whether they are discovered by using biblical cross-references and a Cruden; or whether they are found by the more esoteric methods of modern biblical scholars who are able to read the original languages, a major problem remains. It is all very well to discover biblical passages that appear to be interconnected, but it is another matter to know how to recognize which of these connections are significant.

For each individual this process of recognizing the significance of the connections is different. There are often several possible layers of meaning in scriptural passages. We may not be able to recognize them all, or we may not wish to. The cry of recognition that arises sometimes in conversations: 'Oh, that reminds me of so-and-so'-seldom arouses the same response in everyone present. Some connections are clear and easy to recognize, but if similarities are very subtle, or if they depend on special inside knowledge, or if

5 For further discussion see *Goulder* (1974), pp. 171-201.

they disturb long-held assumptions on any subject, the recognition
can be hard to achieve.

Take, for instance, the story in Luke's gospel about Anna the
prophetess. We gave this some attention in chapter 10, but did not
begin to cover all the implications of this passage:

> There was a prophetess, too, Anna the daughter of Pha-
> nuel, of the tribe of Asher. She was well on in years. Her
> days of girlhood over, she had been married for seven years
> before becoming a widow. She was now eighty-four years
> old and never left the Temple, serving God night and day
> with fasting and prayer. She came up just at that moment
> and began to praise God; and she spoke of the child to all
> who looked forward to the deliverance of Jerusalem.
>
> *Luke 2:26-38*

In chapter 10 we chose to recognize the importance of Anna by
emphasizing how she comes from the tribe of Asher. Others would
recognize the importance of this passage by analysing the numbers
cited: '. . . she had been married seven years before becoming a
widow. She was now eighty-four years old.' It is possible to
construct out of these figures a conviction that Luke is dealing with
symbolic numbers that make the time precisely right for seeing the
'redemption of Israel'. This kind of understanding is reached by
relating this passage to a recitation of numbers and dates that appear
in a speech of the angel Gabriel in the book of the prophet Daniel.
The angel speaks of the redemption of Israel coming within a
pattern of weeks, that are taken to mean years, and each number can
be said to be charged with significance.[6]

Two questions emerge from this: whether or not we find this
kind of arithmetical analysis helpful, and whether or not we
recognize its validity. A great many people find it both helpful and
valid and use it as a means of recognizing a valid scriptural
connection. On the other hand it is such a complex form of analysis
that many people prefer not to tangle with it at all, on the grounds
that it yields little for the amount of mental effort required to work

6 Daniel 9:24-7.

it out. In this way a decision can be reached not to recognize, or at least not to emphasize, a possible means of connecting Anna's story to the book of Daniel.

A simpler scriptural relationship within the story of Anna is to note that the name Anna is a different rendering of the name Hannah. This calls to mind the Hannah who frequented a sanctuary of Yahweh a thousand years before the time of Anna the prophetess who, in her turn, also frequents a sanctuary of Yahweh. Hannah awaited the redemption of Israel through Samuel, her miraculously conceived son who was dedicated to God from the womb; Anna the prophetess waits for the redemption of Israel through Jesus, the miraculously conceived and specially dedicated son of Mary. If we decide to recognize the parallel between Anna and Hannah, this recognition is strengthened by an awareness that there are many other possible connections between Luke's gospel and the story of Hannah. These include the parallel songs of Hannah and Mary, as well as the miraculous conceptions of children by two women who should not be able to conceive. If, on the other hand, we choose not to recognize this connection between the names Hannah and Anna, perhaps on the grounds that such a connection is too slight to be important or is entirely coincidental, such a choice may be questioned, but in the end we are all free to decide for ourselves. As with the numerological connection to the book of Daniel, this connection of Anna's name to Hannah can be accepted or rejected.

In this way, the story of Anna the prophetess provides two examples of biblical connections in which the process of recognition can be observed in action. The connections involved are slight ones. No points of great theological or historical significance hang on such questions, that is why they are useful here. In thinking of how we recognize or do not recognize even the slight connections it becomes clear that personal predilections play a part in this process of recognition, and it also becomes clear that these predilections can sometimes stand in the way of recognition. For example, if a reader finds the whole subject of numerology distasteful, the possible connection between the book of Daniel and the story of Anna is unlikely to appeal. Equally, if someone is determined to believe that names have no significance, the similar names of Anna and Hannah will mean nothing.

No one can dictate whether any particular set of biblical passages should or should not be recognized as valid. This applies with minor connections like the ones above, and also with major connections, like the miraculous conceptions of Mary and Hannah and Sarah, the dreams of the two Josephs, and the stars found in gospels and scriptures alike. Connections between biblical passages enjoy every shade of credibility, and there can be hundreds of criteria on which to base a recognition. Such decisions are up to the individual, once the passages have been read and the possible connections considered. In the preceding chapters we have outlined a great number of biblical connections that we have recognized and found helpful in trying to understand the background and origins of the birth stories in Matthew and Luke's gospel. There are many more listed in the tables at the back of the book. Not everyone will choose to recognize all these connections or will judge them all to be valid. Some connections might be rejected as far-fetched or irrelevant, and some might be accepted when it is far from clear what such an acceptance really implies.

In discovering and trying to assess biblical connections, a degree of self-confidence is necessary. There is no reason to be intimidated by the biblical scholars who are the experts in this area; they are by no means always right and the best of them will always say so. They are not the only people who can assess the evidence. Of course scholars do have expertise, sometimes great expertise, and it is foolhardy and arrogant to ignore what they say just because it can be difficult to understand, or because it raises awkward questions, or because it upsets our preconceived ideas. What the scholars have to say needs to be taken seriously and assessed carefully, but again we are all free to make up our own minds. Equally, there is no reason to be intimidated by religious propaganda in this area. Obscurantists and other extremists have been known to threaten with hell fire and excommunication when perfectly reasonable questions are asked about a biblical text. But such people have no monopoly on interpreting the text, and there is no reason to submit to any form of spiritual bullying. Anyone who is interested and motivated can learn about biblical connections, and learn to assess the evidence. Naturally all of our assessments in this area, as in every other area, are partial, and subject to error and frequently in need of revision. That being understood, we can welcome our own discoveries and live at ease with the ability to assess such discoveries for ourselves.

Epilogue

It is perfectly natural to turn to this final section of the book in search of conclusions. After twelve chapters of examining the birth stories of Matthew and Luke and seeing how these stories are related to stories in the Hebrew Scriptures it is not unreasonable to hope for a succinct summary of what all this means. Yet we are reluctant to declare firm and final conclusions. In the Introduction we stated that our aim was to reveal evidence about how the birth stories were written, and that this evidence could be assessed by every reader individually. We believe this to be true. Everyone can assess the evidence in this book for himself or herself. We have already indicated in chapter 11 our mistrust of the tendency to draw absolute conclusions about the birth narratives, and we do not intend to ignore what we have said by proposing our own absolute conclusions. All we can do here is to try to summarize the material we have covered and try to respond to one particular problem this material gives rise to.

To state the obvious, the birth stories are profoundly influenced by the scriptures. They come out of a tradition which we earlier called the 'looking-glass world' of the Hebrew Scriptures; a tradition in which one text is reflected in another text. This happens to such an extent in the birth stories that almost every incident and every character described by Matthew and by Luke has a strong precedent in the scriptures. Time and time again in the birth stories, the precedents of the Hebrew Scriptures seem to shape and form the stories told by Matthew and Luke. Because their gospel stories seem so much like reruns of other earlier stories, a very logical question arises. What really happened when Jesus was born?

The answer is simple. We do not know what really happened when Jesus was born. It is doubtful if anyone knows. This is not at all surprising. Often we do not know what has really happened in our own lives, and we certainly cannot always claim to know what really is happening in the world around us. Hard facts cannot always be known despite the best efforts of news reporters, diarists, archivists, or gospel writers. The desire to know the full and factual details of any reported event is understandable, but our grasp of facts is always fragile. Our own memories can let us down; diaries and journals are highly selective in how they recall events, and reports in the news media or in history books are subject to bias and distortion.

The gospels were never intended as factual reports about what really happened. Cross-examining the birth stories in a rigorous search for hard facts is to misunderstand the very purpose of these stories. Matthew and Luke are declaring their beliefs about Jesus, and telling stories to spread the word about Jesus. Their writing is lively, and committed, and complex. Their stories about Jesus's birth do not respond well to the thirst for hard facts. They do respond well to detailed study linking them to their origins in scripture. Seen in this way, the stories become richer. Seen as imperfect factual reports, the stories are impoverished.

The birth stories are an introduction to the gospels that follow. Like all good introductions, they were almost certainly the last sections of the text to be written. When Matthew and Luke were writing these stories they already knew what followed. They already knew the stories of the life and of the death and of the resurrection of Jesus. They were part of the new religion which was taking shape around these stories of Jesus, and they were writing at a time when that new religion was under stress. The gospels filled a need to know more about Jesus. The members of the emerging

Christian church had to be reminded and reassured about the importance of their leader, who he was, and what his role was. The birth stories of Matthew and Luke assert all of this clearly and repeatedly. They are attractive and memorable stories which set the stage for all the other stories about Jesus. They do this by establishing the identity of Jesus through what were seen as vital links with the Hebrew Scriptures.

In the book of Isaiah there is a passage that reads: 'For precept must be upon precept, precept upon precept; line upon line, line upon line; here a little, and there a little.' (Isaiah 28:10, AV.) Although it is unimportant in its original context, where it is little more than a rhetorical device, we have found this passage is useful because it is a reminder of how a text takes shape. For our purposes here, it can be understood almost as a catchphrase indicating how the birth stories took shape. They emerged from layer after layer of stories in the Hebrew Scriptures; precept upon precept, line upon line, taken from many different places. These birth stories of Matthew and of Luke are rich and strange and very ancient, part of a world of text that is foreign to most of us today. We hope that in this book we have at least opened out that world of text and provided access to some of the stories and traditions beyond the all-too-familiar Christmas-card images of the birth at Bethlehem.

Chronology

Unless otherwise indicated, all dates are BCE. The dating of documents refers to the time when they began to take the form now known to us.

PEOPLE AND EVENTS	DATE	THE WRITTEN RECORD	DATE
Lamech and his two wives	unknown	Genesis 4:23–4	c. 950–750
Abraham to Canaan	c. 1850	Genesis 12	c. 950–750
Hyksos pharaohs Hebrews in Egypt	1720–1560	Genesis 37–50	c. 950–750
Hammurabi in Babylon	c. 1725	Hammurabi's code	c. 1700
Tamar and Judah	c. 1700	Genesis 38	unknown
Building of Pithom and Rameses Hebrews enslaved	1290	Exodus 1:6–14	c. 950–750

Exodus from Egypt	*c.* 1250	Exodus 1-15	assembled *c.* 625
Crossing of Red Sea		older sources	
Miriam the Prophetess			
Balaam and his donkey	*c.* 1220	Numbers 22-4 oracles	*c.* 950-750 very early
Joshua invading Palestine Rahab Jericho Crossing of Jordan	*c.* 1220-1200	Joshua 1-10	before *c.* 750 sources assembled *c.* 550
Greeks beseige Troy	*c.* 1200	Homer Odyssey	?800-600
Wife of Manoah Samson	*c.* 1175	Judges 13 older sources	*c.* 650
Ruth and Boaz	*c.* 1125	Ruth	*c.* 625
Hannah conceives	*c.* 1070	1 Samuel 1-2	before *c.* 750
Death of Eli	*c.* 1050	1 Samuel 4	
Samuel	*c.* 1070-1000	1 Samuel 1-25	assembled *c.* 625
Samuel annoints David king	*c.* 1010	1 Samuel 16	
David king, unites the tribes	*c.* 1010-970	1 Samuel 16-2 1 Kings 2	assembled *c.* 625
Solomon king	970-931	1 Kings 1-12	*c.* 625
Temple built		Psalm 72 Ps. 72 rewritten	*c.* 730 *c.* 450
Queen of Sheba visits	970-931	Song Song rewritten	before *c.* 750 450-300
The Kingdom divides	931	1 Kings 12	

Abijam king	913–911	1 Kings 15:1-8	before *c.* 700
		2 Chronicles 1-2	*c.* 350
Elijah the prophet	*c.* 875–850	1 Kings 17 – 2 Kings 2	*c.* 625 [assembled]
Elisha the prophet	*c.* 850–?	2 Kings 2-13	*c.* 625 [assembled]
Hosea, Micah and Amos	*c.* 750	Amos [core only]	*c.* 730
		Micah [core only]	before 700
		Hosea [core only]	before 721
King Uzziah dies Isaiah's vision	740	Isaiah 6	
Isaiah prophet in Jerusalem	740–698	Isaiah 1-39 [core only]	before *c.* 698
Isaiah oracle to Ahaz	734	Isaiah 7	
Assyria conquers Samaria Northern kingdom of Israel collapses	720	2 Kings 17	*c.* 625 [assembled]
Josiah king 'Book of Law' found in the temple	640–609	2 Kings 22 Deuteronomy (core only)	*c.* 635 *c.* 650
Nebuchadnezzar king in Babylon	604–562		
Pharoah Necho king in Egypt	610–595	2 Kings 23:29-34	
Nebuchadnezzar conquers Jerusalem Jehoiachin and first deportation	16 March 597	2 Kings 24	
Nebuchadnezzar destroys Jerusalem	587	2 Kings 25 cf. 2 Chronicles 36	*c.* 550 *c.* 350
Second deportation		cf. Jeremiah 39	various dates to 586

Second Isaiah poet in exile	*c.* 587–520	Isaiah 40–55	
Cyrus of Persia conquers Babylon	538	Isaiah 44:28–45:1	
Zerubbabel rebuilds altar Foundations laid for second Temple	538–537	Ezra 3	*c.* 350 [assembled]
Work recommenced on second Temple	August 520	Haggai [core]	contemporary
Temple rebuilding encouraged	October 520	Zechariah [core]	contemporary
Completion of second Temple	515	Ezra 6	*c.* 350 [assembled]
New walls built for Jerusalem	445–443	Nehemiah 3	
Law, Prophets, many psalms, well advanced	*c.* 400		
Persia fading; Jerusalem restive; Ezra, Nehemiah, and Chronicles started	350	Coins stamped YDH [= 'Judah']	
Death of Plato	348		
Reign of Alexander the Great	336–323		
Pharaoh Ptolemy Philadelphus: Greek version of scriptures started	285–246	Septuagint: work on Greek translation slow	*c.* 250–100
Mattathias rebels against Greeks	167	1 Maccaabees 2:17–25 cf. Daniel	*c.* 167

Judas Maccabeus leads rebellion Independence Treaty with Rome	166–160	1 Maccabees	c. 100
Pompey takes Jerusalem for Rome	63		
Life of Virgil [Eclogues]	70–19		
Herod puppet king in Jerusalem Massive building includes new temple	37–4		
Jesus born	?6	Matthew 1-2 Luke 1-2	c. 80 CE c. 85 CE
Herod dies Revolt in Jerusalem	April, 4		
Quirinius takes census Revolt	6-7 CE	Luke 2 Acts 5	c. 85 CE
Jesus in temple as a youth	c. 8 CE	Luke 2	
Jesus baptized by John the Baptist	c. 26 CE	Luke 3:23	
Jesus is killed	c. 30 CE	Luke 23, and all the gospels	
Conversion of Paul	c. 33-4 CE	Acts 9	c. 85 or earlier
Flavius Josephus, Jewish historian	c. 38-100		
Paul writes first letter to Thessalonica	50-51 CE		

Life of Nero	37–69		
Persecution of Christians in Rome	64 CE		
Peter and Paul killed		Mark	c. 64 CE
Jerusalem rebels	67 CE		
Siege of Jerusalem by Romans	67–70 CE	Josephus: Wars of the Jews	78 CE
Jerusalem conquered and destroyed	August 70 CE		
Life of Plutarch	c. 46–119 CE		
Rabbis using Jamnia	c. 80 CE	Matthew writing	c. 80 CE
Birkhath-ha-Minim	c. 85 CE	Luke writing	c. 85 CE
		John writing	c. 95 CE
Life of Papias, very early bishop	c. 60–130 CE		
Life of Suetonius, author of The Twelve Caesars	c. 69–?	Aquila's translation of the Hebrew Scriptures	c. 140 CE
Ptolemy the astronomer	c. 150 CE	Protevangelium of James	c. 150–200 CE

There are many hundreds of surviving New Testament documents. They range from very small fragments to nearly complete Bibles. A few of these date back to within a century of the writers of the New Testament. For a full list of these and their present location, see Nestle-Aland, *Novum Testamentum Graece*, Stuttggart, Deutsche Bibelstiftung, 1981, pp. 684–716. The volume has an introduction in English.

The earliest known fragments of Greek manuscripts for the New Testament date from *c.* 200 CE and the earliest manuscripts for the complete Bible, such as Codex Sinaiticus, Codex Alexandrinus and Codex Vaticanus, date from *c.* 400 CE.

Tables

Ancient Use of Ancient Sources

The numbering of verses and chapters can differ from Bible to Bible. We have followed the numbering system used in the New Jerusalem Bible as closely as possible. The differences between Bibles are seldom great, but they can lead to confusion. If such confusion arises the best solution is to read the verses surrounding the Biblical references in question.

If possible it is best to read the whole context of any reference used even where there is no problem of verification. This usually gives a better sense of the passage.

There are useful introductions and footnotes throughout the New Jerusalem Bible which are usually very helpful when more information is needed. We can recommend them for quick reference. The marginal notations of the NJB are also useful in cross-referencing biblical passages.

Luke's genealogy is not included in this tabulation. See chapter 3 pp. 29-32 and Luke 3:23-28.

Abbreviations for books of the Bible listed in the tables:

Gen.	Genesis	Song	Song of Songs
Exod.	Exodus	Wisd.	Wisdom
Lev.	Leviticus	Ecclus.	Ecclesiasticus (or
Num.	Numbers		Sirach)
Deut.	Deuteronomy	Isa.	Isaiah
Josh.	Joshua	Jer.	Jeremiah
Judg.	Judges	Ezek.	Ezekiel
1 Sam.	1 Samuel	Dan.	Daniel
2 Sam.	2 Samuel	Hos.	Hosea
1 Kgs.	1 Kings	Mic.	Micah
2 Kgs.	2 Kings	Hab.	Habakkuk
1 Chr.	1 Chronicles	Hag.	Haggai
2 Chr.	2 Chronicles	Zech.	Zechariah
Neh.	Nehemiah	Mal.	Malachi
Tb.	Tobit	Mk.	Mark
Jdt.	Judith	Lk.	Luke
Macc.	Maccabees	Rom.	Romans
Ps./Pss.	Psalms		

Table I

The Birth Stories

TEXT	EVENT	POSITED TEXTUAL SOURCES
	The Genealogy	2Sam.7:12-29;

Matthew

TEXT	EVENT	POSITED TEXTUAL SOURCES
1:1	David/ Abraham	Gen.12:1-4; 15:1-6; 17:1-8 Gen.22:11-18; Ps.132:11f.; cf.1Sam.16:1-14
1:2	Isaac, angel appears Jacob (Israel) Judah Tamar	Gen.21:1-8; 26:1-5 Gen.25:19-28; Gen.28-30; 35:10f Gen.29:35 Gen.38
1:3-4	Perez	Gen.38:27-30; Ruth 4:12; 18-22
1:5	Rahab	Josh.2
1:5	Salmon/Boaz/Ruth	Ruth, and especially 2:1; 4:1-13

1:6	Uriah's wife (Bathsheba)	2Sam.11:2-4; 12:7-11; 1Chr.20:1f.
1:7	Rehoboam/Abijah	1Kgs.11:43; 2Chr.11:20-22
1:8	Asa	1Chr.3:10
1:9	Uzziah/Ahaz	2Kgs.15:7,13,18,32,38;16:20; Isa.6:1; Isa.7
1:1	Josiah	2Kgs.22:1-23:30; cf.1Kgs.13:2
1:11	Jechoniah	2Kgs.23:34-7; Jer.22; 2Chr.36:1-10
1:12	Shealtiel	1Chr.3:17; cf. 1Chr.1-12
1:13	Zerubbabel	Ezra 2:2; see also ch. 3-4
1:14-15	Eliakim, Azor, Zadok, Akim, Eliud	2Sam.8:17; 15:24; 20:25; 1Chr.6:3; 2Kgs.18:18; Isa.22:20-25
1:16	Matthan (Mattathias)	1Macc.2:17-25
1:17	genealogical patterns	cf.1Chr.1-8
	Joseph	**Gen.38, especially v. 26**
1:19	righteous man/ public example	Gen.6:9; 20:1-16; Deut. 24:1-4; Gen.13, esp. v. 26
1:20	Annunciation Joseph's first dream about Mary (cf. Luke 1:26-38)	Gen.37 especially v. 5-11 and 19f.; Gen.40-41; 42:5-7 (These apply to all four of Joseph's dreams.)
1:21-3	give birth to a son (cf. Luke 1:31)	Gen.17:19; cf. Rom.4:19ff Isa. 9:5-7
1:23	quote from prophet (virgin [?] shall conceive)	Isa.7:14
	The Magi	**Gen.25:19ff; cf. Gen.41 and Dan.2**
2:1	Herod=Esau/Edom	Gen.25:19-34; Gen.27 all See also Mal.1:1-5
2:2-3	The Magi/homage	Gen.27:29; 37:9-11; Isa.60:1-7
2:4	magi before king	Gen.41:8; Num.22-4; Jer.36:21ff.

2:5-6	quote from prophet	Micah 5:1; cf.Gen.35:16-20; Ruth 1:1-16; 1Sam.16:1-13; 2Sam.5:2
2:7-10	star/homage	Gen.37:9-11; 42:5-7; 43:26; Num.24:15-20; Isa.60:3-4
2:9	guide to the place	Exod.13; 21f.
2:11-12	gifts: gold etc.	1Kgs.10:1-25; Ps.72:10-11,15; Isa.60:5-6; Song 1:3; 3:6
2:13-14	Joseph's second dream about Egypt	Gen. 27:41-5; Num.24:2; Judg.2:1; 6:12-13; Ps.34:7
2:15	quote from prophet (out of Egypt)	Hos.11:1; cf.Exod.3-15 and especially Exod. 3:7-8; 4:22; 5:1f.; 7:26; Num.23:22; Deut.4:37
2:16-17	babies killed	Exod.1:15-22
2:18	quote from prophet (Rachel weeping)	Jer.31:15; cf.Gen.35:16-20
2:19-23	3rd and 4th dreams leave Egypt go to Nazareth	Exod.3:7-12; Num.24:22; Jer.44:28
2:20-21	'who threaten . . . are dead . . .' travel with donkey [?]	Exod.4:19 Exod.4:20
2:23	quote from prophet [?] (Nazarene [?]) choice of two puns: [both in Hebrew]	[a] Isa.11:1 [b] Judg.13:5-7

Luke

1:1-4	Prologue	2Macc.1:1-9 and the preface to Sirach.
1:5-25	***Elizabeth And Zechariah***	***Gen.15-22***
1:5	Herod (an Edomite) Zechariah	See above Matt.2:1-10 Lev.21:1-24; Neh.12:4; 1Chr.16:4-6; 24:10-11

1:6-10	Zechariah and Elizabeth	Gen.18:1-15; Exod.6:23; 30:7-9; Deut.6:1,17,25; 1Sam.1:11
1:6,	right before God	Gen.26:5 cf.6:9f.; cf.30
1:7	barren	Gen.11:30; 25:19-28,29:31ff., 30:1-24; Judg.13:2-4; 1Sam.1:1-21
1:11-22	***Zechariah's Vision***	***Judg.ch.13 and Dan.10:1-19***
1:10-13	Angel appears (Luke 1:26-38)	Gen.15:1; 16:7-12; 18:1-15 Judg.13:3-7; Tob.1-5; Dan.10:7-10
1:11	at incense hour	Exod.30:6-8; cf.Abraham in Gen.15 and 18
1:13-17	child promised:John	Gen.17:19; Lev.10:9; Num.6:1-8 Judg.13:3-5,24f.; Isa.7:14; 49:1; Jer.1:5; Mal.3:1; 4:5-6; 3:23-4
1:15	the nazirite/ like Elijah	Num.6:2-4; Judg.13:5; cf. all of Malachi and Ecclus.48
1:18-25	disbelief/pregnancy	Gen.17:17-20; 21-2; Ezk.3:24-7
1:18	more doubts	Gen.15:8; cf.17:17; and 18:11ff.
1:20-22	speechless	Dan.10:15
1:25	take away reproach	Gen.16:13; 30:23; cf.Lk.1:58 below
1:26-56	***Mary:***	***1Sam.1-3; cf.Exod.15:20f.; Judg.13***
2:26-38	Annunciation (see Matt.1:20-25) (see Luke 1:11-20)	Gen.15:1-6; 18:1-15 Gen.25:19-28; Judg.13:1-20 Isa.chh.7-9
1:28	'highly favoured'	Dan.9:21-3; 10:18-19
1:30	'favour or 'grace'	Gen.6:8; 19:19; Judg.6:17
1:31	'to conceive . . . Jesus'	Isa.7:14; cf.Gen.16:11 (cf. Matt.1:21)
1:32-3	'most high etc.'	Gen.12:2-3; 14:19; 2Sam.7:13-17; Dan.713f.; Isa.9:6f.; Jer.23:5f.; Ps.86:9
1:34	'how can this come about . . .?'	Gen.17:17-19; 18:12-14; 25:19-28; 29:31f.; 30:1-24; Judg.13:2-4;

	(miraculous	1Sam.1:1-21
	conceptions)	
	see Luke 1:7ff.	
	'. . . I have no	
	knowledge of man . . .'	Judg.11:34–40; Tob.3:14f.
1:35	the cloud	Exod.13:21f.; 24:16-18; 40:34-8;
		1Kgs.8:10-13; Hag.2:6-7
1:35-7	'. . . nothing	Gen.18:14; Judg.13:2; Ps2:7
	impossible . . .'	
1:36-8	divine promises	Deut.7:12-14
	trustworthy	
1:38	trusting response	Gen.15:6
1:40-4	child 'leaps'/older	
	serves younger	Gen.25:22f.
1:42ff.	greeting/blessing	Gen.14:19; 30:2; Judg.5:24; 6:12;
	blessed among women	Judith 13:18
	fruit of womb	
1:43	the Lord/king comes	2Sam.24:21, and see Lk.2:1 below
1:45-56	***Mary's Song***	***1Sam.2:1-10; (cf.Joel 2:21-7)***
	[Magnificat]	***and Acts 13:16ff. also by Luke***
		[See also Table III below.]
1:46-7	rejoicing in God	Tob.3:11; 8:6f.; Ps.103:1; Hab.3:18
1:48	call me blessed	Gen.30:13; Mal.3:12
1:48	humiliation[1]	Gen.29:32; Tob.3:12f.
1:49	great things	Pss.71:19; 103:1
	Holy is his name	Pss.111:9; 126:2f.
1:50	faithful love	Pss.88:11; 103:1,17; Hos.2:4ff.
1:51	power of his arm	Deut.4:34; Pss.98:1f.; 118:16;
		Isa.52:10; Jer.27:5
1:52f	raised the poor	Pss.138:6; Isa.61

---

1 The word 'humiliation' is sometimes translated 'misery', as in Gen.29:32. As with the other problems of translation this has come from the Hebrew into the Greek and on into English.

1:51-3	filling the hungry	Exod.6:6; 1Sam.2:7-8; Isa.40:29-30; 41-17; 42-7; 61:1-3
1:54-5	according to promises	Gen.12:1-7; 13:14-17; 22:15-18 Ps.98:3; Isa.41:8-12; 42:1-4; 49:1-7
1:56	three months	2Sam.6:11
1:57-80	***Birth of John***	***Gen.15-22***
1:57	she bore a son	Gen.21:1f.
1:58	friends rejoice pun on 'Isaac'	Gen.21:6; 30:22-4; see NJB notes pp. 36,41; cf. Lk.1:25 above
1:59-66	child named/ circumcised	Gen.21:3-4; cf. Gen.17:12; Lev.12:3
1:63	writing tablet	Isa.8:1
1:68-79	***Zechariah's Song*** ***[Benedictus]***	***1Kgs.1:48 with 2Sam.22:2ff. (Ps.18)*** ***Tob.3:1-6; 8:7-18; 11:14f.;*** ***Tob.13; cf.Ps.106*** [See also Table III below]
1:68	blessed be the Lord who visited and saved	1Kgs.1:48; cf.Gen.12:2; Gen.21:1; Exod.6:6; 2Sam.22:3
1:69	deliver:--	
1:71	and save	2Sam.22:18; Ps.110:9
1:74	from enemies	
1:71-3	promise to Abraham /David	Gen.15:1ff.; 2Sam.22:51
1:72	'faithful love'	2Sam.22:51; cf.Lk.1:50 above
1:74-5	deliverance again	Gen.22:16-18; Mal.3:20-23
1:76	prepare a way	Mal.3:1
1:78	'dayspring'	Mal.3:20; Zech.3:8
1:78	'faithful love' again	see notes NJB, p.1501
1:79	light the darkness/ guide our feet	2Sam.22:17,29,32f.; Ps.119:105; Isa.9:1; 42:6f.; 49:6f.; 59:9; Zech.6:12

1:80	the child grew	Gen.21:20; Judg.13:24f.
2:1-20	**Birth of Jesus**	**1Sam.1:1-2:11**
2:1-5	to Bethlehem	Gen.35:19; Mic.5:2; 1Sam.16:1-13
2:1	census	Exod.30:12; 32:32-3; 2Sam.24, and see Lk.1:43 above, cf.1Chr.21:1-5; 2Chr.3:1-3
2:3-5	to home town/district	Gen.35:1; 16-20
2:6	shepherds	1Sam.16:11; Mic.5:3-5
2:7	swaddling clothes/ in manger	Wisd.7:3-6; Jer.14:8
	ox and ass [?]	Isa.1:2-3
2:9	angel of the Lord	Gen.16:9ff.; Num.22:22; Judg.2:1,4; 6:11; 13:3; 2Kgs.19:35; Zech.1:12; 12:8
2:12	sign	Isa.7:14
2:13-14	heavenly host	Ps.118:26; Isa.6; 9:6f.; Ezek.3:12f.
2:19	pondered in heart	Gen.37:11; cf. Lk.2:51 below
2:21-8	circumcision	Gen.17:12-14; Lev.5:7; 12:2-6
2:22-40	**At the Temple:**	**1Sam.1:19-2:11**
2:22	'purification'	Lev.12:2-4; cf. Num.18:16
2:22-3	presentation	Gen.22:1; Exod.13:1-16; 22:29; Lev.5:7; 12:8; Num.3:11ff.; 1Sam.1:21-8; Neh.10:36
2:25-8	spirit poured out	Joel 3:1ff.; Zech.12:10 cf. Acts 2:17ff.
2:25	a good man	Gen.6:9
2:26	see saviour and die (see Lk.2:29 below)	Gen.46:30
2:29-32	**Simeon's Song [Nunc Dimittis]**	**Isa.40:1-5; 42:1-5** [See also Table III below]
2:29-32	joy after sadness	Gen.46:30; Isa.40:1
2:30	salvation seen	Isa.40:5

2:31	prepare ... let all see	Isa.40:3-5
2:32	light for gentiles	Isa.6:5b; 42:6f.; 49:6; 52:10; 60:3
2:33-5	sad oracle	Ps.22:16-21; Isa.8:13-17; Jer.15:10
2:36-8	Anna (=Hannah)	1Sam.1ff.; Judith 8:4-8; Isa.40:2; 52:3,9
2:36	tribe of Asher	Gen.30:9-13; Deut.33:24f.; Josh.19:24f.
2:38	the numerology	Dan.9:24-7
2:39	redemption of Israel	Isa.40:2; 52:3,9
2:40	growing up	1Sam.2:18-26
2:41-52	temple at Passover	Exod.12:1ff.
2:43	at twelve years old	1Sam.3
2:51f.	pondered in heart	1Sam.2:26; cf. Lk.2:19 above

Table II

The Hebrew Scriptures

This table sets out four samples of the sort of evidence that indicates how writers in the Hebrew Scriptures use and adapt the work of their predecessors. This table can also be used to compare the methods of writers in the Hebrew Scriptures with the methods of one or other of the New Testament writers.

Table II provides only a few small samples out of a great mass of evidence. The samples were chosen because they are reasonably easy to comprehend in almost any English translation without any knowledge of the original languages, and with very little knowledge about the writers or their history. Dates for both the events and the writings can be found in the chronology.

Crossing the Waters

SAMPLE PASSAGE	SUBJECT MATTER/EVENT	POSITED SOURCE
Joshua		*Exodus*
3:14-17 (cf.2Kgs.2:7-16)	crossing Jordan/ Red Sea	14:21-2
4:9-24	crossing the water: cloud leads/follows ark leads/follows	14:19-20
5:12	manna ceases/starts	16
5:2-9	Joshua circumcises all Israel/Moses's wife circumcises his son	4:24-6

David's Census

SAMPLE PASSAGE	SUBJECT MATTER/EVENT	POSITED SOURCE
1Chronicles		*2Samuel*
21:1	David moved to take census by Satan or Jahweh	24:1
		cf.Job 1:6-12
15:1-26	David has ark carried into Jerusalem	6:1-19
2Chronicles		*1Kings*
13:1-22	These 22 verses are derived from 8 verses which are expanded thus:	15:1-8
13:3	census statistics	2Sam.24:1-4,9
13:4-12	pattern of speech content of speech	Judg.9:7-20 1Kgs.12
13:5	salt	Lev.24:1-9

13:8-10	idols	Ju.17:1-6 cf. 1Kgs.12
13:10-12	Levites etc.	Lev.24:1-9
13:13-18	ambush	Judg.9:25-41; cf. Josh. 8:1-25

NB Judges, Joshua and Leviticus: various dates to 550 BCE.

King Jehoshaphat's Story

2Chronicles		1Kings
17-20	Ahab's war incorporated into Jehoshaphat's story	22:41-51
17:3-6 (cf.2 Chr.14:1-6)	Jehoshaphat like David	15:10-15; 22:41-5
17:5 (cf.2 Chr.1:11-17)	Jehoshaphat receives riches	5:1,6
17:11 (cf.2 Chr.9:13-14)	Arabs brings gifts	10:14,15
17:10 (cf.2 Chr.1:1)	Jehoshaphat secures kingdom	2:44-6

| 2Chronicles | | 1Kings |
| 20:6-12 | Jehoshaphat's prayer like Solomon's | 8:22-61 |

King Abijah's Story

2 Chronicles Ch.13	*1 Kings 15 and Other Sources*
In the eighteenth year of King Jereboam, Abijah became king of Judah and reigned for three years in Jerusalem. His mother's name was Micaiah daughter of Uriel of Gibeah.	In the eighteenth year of King Jereboam son of Nebat, Abijam became king of Judah and reigned for three years in Jerusalem. His mother's name was Maacah descendent of Absolam. In everything he follwed the sinful

	example of his father before him; his heart was not wholly with Yahweh his God, as the heart of David his ancestor had been. However, for David's sake, Yahweh his God gave him a lamp in Jerusalem, with a son to succeed him, so keeping Jerusalem secure; for David had done what Yahweh regarded as right and had never in all his life disobeyed whatever he had commanded him (except in the matter of Uriah the Hittite).
	The rest of the history of Abijam, his entire career, is this not recorded in the book of the Annals of the Kings of Judah?
When war broke out between Abijah and Jeroboam Abijah took the field with an army of four hundred thousand picked warriors, while Jereboam took the field against him with eight hundred thousand picked warriors.	Abijah and Jereboam made war on each other.
2Chr.13:1-3	1 Kgs.15:1-7
	Joab gave the king the census results for the people; Israel had eight hundred thousand fighting men who could wield a sword, and Judah five hundred thousand.
	2 Sam.24:9
Abijah's speech. 2Chr.13:4-12	cf. Judg. 9:7-20/1Kgs. 12
by an inviolable covenant (of salt)	You will put salt in every cereal offering that you offer, and you will not fail to put the salt of the covenant of your God on your cereal offering ....
v.5	Lev.2:13

Yet Jereboam son of Nebat, the slave of Solomon son of David, rose in revolt against his master. Worthless men, scoundrels, rallied to him . . .

2Chr.6:7

. . . you propose to resist Yahweh's sovreignty as exercised by the sons of David because there is a great number of you and you have the golden calves that Jerboam made you for gods!

2Chr.13:8

But for our part, our God is Yahweh, and we have not abandoned him; our priests are sons of Aaron who minister to Yahweh, and

. . . . Abimelech paid violent adventurers to follow him.

Judg.9:5

In the highlands of Ephraim there was a man called Micayehu . . . (he) returned the money to his mother.

His mother then took two hundred silver shekels and gave them to the metal worker. With them, he carved a statue (and cast an idol in metal) which was put in Micayehu's house.

Judg.17:1-4

Jereboam thought to himself, 'As things are, the kingdom will revert to the house of David. If this people continues to go up to the Temple of Yahweh in Jerusalem to offer sacrifices the people's heart will turn back again to their lord, Rehoboam king of Judah, and they will put me to death.' So the king thought this over and then made two golden calves; and he said to the people, '. . . . here is your God, Israel . . .' He set one up at Bethel, and the people went . . . all the way to Dan to worship the other.

1Ki.13:26-29

. . . 'Order the Israelites to bring you crushed-olive oil for the lamp-stand, and keep a flame burning there continually. Aaron will keep

those who serve are Levites;
morning after morning, evening
after evening, they present burnt
offerings and perfumed incense to
Yahweh, they put the bread of
permanent offering on the clean
table and nightly light the
lamps . . .

See how God is with us, at our
head, and his priests with
trumpets to sound the alarm
against you! Israelites, do not
make war on Yahweh, God of
your ancestors, for you will not
succeed.

2Chr.13:10-12

it premanently in trim from evening to morning, outside the cur-
tain of the testimony in the Tent of
Meeting, before Yahweh. This is a
perpetual decree for your descendants: Aaron will keep the
lamps permanently trimmed on
the pure lampstand before Yahweh. You will take wheaten flour
and with it bake twelve loaves . . .

Lev.24:1-5

Now Jereboam had sent a party
round to ambush them from the
rear; thus the main force con-
fronted Judah and the ambush lay
to their rear. And when Judah
looked round, they found themselves being attacked from front
and rear. They called on Yahweh,
the priests sounded the trumpets,
and the men of Judah raised the
war cry and, as they raised the
cry, God routed Jereboam and all
Israel before Abijah and Judah.

2Chr.13:13-16

Israel then positioned troops in
ambush all around Gibeah. On the
third day the Israelites marched
against the Benjaminites and, as
before, drew up their line in front
of Gibeah. The Benjaminites sal-
lied out to engage the people and
let themselves be drawn away
from the town. As before, they
began by killing those of the people who were on the roads . . .

All the Israelites then
retreated and reformed . . . while
the Israelite troops in ambush
surged from their positions to the
west of Gibeah . . . the battle was
fierce . . . Yahweh defeated
Benjamin . . .

Judg.20:29-35,
cf.Judg.9:25-41; Josh.8:1-25

The rest of the history of Abijah, his conduct and his sayings, are recorded in the midrash of the prophet Iddo. When Abijah fell asleep with his ancestors, he was buried in the City of David; his son Asa succeeded him.

2Chr.13:22f.

When Abijam fell asleep with his ancestors, he was buried in the City of David; his son Asa succeeded him.

1Kgs.15:8

Mary's Song	Hannah's Song
My soul proclaims the greatness of the Lord	My heart exults in Yahweh,
and my spirit rejoices in God my Saviour;	in God my strength is lifted up,
because he has looked upon the humiliation of his servant.	my mouth derides my foes, for I rejoice in your deliverance.
Yes, from now onwards all generations will call me blessed,	
for the Almighty has done great things for me,	There is no Holy One like Yahweh, (indeed, there is none but you)
Holy is his name,	no Rock like our God.
and his faithful love extends age after age to those who fear him.	. . .
He has used the power of his arm,	The bow of the mighty has been broken . . .
He has routed the arrogant of heart.	

He has pulled down princes from
　　their thrones and raised high the
　　lowly.
He has filled the starving with good
　　things, sent the rich away empty.
He has come to the help of Israel his
　　servant, mindful of his faithful
　　love
— according to the promise he made
　　to our ancestors —

of his mercy to Abraham and to his
　　descendants for ever.

Luke.1:46–55

The full fed are hiring themselves
　　out for bread
but the hungry need labour no more;
. . .

He raises the poor from the dust,
he lifts the needy from the dunghill
　　to give them a place with princes, . . .

He safeguards the steps of his
faithful
he endows his king with power,
he raises up the strength of his
　　Annointed.

1Samuel.2:1–10

Zechariah's Song

Blessed be the Lord, the God
　　of Israel,

for he has visited his people,
　　he has set them free,
and he has established for us a
　　saving power
in the House of his servant David,

just as he proclaimed,
by the mouth of his holy prophets
　　from ancient times,

David's Song[1]

'. . . . when Yahweh had delivered
him from all his enemies and from
. . . Saul'

(inscription to 2 Psalm 18)

Blessed be Yahweh, the God of
Israel, for setting one of my own
sons on the throne . . . 1Kings 1:48

(cf.Psalm 106:48)

. . . my Saviour, you have saved me . . .
I call to Yahweh who is worthy of
praise, and I am saved from my foes.

Psalm 18:1,3

cf . . . which God proclaimed,
speaking through his holy prophets

Acts 3:21 (cf.: Deut. 18:15)

1 2 Samuel 22; 1Kings 1:48; Psalm 18.

that he would save us from our
    enemies
and from the hand of all those
    who hate us,

He reached down . . . snatched me
    up,
pulled me from the watery depths,
rescued me from my mighty foe,
from my enemies who were
    stronger than I.

                   Psalm 18:16f.

Simeon's Song

Now, Master, you are letting
    your servant go in peace
as you promised;

for my eyes have seen the
    salvation

which you have made ready in
    the sight of the nations;

a light of revelation for the
    gentiles

and glory for your people
    Israel.

                   Luke 2:29-32

A Song of the Exiles

'Console my people, console them,'
says your God.
'Speak to the heart of Jerusalem and
    cry to her

that her period of service is ended,
that her guilt has been atoned for,
that, from the hand of Yahweh, she
    has received
double punishment for all her sins.'
    A voice cries, 'Prepare in the
    desert
a way for Yahweh.
Make a straight highway for our God
Across the wastelands.
Let every valley be filled in,
every mountain and hill be levelled,
every cliff become a plateau,
every escarpment a plain;
then the glory of Yahweh will be
    revealed

and all humanity will see it together,
for the mouth of Yahweh has
    spoken.'

                   Isiah 40:1-5

and show faithful love to our
   ancestors,
and so keep in mind his holy
   covenant.

Luke.1:68–72

He saves his king time after time,
displays his faithful love for his
   annointed,
for David and his heirs for ever.

Psalm.18:50

Bibliography

The editions referred to here are those most readily available at the
time going to press.

Abbreviations for versions of the Bible:

AV	Authorized Version
JB	Jerusalem Bible
NEB	New English Bible
NIV	New International Version
NJB	New Jerusalem Bible
RSV	Revised Standard Version

Bibles and Apocryphas

Authorized Version [also known as the King James Bible], first
   published 1611

Good News Bible, USA/UK, American/British Bible Society, 1966
   (New Testament), 1976 (Old Testament)

Jerusalem Bible, New York, Doubleday & Company, 1966

New American Bible, Kansas, Catholic Bible Publishers, 1970

New English Bible, Oxford, Oxford University Press, 1961 (New Testament), 1970 (Old Testament and Apocrypha)

New International Version, New York, International Bible Society, 1978

New Jerusalem Bible, New York, Doubleday and Sons, 1985

Novum Testamentum Graece [Greek New Testament], ed. Nestle-Aland, Stuttgart, Deutsche Bibelstiftung, 1981

Revised English Bible, Oxford, Oxford University Press, 1989

Revised Standard Version New York, Thomas Nelson & Sons, 1946 (New Testament), 1952 (Old Testament), 1957 (Apocrypha)

Other Sources

Birth Narratives, The, Toronto, CBC [Ideas transcript; broadcast prepared and presented by Margaret Horsfield], 1987

Brown, Raymond E., *The Birth of The Messiah*, New York, Image Books, 1979

Caird, G.B., *Saint Luke*, edited by D.E. Nineham, Hammondsworth, Middlesex, Penguin Books [Pelican New Testament Commentaries], 1963

Cruden's Complete Concordance to the Bible, ed. Alexander Cruden, Cambridge, Lutterworth Press, 1977

Ellis, Peter F., *Matthew: His Mind and Message*, The Liturgical Press, Collegeville, Minnesota, 1974

Eusebius, *A History of the Church From Christ to Contantine*, trans. G.A. Williamson, Harmondsworth, Middlesex, Penguin Books [Penguin Classics], 1981

Fenton, J.C., *Saint Matthew*, Harmondsworth, Middlesex, Pelican Gospel Commentaries, Penguin Books, first published 1963

Fitzmeyer, Joseph A., *The Gospel According to Luke*, New York, Doubleday and Co., Garden City, 1981

Frye, Northrop, *The Great Code*, Toronto, Academic Press Canada, 1982

Gaston Lloyd, 'Sola Scriptura', *Bulletin of the Canadian Society of Biblical Studies*, vol.47 (1987), pp. 3–18

Goulder, M.D., *Midrash and Lection in Matthew*, London, SPCK, 1974

——, *Luke: A New Paradigm*, 2 vols, Sheffield, JSOT Press, 1989

Guilding, Aileen, *The Fourth Gospel and Jewish Worship*, Oxford, Clarendon Press, 1960

Hastings, James (ed.), *A Dictionary of the Bible*, New York, Charles Scribner's Sons, 1902

Holtz, Barry W., *Back to the Sources*, New York, Summit Books, 1984

Josephus, *The Jewish War*, ed. by Gaalya Cornfeld, Grand Rapids, Michigan, Zondervan Publishing House, 1982

——, *The Works of Flavius Josephus*, trans. William Whiston, Edinburgh. The Excelsior Edition, n.d.

Justin Martyr, *The Dialogue with Trypho*, trans. A. Lukyn Williams, London, SPCK 1930

New Testament Apocrypha, trans, E Hennecke, ed. W. Scheemelcher, London, Lutterworth Press, 1963

Nineham, Dennis, *Saint Mark*, Harmondsworth, Middlesex, Penguin Books [Pelican Gospel Commentaries], Penguin Books, 1963

——, *The Use and Abuse of the Bible*, SPCK, London, 1976

Plutarch, *The Lives of the Noble Grecians and Romans*, trans. John Dryden, The Modern Library, New York, n.d.

Sanders, E.P., *Jesus and Judaism*, Canada, SCM Press/USA, Fortress, 1985

Suetonius, *The Twelve Caesars*, trans. Robert Graves, Harmondsworth, Middlesex, Penguin Books, [Penguin Classics], 1957

Thucydides, *The Peloponnesian War*, trans. Rex Warner, Harmondsworth, Middlesex, Penguin Books [Penguin Classics], 1954

Vermes, Geza, *Jesus the Jew*, Canada, SCM Press/USA, Fortress Press, 1973

——, *Jesus and the World of Judaism*, SCM Press/USA, Fortress Press, 1984

Virgil, *Ecologues*, trans. Lee, Guy, Harmondsworth, Middlesex, Penguin Books, [Penguin Classics], 1984

——, *The Aeneid*, trans. W.F. Jackson Knight, Harmondsworth, Middlesex, Penguin Books [Penguin Classics], 1956

General Index

Index to
Biblical Quotations

The Old Testament

Genesis
4 : 23-4 *(32)*
15 : 1-5 *(21-2)*
18 : 1-15 *(67)*
22 : 11-13 *(22)*
25 : 29-34 *(86)*
27 : 41-5 *(89)*
30 : 22-4 *(69)*
35 : 10-11 *(22)*
37 : 5-10 *(82)*
37 : 19-20 *(83)*
38 : 6-7 *(12)*
38 : 8-10 *(12)*
38 : 15-18 *(13)*
38 : 24-6 *(14)*
41 : 17-24 *(83-4)*
41 : 39-40 *(84)*
42 : 5-7 *(84)*
46 : 30 *(140)*

Exodus
1 : 7-11 *(85)*
1 : 15-22 *(88)*
2 : 2-4 *(90)*
3 : 23-5 *(80)*
5 : 7-12 *(90-91)*
4 : 19-20 *(91)*
14 : 21-2 *(149*
19 : 16-20 *(151)*
24 : 16-18 *(74)*
40 : 34-8 *(75)*

Numbers
22 : 5-6 *(123)*
22 : 12-19 *(124)*
24 : 15-17 *(122)*
24 : 15-19 *(81)*

Acknowledgments

We would like to thank many people for their help and encouragement. The Benedictine Sisters in Nanaimo British Columbia provided the opportunity and the motivation for the lecture which sparked off the radio documentaries which in turn sparked off this book. We are grateful to them. Equally, warm thanks are due to the *Ideas* programme at CBC Radio in Toronto, especially to Sara Wolch and to Bernie Lucht. Our thanks are also extended to all scholars who agreed to be interviewed for the ideas programmes.

Many people kindly helped to compile the tables and check the text in this book, and we thank them: Betty Bibbs, Barbara Cowling, Nancy Dalby, Joan Dowsley, Patricia Kahr, Ann Hill, Dorothy Hutchinson, Lois Jane McTaggart, Ruth and Don Meadows, Harry Johnson, Shirley Rokeby, Malcolm Roberton, Marjorie Sandercock, Madge Taylor and Sidney Vivian. We also thank the Vancouver School of Theology, the faculty and the library staff who have always been most helpful.

Because this book has been written in many places including London, Nanaimo and Toronto; mid-air, mid-sea and on Protection Island, various marvels of technology have come to our aid. These include computers and jet aircraft, FAX machines and telephones, and most important of all a set of handmade oars and a rowboat.

About the Authors

Margaret Horsfield

Margaret Horsfield was born in Port Alberni, B.C., and received her B.A. from Simon Fraser University. She moved to England in 1977, where she completed her M.A. in Shakespeare Studies at the University of Birmingham. She went on to become a broadcaster and writer for BBC Radio in England and the CBC in Canada, and her projects have taken her from the scaffolding around Big Ben during that famous landmark's repairs, to the golden triangle in Thailand and Inuit hunting grounds on Baffin Island, from a live volcano off Iceland to a sundance ritual on the Canadian prairies.

In recent years many of her programs have been on theological subjects, and she has made the rounds of synagogues, bishops' palaces, art galleries and cathedrals in the course of her research.

A casual discussion about Christmas-cards sparked the idea for this book, and led to a summer of writing on Protection Island in collaboration with her father.

Peter Horsfield

Peter Horsfield was born in Victoria and went from school to sea, where he trained to be a navigator and a mate. For one short season he was master of a sailing vessel on Hudson Bay, but most of his seafaring was spent watchkeeping on cargo ships in wartime convoys crossing the North Atlantic.

He later became an Anglican clergyman and for over twenty years he and his wife Anne worked in various parishes in British Columbia; they later lived on Gabriola Island, working as volunteers with an ecumenical church group. Throughout his rather diverse career in the ministry Peter Horsfield has held a number of eclectic jobs: he has worked as a ferry mate, a building contractor, and a designer of water cisterns, solar panels and irrigation systems.

Peter and Anne Horsfield now live in Nanaimo, within rowing distance of their daughter Margaret's cottage on Protection Island. Ostensibly retired, they remain more active than ever in the community, and devote much of their leisure time to the cultivation of their beautiful flower garden.